A QUESTION OF GUILT

by

James Taugner

To my grandson Jeff

James Taugner

ISBN 0-7414-0673-X

Published by:

INFINITY
PUBLISHING.COM

Infinity Publishing.com
519 West Lancaster Avenue
Haverford, PA 19041-1413
Info@buybooksontheweb.com
www.buybooksontheweb.com
Toll-free (877) BUY BOOK
Local Phone (610) 520-2500
Fax (610) 519-0261

Printed in the United States of America

Printed on Recycled Paper

Published June, 2001

A QUESTION OF GUILT

Chapter 1

He rolled down the window of the van and settled back in his seat to wait, his right hand absently stroking the knife in the sheath attached to his belt. Finally, after ten months and obeying all the rules -- an eternity for someone like him -- his parole from Joliet Correctional had been granted, and now payback time was here.

The van was parked in a spot that gave him a clear view of the building and adjoining parking lot. A huge elm tree between the curb and the sidewalk cast a shadow of protection from the nearest street light, assuring him that he blended in with the surroundings. It was eleven-fifteen, and if the rest of his information was correct, the festivities inside should break up soon.

A fire door opened, and he saw two young men in formal attire come out for a cigarette break. A moment later they were joined by a young woman dressed in an evening gown. One of the men offered her a cigarette and lit it for her. He could hear voices, punctuated by occasional laughter.

He knew their kind, young and carefree, the products of northwest side middle-class homes, who never had to scratch and claw for the basic comforts the way he did. From the beginning, he was denied access to their tight little social circles; indeed, they had disavowed his existence. And later, as a delinquent high school dropout with an arrest record, he was treated as though he were a leper. If they noticed him at all, it was with a look of snobbish disapproval.

He made a face and spit out the window. Stuck-up bastards, every one of 'em. Them and their tight little circles. Think they shit Hershey bars.

Watching them smoke made him reach for his cigarettes. He used the dash lighter and cupped his hand over the glowing ember of the cigarette. The fire door opened again, and he saw them reenter the building. He reached under the seat for a bottle of vodka, took a swig, swished it around in his mouth and spit it out the window, a cleansing farewell gesture. Then he gulped several ounces and put the bottle away.

He slouched down and picked at one of the calluses on his hands, a preoccupation that brought back the memory of a recent pickup he had met in a bar and brought to his apartment. She had commented on the roughness of his hands on her body, saying it was a badge of honest labor. He remembered trying not to laugh.

Dumb bitch. What if he'da told her he got 'em from years of pumpin' iron? Hey, dummy, *burglars* don't get *calluses.*

He grinned. She'da freaked out.

Finally, in a blaze of light, the front doors swung open, and he came to full alert when the sounds of excited squeals and the chattering of couples shattered the silence of the balmy May night. He watched them spill forth onto the concrete steps and walkway, some heading directly for the parking lot, others stopping to form groups.

He knew that, from this distance and in the limited light, all the men would look alike, so his eyes searched the crowd for the peach-colored gown his mark's date was wearing. And on the possibility that he might miss them, he had pinpointed the spot where the Buick was parked; either way he was sure to locate them. When the groups broke up, he finally spotted the couple walking toward the parking area.

Then, when he saw their car approaching the apron to the street, he started his engine. If he had figured correctly, they should turn in the same direction he was facing. From information gathered, he had formed a profile of his mark: a 'goody-boy' who would take his date home at a reasonable time.

He watched the car reach the street, smiled when it turned in the predicted direction, and pulled his van out into the traffic. Four vehicles separated him from the Buick, but the seats in the van gave him a height advantage that allowed him to remain at a safe distance. When they reached Northwest Highway, the car ahead bore right, while the others signaled for a left turn. It took a few minutes of stop-and-go to get through the intersection, but he never lost sight of the target car. Half a mile on, their right turn signal started blinking. But he knew where they were going and continued on until one street beyond them before making his turn.

The area was residential, and the streets were empty at this time of night. He turned right at the next intersection and proceeded to the street they had taken, then he switched off his lights, turned left, and pulled in at the curb behind the first parked car. He could see the Buick halfway down the block, in front of her house, the one with a front porch light burning.

He lit a cigarette and settled back to wait. He had been tracking the Buick since eight o'clock that evening, when it left to pick up his mark's date and then on to the dance, where he broke off to get something to eat and kill some time. Now he had to wait again, while they said goodnight. But it was worth it; in another hour, at most, he would know satisfaction.

Twenty minutes later, he saw his mark get out of the car and escort his date to her door. He reached over and rolled the window down on the passenger side, then he opened the console and took out a pair of latex gloves, a patch of first aid gauze, and a small bottle of liquid, which he used to saturate the gauze.

When he saw the Buick pull away, he put on the gloves and followed with his lights off. He hung back until the car turned at the next street to circle back to the highway, then he switched on his lights and brought the van up until it hit the bumper of the Buick, a move he hoped would look like an accident and make the driver stop to investigate. Instead, he saw it swerve, then brake and turn at the next street. He figured the driver thought he was a carjacker.

He followed it through the turn, and, with no parked cars to hinder him, he swung wide and floored the accelerator until he drew ahead of the car and could force it over to the curb. Then, in rapid succession, he threw the shift lever into park, grabbed the gauze, got out, and went around to the rear of the van.

He waited there until he saw the other driver get out and close the door, then he rushed him, pinning his arms behind his back. He counted on a struggle, with heavy breathing, so, while holding him with one powerful arm, he clamped the gauze over his victim's face with his other hand and held him until he went limp.

After a few more seconds, to let the vapors take full effect, he maneuvered the unconscious body onto his shoulders, carried it to the rear of the van and dumped it inside.

With the lights out again he drove to the end of the block and turned into an alley. There, letting the engine idle, he crawled into the back, switched on a six-volt lamp for light, and tied the victim's wrists and ankles with rope, then sealed the mouth closed with duct tape. All the while the only sounds were those of the purring engine and the faint crackling noise from the disposable plastic drop cloth on the floor, which later would be discarded along with any incriminating material.

He drove out of the alley and worked his way through the side streets to Milwaukee Avenue, picked up Elston and took it to Central, then turned north to a wooded area adjoining a golf course. The woods were closed to the public after dark, but the small parking area had an outcropping of bushes that would hide his slate-gray van from passing cars on the road.

When he opened the rear door, he found his captive awake and struggling at his bonds. He considered putting him to sleep again, but decided against the idea. He wanted him awake.

He reached in, grabbed one ankle, and pulled until the victim's body was hanging, face up, halfway over the bumper. Then he got under him and used both arms to bend the man's back over his powerful shoulders so that struggling would be painful.

Swaying only slightly, he took a footpath through the trees to a spot behind an overgrowth of tangled vegetation where he let his burden drop to the ground. As he watched his victim struggle to a sitting position, he got down on his knees and took a penlight from his shirt pocket. He turned the beam on the young man's face for a moment, then he turned it on his own and held it there. His lips drew away from his teeth in a vicious smile, and his voice came out as a growl:

"*Remember me*?"

He shined the light on the other's face, and the wide-eyed shock he found there answered his question. He pressed the end of the penlight into the ground between them so the light illuminated both their faces.

"I remember you, too, *Asshole*. Spent ten months in a cell 'cuz of you . You and your big mouth. Just had to play the hero, didn't cha? Didja think I'd let ya get away with it?" He waited for a reaction, but saw only a worried frown. "Didn't anyone tell ya about me? No? Too bad. The word's out on the street -- ya shoulda listened. Because *nobody*, but *nobody*, messes with me and gets away with it!"

His hand moved to the sheath inside his waistband and removed the hunting knife. Even in the poor light, the glint of the blade was bright and sinister. He saw his captive struggling at the ropes, stirring up the dust around him.

He liked watching him squirm, would love to prolong the torture. But it was time. He accomplished what he had intended, to see the victim's terror, to make him know why he would die and who would kill him. To prolong the pleasure was not only pointless now; it was also dangerous.

He straddled the man's legs and held his head down against the ground. Then he raised the knife and plunged the blade into the right side of the chest, pulled it out and stabbed again and again, working down to the lower abdomen where the knife caught on something and had to be pulled with all his strength to remove it.

He stopped the attack and wiped the knife clean on the victim's clothing, returned it to the sheath, put the penlight away and stood up. The odor of the fumes still hung in the air around him, and he remembered that the gauze was still in his pocket. He threw it into a nearby bush and walked away.

CHAPTER 2

Sunrise invaded the room, forcing the charcoal shadows of night into hasty retreat. The disturbing light stirred Paul to waking, and he lay still for a moment, trying in vain to recapture his dream.

It was Sunday, his day to relax, but that did not include sleeping half of the morning away. He was on his left side, facing away from his wife, and to verify that she still slept, he reached around and touched the small mound of blanket that covered her sleeping form, then got up and went to the wall-length closet for his clothes.

Ignoring the unused robe that she had bought for his birthday, he chose a well-worn pair of jeans and a cotton sport shirt. She gave him the robe so that he would have something to relax in when he first got up, but he never was comfortable in it. He told her he was sorry -- but all his life -- when he got up, he got dressed; a robe made him feel lazy, sloppy.

He closed their bedroom door quietly behind him and walked to the head of the stairs, where he stopped and listened to the silence. The faint morning light filled the hall with contrasting shades of gray, from dark, to pearl, to almost white. He liked being the first one up; the soft light and rocklike stillness of the house evoked in him a primal sense of peace and security, the same way, he imagined, that early man must have felt for his cave.

A compelling pressure in his bladder broke the spell, and he started down the stairs to the half-bath on the first floor. But when his eyes were even with the floor of the upper level, he noticed the door to his son's bedroom was open. It was not like Kevin to leave his door open. *Ever.* Suddenly a vague uneasiness replaced Paul's former discomfort, and he walked back up, then down the hall.

Although he knew it was silly, the thought of peeking into his son's room made him feel like a spy. No doubt Kevin would consider it a breach of trust. His eyes swept the room, and when he saw his son's bed, he felt a tendon contract deep in his groin. The bed was empty.

He entered the room and stared at the undisturbed bedspread, the mound of plumped-up pillow, and suddenly that previous aura of solid security deserted him, leaving fear in its wake. Kevin never stayed out all night without letting them know; he always called if he were going to sleepover at a friend's house.

The previous night, with its festive preparations, flashed across his memory and with it came a vision of his son, standing impatiently for Joan's inspection. "Don't look so pained," she had said. "You're not just on a date, you know -- you're taking your girl to the prom. I wouldn't be your mother if I didn't want you to look your best".

With that still in mind, Paul left the room, closing the door behind him and went downstairs. He used the bathroom, then moved to the kitchen and plugged in the coffee maker. His wife would be up before long, and, so that nothing should look out of the ordinary, he opened the kitchen blinds and then the living room drapes. He went out onto the lawn for the morning paper and brought it back to the kitchen where he separated the sections, putting Joan's favorite Sunday supplements on her side of the table and the front section on his. Then he set their places with cups, saucers, spoons and paper napkins, diet sweetener and powdered creamer for her and sugar for him. This was the routine whenever he was up first.

When the red light in the base of the electric percolator blinked on, he poured coffee for himself and opened the paper to the headlines. His eyes moved over the printed words, but his mind was preoccupied. He leaned back and stared at the ceiling, searching for rational answers. But, before one could form, he heard the soft rustle of his wife's satin robe as she entered the room. He looked down quickly and pretended to read.

She leaned over him and kissed his cheek. "Mor -- ning." The usual musical lilt she gave to the word was there, but just above a whisper now.

Paul looked up and smiled. "Good morning, sleepyhead."

Joan moved away to pour coffee for herself, then sat down across from him. "I had trouble getting to sleep last night. Couldn't help wondering how the dance turned out. Wish I could have seen Kevin and Kim together." She sipped her coffee. "Did I tell you? She came over the other day when Kevin wasn't home, to show me the new dress she bought for the prom."

"No, you didn't."

"I made her try it on for me, and, Paul, I swear, you wouldn't believe how beautiful she looked."

"Yes, I would."

"She was so excited. She asked me, over and over, if I thought Kevin would like it. It made me happy for Kevin -- she's such a sweet thing."

"He's a lucky guy."

"Not so loud."

"Why are you whispering?"

"I don't want to wake Kevin. He must have got home awfully late last night. I didn't hear him come in -- and I was awake a long time."

Paul was staring at the front page.

"Did you hear him?"

He looked up. "What?"

"Did you hear him come in?"

"No."

He knew he was stalling and chided himself for it. She was going to know eventually, but he hated to start her worrying sooner than necessary. Besides, he expected to see Kevin come dragging in any minute now with some wild explanation. Kevin is good at that; he has a fertile mind.

Paul knew he handled stress better than Joan; he did it so well that there were times when she accused him of being unfeeling, callous. He preferred the term, 'nerves of steel'. And now, as if to confirm that quality, he found he was actually reading and digesting the news item that just moments before would not register in his mind at all.

Joan put aside the section she had been reading and refilled their cups "What do you want for breakfast?"

Paul looked up and made a face. "Oh, I don't know. I'm not really hungry. Maybe just toast for me."

She gave him a quizzical smile, her head tilted, one eyebrow arched. "What's this? I thought after that little session we had in bed last night, you'd wake up ravenous. How did I fail?"

He grinned. "And I should think you'd have had no problem going to sleep for the same reason. So, who failed?"

She shook her head and laughed. "Okay, we're even. Nobody failed."

Paul lowered his head to the paper again, but not to read. Instead his eyes followed Joan covertly as she moved about the kitchen. He decided Kevin wasn't the only one in this family with a pretty girl; the old man was doing all right, too. He knew of no one else with a prettier forty-three-year-old wife. And, at maybe ten pounds heavier than when they first married, Joan's figure was even better now; soft swelling curves had replaced former protruding angles.

Although she admitted to having a few, there were no gray strands in her light brown hair that he could see. Her face still was unlined, but Joan mentioned that she was beginning to show her age in her neck. “No matter what they do with make-up,” she once said, “you can always tell a woman's age by her neck”. He had done a brief study of this theory and agreed that it had some merit. But he saw his wife as the exception to the rule.

“Move the paper; your toast is ready.”

Paul put the paper onto the counter behind him and stared at the food. By now even his ‘steel’ nerves were beginning to fray. But fear, he knew, was contagious, and somehow he must go through the motions. He chewed the toasted bread slowly and used the coffee to help swallow it. Joan ate a soft boiled egg and two slices of toast, but still managed to finish before him.

He watched her clear the table and leave the room. When she was out of sight, he listened to her movements, thinking she would go upstairs to get dressed, but the sound of the front door being opened proved him wrong.

He winced, knowing she would see his car wasn't at the curb. Next she'd go out back and look through the garage window and see it wasn't in there either. He closed his eyes and waited. She was back in less than a minute.

“Paul! Your *car* has been stolen!”

He almost laughed. It was just like her to think that, instead of the other possibility.

“Did you hear me? Your *car* is *gone*.”

She frowned when she saw that look of guilt on his face, then her eyes widened in comprehension.

“Oh, my God! Kevin didn't come home last night?”

Paul got up and put his arms around her. “Honey, take it easy,” he said, pressing her head against his chest.

She jerked away from his embrace and stepped back, color rising in her face, eyes flashing.

“You *knew*. You sat there all this time, talking and eating as if nothing was wrong -- and you knew all along.

Damn you! Don't you think I have a right to know what's going on?"

He made a move toward her, but she moved away again. "Joan, please, calm down. I -- "

"How did you know he wasn't home?"

"I saw his bedroom door open, so I looked in and saw his bed hadn't been slept in."

"Why didn't you tell me, Paul? Why did you let me think everything was okay?"

"Because I thought he still might come home before you found out and got all worked up. I didn't want to worry you unnecessarily." He saw the fire in her eyes. "Okay, if he had come home before you found out, you'd have been shocked, of course, but it would have saved you from needless worry. I'm sorry it didn't work out that way."

He watched the flush of anger drain away and lines of worry crease her forehead. She returned to the table and sat down, her hands fluttering like butterflies, from her neck to her face and up to her hair, then down to her neck. Paul sat down across from her.

"He must have had an accident," she said. "For all we know, he could be lying in some hospital, unconscious, right this minute."

"See what I meant? You always think the worst. If that had happened, we'd have heard by now. He's got identification in his wallet; the police would have called."

"Well, *something* happened. Kevin's never stayed out all night without letting us know." She scowled at him then. "And I don't know how you can sit there so calm. I swear, sometimes I think you must be made of ice."

Paul sighed audibly. "Honey, think for a minute. They went to a *prom* last night. Don't you remember what that was like -- how exciting it was? Maybe somebody invited them to a party afterwards. You know how it is today. There's always someone with access to alcohol. Maybe he had a little too much to drink, and one of his friends talked him into sleeping it off at *his* house."

She stiffened in her chair. “Kevin has never done that -- he doesn’t drink.”

“So far as we know.” He saw that she was about to protest. “Joan, wait a minute. You know, as well as I do, that kids experiment. Both of us know Kevin smoked on the sneak for a while, and it took football training to get him to quit. Kids are under a lot of peer pressure. There's always someone there to push you, challenge you. You want to fit in with the crowd, not look like an oddball, or whatever it is you're called today -- *nerd*, I think they call it now. So who's to say what temptations he faced last night. They were all celebrating an important milestone. *Graduation*.”

Joan tilted her head and sighed. “Oh, I know what you're saying. It's just that I like to believe we've taught him some values. I like to think I *know* my son. I just don't believe he'd let himself get drawn into that kind of thing -- and I definitely don't believe Kimberly would either.”

Paul reached across the table and captured her flitting hands in his. “You may be right. I was just trying to offer some plausible reasons.” He glanced up at the wall-clock. “I have to admit, I'm getting a little concerned now myself.”

“We can't just sit here doing nothing, Paul; let's make some calls.” She got the address book from the counter under the telephone and returned to the table. “Let's call Kim and -- ”

“*No*. I don't think that's a good idea, just yet. Let's start with Tommy Reid; he practically lives here anyway. He'd have been there last night, and if anyone knows where Kevin went after the party, he would.” He stood up. “Why don’t I make the calls -- I think I’m calmer.” He watched her nod her head.

Chapter 3

The phone was picked up on the second ring, and Paul smiled when he recognized Tommy's voice. It figured -- with a teenager in the house, who else did he expect?

"This is Paul Becker, Tommy."

"Mr. *Becker*?" The surprise in his voice was obvious. "What ..." He paused, as if unsure of his ground. "Is something wrong?"

"I don't know, Tom. Is there?"

There was another pause. "*No*. I'm just surprised. You never call *me*."

"I guess it would be a shock, at that. Look, Tom, I was just wondering if you might have seen Kevin and Kim leave the dance last night."

"Yeah, sure, Mr. Becker. But I don't understand -- isn't Kevin there?"

"No, he isn't. Kevin didn't come home last night and my wife and I are quite worried."

"Oh, wow! I can't believe it. Kevin wouldn't do *that*."

Joan was pacing back and forth, shaking her head. "I just know something terrible happened."

Paul covered the transmitter. "Please, Joan, calm down, I'm trying to hear Tommy."

She pressed her lips together, but continued pacing.

"Tom, did you hear of anyone suggesting a party, or any kind of get-together that they might have gone to?"

"No. At least none of our friends mentioned anything. I don't know about the others -- they may have -- but Kevin wouldn't go to a party that didn't include us."

"Did he say anything to you before he left?"

"He just said he was going to take Kim home, and he'd see me tomorrow. I mean, today -- oh, you know what I mean."

"Okay, Tom. Thanks for your help."

"Mr. Becker? Please let me know, or have him call me when he gets home. I'm worried now, too."

"I sure will, Tommy. Good-bye." Paul hung-up the phone and shrugged. Joan was looking at him, wide-eyed, anticipating.

"Well?"

He shook his head. "He's as surprised as we are. All he knows is Kevin took Kim home and said he'd see him today."

"There was no party?"

"No party."

"See? I told you."

He shook his head. "I think I'd feel better if there had been."

"What next -- call Kim?"

"I suppose so." He grimaced to indicate his reluctance. "You want to handle this one?"

"I guess it would be better."

He sat down and watched her push the buttons. "Try not to sound panicky, okay?"

She frowned and waved him away. He rose willingly and went out the back door. He imagined how the conversation would go and had no desire to listen.

Spring had been cut short this year by a winter that endured into the third week of April. Today, however, marked the beginning of the first week of May, and the yard was filled with sunshine and the fresh scents of spring.

Standing in the midmorning silence, Paul felt as if he actually could hear the sound of growing things, the rustle of new leaves breaking through, the whispered stirrings of immature blooms. He felt the urge to open a lawn chair and just *sit* there the rest of the day, enjoying this gentle season of renewal -- no cares or worries -- instead, he lingered for a few minutes more, then turned and went back into the house.

Joan was sitting with her elbows on the table, her hands covering her face, and Paul knew at once that nothing encouraging had come of the phone call. He sat down and waited, reluctant to be the first to speak.

Three years before, Paul quit smoking, and, except for withdrawal symptoms during the first month or so, the craving never had returned. Now, suddenly, the urgent need of a cigarette was compelling.

Joan looked up then and shook her head. "Kevin had Kim home by twelve-thirty. She said they sat in the car, talking, 'till about one, then he walked her to her door and said he'd call her in the morning. She's very upset."

"I can imagine. That's why I suggested we call Tommy first. I was hoping he'd have the answer, and we wouldn't have to get her upset, too."

Paul stared at a spot just above his wife's head, but he could see her eyes searching his face for answers. He forced himself to look directly at her, but his mind refused to work the magic words she needed to hear.

"I don't understand," he said, regretting his ineptitude, "everything we've heard says he should have come home -- but he didn't."

"I think we should call the police."

"And what are we going to say? That our son didn't come home from his prom last night? Come on, Honey, they'll laugh at us."

She glared at him. "Are you saying parents don't have the right to report their child is missing?"

"A *child*? Yes. But Kevin's not a child; he's eighteen years old. If you told them your *ten-year-old* didn't come home all night, you'd get their attention, but I can't see them getting excited about Kevin, especially when they hear he went to a prom last night."

She was silent for a moment, as if weighing his words, then she put her hands on her hips and tilted her head, striking a pose that reminded him of a defiant child.

"Well, how long does somebody have to be gone before they're considered a missing person?"

Paul hesitated. He tried to recall reading something in the newspaper concerning a missing person, but it was months back. He shook his head. "I'm not sure. I seem to remember seventy-two hours, but I could -- "

"*Seventy-two-hours*?"

"I could be wrong," he said quickly. "Maybe it was only thirty-six, but it seems like it was a lot more than one night."

"That's *ridiculous*. A person could be hurt and *bleed* to death before then. You could be kidnapped and taken half way across the country in that amount of time." She paused, then added, "That's *crazy*."

"I know it doesn't sound right, at first, but stop and think for a minute. If the police were expected to investigate every time a person stayed out all night without letting someone know, they wouldn't have time for anything else -- that's all they'd be doing."

He knew his argument was sound, but he realized also that cold, hard logic seldom made sense to a worried mother.

The frustration was there in her face, and he felt powerless against it.

When finally she spoke, her voice lacked its former ardor. "So, we just wait?"

"At least until afternoon, but maybe I'll think of something in the meantime. I still think he'll show up."

He wished he had something more to offer. The only other possibility that kept nagging at him would start an argument. The thought had occurred to him that Kevin might have met another buddy of his, perhaps a little more worldly, who could have suggested they complete their graduation into 'manhood', someone who might know of a prostitute they could visit. But, as he turned this over in his mind again, he saw a flaw: an all-night session with one of those 'ladies of the night' was more than Kevin could afford.

The craving for a cigarette loomed again; he needed something to do.

"I'm going to shave and get showered," he said.

"I should get cleaned up and dressed, too, but you go ahead; I'll stick by the phone 'till you finish, just in case."

Paul made his way to the master bath, looked in the mirror a bit ominously, then lathered his face at his side of the double-sink vanity. Joan's side had additional space beyond her sink for a chair and a lighted make-up mirror. As he turned his head to shave his right cheek, he saw the complex array of her toiletry and was amazed, again, at how she managed to keep her side looking neater than his.

He finished shaving and entered the shower. The habitual routine allowed his mind to wander, and he let it drift back to the one possibility that sounded reasonable: the lady-of-the-evening theory. Okay, so they couldn't afford an all-night-stand -- they could have taken the quickie route and then topped off the celebration by getting drunk. He decided that at least it was within the realm of probability.

The telephone in the bedroom rang, and he turned off the water to listen. It rang only twice. He held his breath for complete silence, but heard no conversation, so he figured Joan was on one of the phones downstairs. He finished rinsing, dried himself and got dressed.

When Paul came down, he found Joan sitting on the couch in the living room, staring out the picture window. She wore a frown of fierce concentration, as if by force of will she could make his car appear at the curb with a smiling, carefree Kevin behind the wheel.

"I heard the phone ring when I was in the shower. Who called?"

His voice made her jump, then she turned to him, still frowning. "Just my sister, wanting to know if I can get to the store early tomorrow."

"What's special about tomorrow?"

"The new line of bathing suits came in, and she wants me to help with the displays. You know Cathy." Joan made a conciliatory smile to imitate her sister. "Oh, Joannie, you're so much better at it than I am. You have *such* a *flair* for it. If I do it, one look at the mannequins, and everyone will know all the men have deserted the beach to go fishing."

Paul snickered. "You really are too hard on her, you know. I'm glad you're not my sister."

"So am I," she said, one eyebrow lifting.

"No, really, Catherine's right. She's the business half of your partnership, and she does a good job of it. But when it comes to customer-tempting displays -- the *buy-me* look -- you're an artist, and you know it. I've seen your face when you show me something you've dreamed up -- how proud you are."

She dismissed him with a wave and moved toward the hall. "She probably bribes you to take her side," she said, calling over her shoulder. "I'm going to get out of this robe and cleaned up."

Paul went down to the basement, turned on the light over his drafting table and stared at the drawing he had brought home on Friday night. Something was wrong with the locating mechanism at one station of the automated assembly system his company was installing. The computer 'geniuses' maintained the problem was mechanical and dumped it in his lap. He knew better, and when he found the solution, he intended to cram it down their throats.

He had gone to work for Woodward Engineering right out of the army in nineteen seventy-one as a junior engineer. At that time the company was evolving from tool and die work to designing and building automated assembly systems for companies forced to cut labor costs in order to stay competitive. Ten years ago he was made Chief Mechanical Engineer. It was a privately owned company, and, with no board of directors or vice presidents tripping over one another, his position was held in highest respect. The owner, Fred Woodward, was basically a mechanical engineer, so it seemed natural that their relationship should gravitate into an easy friendship.

Paul studied the drawing now, reviewing the mechanical components, and, finding nothing wrong with the design, he was convinced that the problem was in the electronics. He shut off the light and went upstairs.

Joan had the freezer door open and was studying its contents. "I suppose we have to eat something today -- any suggestions?"

"I don't know." Paul made a face. "Let's keep it simple. Thaw out a couple of steaks -- they're about the easiest aren't they?"

He saw her choose a large porterhouse. "Hey, too big."

"I know. I thought we'd split it. I'll just cut a small piece for me; you can have most of it. How about baked potato and a can of corn?"

"That's good."

He could see the strain taking its toll; her face was pale and drawn even under the fresh make-up. His mind turned to Kevin, and he felt the smoldering anger in his chest grow to glowing embers. It was one thing to have a good time -- hell, he was as tolerant as anyone -- but there was such a thing as carrying it too far. Dammit, why wasn't that kid home?

The telephone rang then, and Joan picked it up before Paul could move. He heard her say hello, then pause.

"Yes," she said, "he's here. What?" She gasped, and her hand flew to her mouth, as if to ward off a blow. "Oh, my God!"

Paul saw what little color she had left drain from her face, turning her make-up garish, almost clownlike. She looked as if she might faint, and his chair tipped over when he jumped up to reach her. He made her sit, then took the phone out of her hand.

"Are you all right?"

She looked at him blankly for a moment, then found her voice. "It's the *police* -- about your car."

Paul could hear the phone talking to itself.

"Hello... Hello....", a voice was saying, "What's going on there?"

He kept one arm on Joan's shoulder and spoke into the phone. "I'm sorry. My wife got upset, and I had to make her sit down."

"Are you Paul Becker?" The voice at the other end was officially impersonal.

"Yes. What's this about my car?"

"It was reported suspiciously parked on Nola Avenue, just off Northwest Highway. Did you leave it there?"

Paul felt a sudden chill. "No, I let my son use it to go to his prom last night, and he hasn't come home. We're terribly worried. That's what got my wife so upset."

"The procedure is to call a tow truck for an abandoned vehicle, but in this case -- a brand new car -- they thought they'd try calling in the vehicle sticker number to see if we could reach the owner. Can you pick it up right now?"

"Yes. My wife has a car. We'll leave at once."

Paul was upset by the officer's lack of interest in the matter of his son's disappearance. Maybe he didn't hear that part or didn't catch the significance.

"Look, officer, my son wouldn't just abandon my car for no reason. Something must have happened. I told you he didn't come home last night, and he's never done that before."

There was no reply for a moment, and Paul clamped his teeth together to keep from voicing his frustration at what he felt was obvious indifference.

"Awwright, Mr. Becker," the officer drawled, "If you want to, you can come to the station, and we'll have someone take your statement."

Paul heard the policeman's tone as condescending, and his frustration turned to rage.

"*Yes*, I *would*," he said, cracking the valve restraining his resentment, "*if* that wouldn't be too much of an *inconvenience*."

Paul got the address of the station house, the officer's name and hung up the phone.

Joan gripped his arm. "What did you find out?"

"Get your keys; we have to pick up my car."

She held on stubbornly. "*Paul*."

"I'll tell you on the way. If we don't hurry, they'll tow it away to some garage the city deals with, and it'll take forever to get it released."

She hesitated, then, sighing, obeyed. He called after her retreating figure: "I'll lock up and met you in the garage."

When he got to her car, the overhead door was open, and he was relieved to see that she was sitting in the passenger seat.

"It's only about a ten minute drive," he said, swinging out into the street.

He had driven her car only once -- the day she bought it -- and he had to look for the button to move the seat back to fit his frame. It was a Chevy Caprice, three years older than his ninety-two Le Sabre, and he could feel the difference. Also, since he had waited until March to buy, his still had that new car smell.

“All right, Paul, I've waited long enough. Are you going to tell me what the police had to say, or not?”

He felt his anger returning. “You wouldn't believe the attitude of that cop.”

“Yes, I would. I could see how furious you were getting.”

“I mean, *really*, all he was interested in was how soon I was going to get that car out of there. He just ignored me when I tried to tell him about Kevin -- as if a car is more important than a human being.”

“Why does that surprise you? You're the one who told me they wouldn't get excited.”

“Yeah, but that was before I found out about the car. Wouldn't you think they'd find it strange that someone would abandon a brand new car, for chrissake?”

“I guess I shouldn't be surprised at anything anymore.” She was silent for a moment, then went on. “So…after we pick up your car, we go to the police station?”

“Yes.”

Chapter 4

Paul thought they should be approaching Nola and slowed down so he could read the street signs. They were headed south on Northwest Highway and, since Nola ended at this point, he knew they had to make a left turn, but he couldn't signal his intentions until he saw the sign. A car honked behind them, then swung around on his right, the driver glaring at Paul as he passed. The street sign came up, but by the time he read the name, it was too late to turn. Cursing softly, he drove on to the next street, made a turn-around in it and went back to Nola.

He drove through the first block, then saw his car about a third of the way down the second. It was parked at a noticeable slant, the right front wheel against the curb and the rear end sticking out at least two feet. A scattering of people were out in front of the well-kept bungalows that lined both sides of the street; two were sprinkling their lawns while several others apparently were just passing the pleasant afternoon in conversation. Only three other cars were parked on the street. He pulled Joan's car in behind his and got out. Joan waited until Paul finished a slow, circular tour of the Buick before joining him.

"Any damage?"

He shook his head. "No, not a scratch."

They saw a balding, middle-aged man approaching from the house next to where the car was parked and, turning to Joan, Paul made a sign to indicate that *he* would do the talking.

The man smiled once quickly. "Afternoon," he said. "I'm the one who reported the car -- you the owner?"

Paul nodded.

"I know how you feel," the man went on. "I had my car stolen two years ago, right out of the parking lot where I work."

Paul decided not to correct the man's assumption. "Did you see or hear anything last night? I mean, when whoever it was abandoned it?"

"I heard the squeal of tires and a couple of car doors slamming, but by the time I got up to look, no one was there. I didn't think any more about it until I got up this morning and saw it still parked here. Then I thought I'd better call the cops."

"I appreciate your calling as soon as you did. The police ran a check on the city sticker and called me. We got here as soon as we could; hope it hasn't been too much inconvenience."

The man made a negative gesture with his hand. "Nah, no trouble. Like I said, I know how it feels when your car is stolen."

Paul opened the door and leaned in to look at the ignition switch. There was no key. He pushed the backrest forward and leaned in to examine the rear passenger compartment, but found nothing. Then, as he moved back, something caught his eye. Stuffed between the velour cushions, where the backrest pivoted over the seat, was Kevin's wallet. Paul looked up and saw the man leaning against the front fender watching him.

Hesitating only a moment, Paul moved the backrest to its normal position and stood up. His pulse had quickened at the sight of the wallet, but he had no desire to involve this stranger in the discovery. He wished the man would go about his business, but Paul knew the situation bred a certain amount of natural curiosity, and he would have to be patient.

"Well, everything looks okay," Paul said, digging into his pocket for his keys.

The man shook his head and smiled, "You sure are lucky. Mine was stripped when I finally got it back. Had to wait for the insurance company to estimate the cost, and then it took three weeks in the shop waiting for parts. One big pain in the ass from start to finish, I'll tell you."

"I can imagine," Paul said, trying to make his smile sympathetic. "Well, thanks again for what you did -- really appreciate it." He got in then and closed the door signaling the end of the conversation.

The car started on the first turn of the engine. He looked down to activate the electric seat control, and, as the seat moved back, it exposed the ring with his spare keys. With his pulse beating faster than ever, Paul made another quick decision, and, using the heel of his shoe, he pushed the keys back under the seat. When he looked up, Joan was frowning at him through the closed window. He pressed a button and the window came down.

"What's the matter?" she asked. "You look pale."

"Nothing." Paul saw the man walking back toward his house. "I was trying to get rid of Mr. 'nosy' -- he was making me nervous."

Her eyes narrowed. "*You*?"

"Yes, *me*," he emphasized, trying not to look guilty. The two recent discoveries had rattled him. He needed time to think.

"Well," she said, "what are we going to do? Should I follow you to the police station?"

"I don't think that's such a good idea. I think it would be better if you went on home where you can listen for the phone."

She sighed in resignation. “I guess you’re right -- Kevin could be trying to reach us. Someone should be home, just in case.”

He reached out and squeezed her hand. “I'll be home as soon as I can.”

Paul watched her walk back to her car, then waited until she pulled away before reaching behind him for the wallet. He flipped quickly through the compartments, finding the usual photographs and personal items, including Kevin's driver's license. The bill compartment contained twenty-six dollars. Deciding that nothing seemed to be missing, he put the wallet into the side pocket of his jeans, shifted into drive and drove off.

He was not, by nature, a deceptive man; he seldom lied, and on the rare occasions that he did, it was only to spare the feelings of others. Now he was lying by omission by not divulging his findings to Joan, and he felt a crack opening in his usual calm. He could see this in his trembling hand when he moved the climate control lever to the fresh air position, and he wondered what had happened to his ‘nerves of steel’.

He turned into a shopping center at the next intersection and drove slowly through the parking lot until he found a convenience store, where he stopped to buy a package of cigarettes and a disposable lighter. He waited until he was back in the car to open the pack and light up.

Leaning back in the seat, he took the first drag of smoke into his lungs, then another quickly followed. His bloodstream absorbed the nicotine and delivered it to his brain with a speed that amazed him. A spell of dizziness, followed by a quick euphoria swept over him and, like an insistent salesman, the old addiction again had its foot in the door of his resolve. Halfway through the cigarette, the tremor in his hands had diminished to a degree that he felt at ease enough to restart the car.

The area was familiar to him, and in a matter of minutes he had found the police station. He parked in a visitor's space and walked around to the front entrance. The station house was built of stone and brick, in the style of the late twenties, but the remodeled interior was all metal and glass.

After stating his business at the front desk, Paul was directed to a large room containing half a dozen desks, most of them unoccupied. He scanned the nameplates until he found the one that read 'Kelsey', the officer who had called him earlier about the car. The man looked up when Paul approached.

"I'm Paul Becker," Paul said. "I'm here about the abandoned car."

"Have a seat," Kelsey said, indicating the visitor's chair next to his desk. He opened a drawer, took out a form and rolled it into his typewriter. "I need your driver's license and owner's registration."

Paul dug into his pocket and produced the documents, then watched as the officer transferred information to the form. Typing with two fingers and having to adjust the line spacing to the blank spaces on the form made the process slow and cumbersome. Feeling tension building again, Paul reached for his cigarettes, then paused.

"Is it okay if I smoke?" he asked.

Kelsey gave him an impassive stare and shrugged. "I don't care -- doesn't bother me."

Paul lit a cigarette and looked around at the empty desks nearby for an ashtray. Finding one, two desks away, he made a mental note to return it before he left. He drew in smoke and thought about the ease with which he had fallen back into these old familiar reflexes; just a feather touch on the trigger was all it took and the trap had sprung, as if his three years without a cigarette had never happened.

"When did you first notice your car was stolen?"

Paul found it hard to believe Kelsey's question. He studied the officer's raised eyebrows, the expectant expression and felt the anger start to rise from his stomach up into his chest, increasing his need for oxygen. The son-of-a-bitch didn't even remember their conversation on the phone. He took a deep breath and tried to make his voice sound controlled.

"The car *wasn't stolen.* I told you on the phone, I let my son borrow it last night to take his girlfriend to their Prom, and now Kevin's *missing*"

Kelsey raised his hand, palm outward. "We don't know that to be a fact," he said. "It's too soon. A lot of things could have happened. *Believe* me, I know how these young kids are today."

Paul clamped his teeth together, took Kevin's wallet out of his pocket and threw it across the desk. It landed in Kelsey's lap. "Look at that," he said. The keys followed with less vigor and stayed on the desktop.

Kelsey glared at him, then retrieved the wallet and began to examine its contents. His eyebrows arched again as he counted the money.

Paul pursued the offensive without waiting for a response. "Are you going to sit there and tell me that my son would hide his *wallet* in the seat cushions, put the *keys* under the seat and then *walk away*? To do *what*? To bum around with no money or wheels? *Fat chance.* "

Kelsey took a deep breath, then his cheeks ballooned as he exhaled through compressed lips. Paul folded his arms across his chest and waited. Kelsey picked up the keys, jiggled them in his hand, then looked back at the wallet again, his jaw muscles working as though he were chewing a piece of gristle. Paul thought he could almost see him thinking. "Well, I guess this puts a new light on things, doesn't it?"

"I would say that, yes."

"In view of the evidence, I have to admit there's some possibility of foul play here."

Paul's mouth smiled, but not his eyes. "Well, well, it looks like I finally have your attention."

Kelsey's face made an attempt at atonement. “Look, Mr. Becker, it's nothing personal. It's just that we get reports of missing kids all the time. Parents call -- or come in -- all excited their teen-ager didn't come home last night, and in almost every case the kid finally comes home, safe and sound. Usually it's because they split up with their sweetheart or had a fight with their parents and want them to worry. You know -- get even.”

He went to a file cabinet and returned with another form. “I'll send out a 'missing' report.”

“Good,” Paul replied.

Kelsey produced a legal pad and looked at Paul. “There's no point in making you wait while I type the whole thing out; I'll just jot down the necessary information and do the rest when you leave.” He took Kevin's driver's license out of the wallet. “Do you happen to have a recent photo of him with you?”

Paul reached for his wallet. “As a matter of fact, I do. My wife took it about a month ago.”

Kelsey examined the photograph. “He's a pretty big fella.”

“Yeah, he had no trouble making the football team.”

“How tall is he, and what's his weight?”

“Five-ten,” Paul answered, beaming. “Two more inches and he'll be looking me straight in the eye. And, ah -- let's see, it seems to me he was a hundred and fifty, the last I heard.”

“Any distinguishing marks, scars?”

Paul searched his memory. “Oh, yeah -- a scar on the back of his left wrist, a cleat mark. Got it last spring, sliding into second base.”

“All around athlete, huh?”

“Yes, and I'm glad. We need to get more kids interested in sports -- helps work off some of the energy and keeps 'em out of trouble.”

“That's the truth.” Kelsey made notes and looked again at Kevin's driver's license. “Is he still eighteen?”

“Yes, he'll be nineteen in August.”

Kelsey checked over his notes and looked up. “That should be it for now. If we need anything more, I have your phone number.” He gave the wallet and keys back to Paul. “I'll have to keep the photo.”

“That's okay,” Paul said, getting up. “How long does it take to get this report spread around?”

“We do it electronically. It'll go to missing persons and headquarters, then out to every precinct. Shouldn't take more than an hour, hour and a half at most.”

Relieved of most of his hostility now, Paul managed to smile as he shook Kelsey's outstretched hand.

The sun was just starting to set when Paul began the drive home. He found it hard to believe the day was ending already. The first truly beautiful day of the season and it was gone without his hardly having noticed. Kevin had mentioned that he wanted to discuss his college choice, and Paul had promised to spend the day with him. Kevin's 'B+' average gave him the advantage of being able to pick and choose; he had been accepted by two prestigious schools already, and there was still one more to be heard from.

Paul remembered how reluctant Kevin had been about discussing his choice of studies. It was only after his insistent prodding that Kevin agreed to talk, and then it came to light that he was worried Paul would be disappointed. He wanted to be a computer engineer and would not be following in his dad's footsteps. It was also discovered that his fear of disapproval had been reinforced on several occasions by Paul's disparaging remarks about the computer engineers with whom he worked.

The memory of the conversation brought back the agony Paul had felt that day at having to face a truth about himself, one that he had been denying for a long time.

"Kevin," he had said, "when I try to make those guys look stupid, I'm covering up my own fear -- fear of losing control. In my field, right now, I'm a dinosaur."

He remembered the shock on Kevin's face. Then he had gone on. "That's right, I *am*. I can see the day coming when the computer will take over the actual designing function. And if I don't catch up with the state of the art, I'll find that I've become obsolete."

He lit a cigarette and consoled himself with the thought that the disclosures he made that day, painful though they were, had brought them to a closer understanding than ever before, especially when he said that he thought Kevin had made a wise choice, that electronics was the future.

Chapter 5

On command the garage door opened, and Paul pulled his car in next to Joan's. He shut off the engine and signaled the door to close, but made no move to get out. A barely audible ticking sound coming from under the hood was all that could be heard above the silence. Leaning back against the headrest with his eyes closed, he debated with himself for a minute. Then, having reached a decision, he locked Kevin's wallet in the glove compartment, removed the keys from the ring and put them in his wallet.

Joan met him at the door. "So? How did it go?"

"It took a while, but I convinced him to file a missing person report."

Her face seemed to crumble with the finality of his words, as if a door had slammed on the possibility of any benign explanation. Paul drew her into his arms and groped for the right things to say, but he never had been any good at offering words of comfort. He dreaded wakes and funerals for this very reason; they always left him feeling awkward and tongue-tied. His only thought now was to maintain hope in her, though he had very little of it himself right now.

"There's still a chance that everything will turn out all right. Just because we filed a report doesn't rule out the chance that he's still okay." He reached under her chin and tilted her head up to look into her eyes. "Honey we mustn't stop hoping." He kissed her lips briefly. "Together, we'll weather this thing."

She pulled away, and he saw her eyes dart to his shirt pocket. He held his breath and waited, but she said nothing. Then she smiled sadly and moved to a seldom-used kitchen cabinet where she dug into the inner reaches and produced an ashtray. She brought it to the table, then sat down.

"I did some thinking while you were gone, and…oh, I don't know...." She seemed embarrassed. "Do you think he could have been kidnapped?"

Surprised by her question, Paul sat down and took her hand. His first impulse was to laugh, but knowing that would only anger her, he checked himself. Normally Joan was quite levelheaded, so he was unprepared; he had to remind himself that the emotional impact of their situation might very well skew her judgment.

"Okay," he began cautiously, "let's talk about that."

Watching for a reaction from her, he reached for his cigarettes, tapped one out and lit it. When there was no response, he silently blessed her and went on. "I guess you could say we're pretty comfortable, financially. We don't have a mortgage on the house any more, I paid cash for my car, and between us we make enough to live well and still have some to invest for our future." He nodded in agreement with himself. "Yeah, we're doing all right. But I certainly wouldn't call us *rich* by *any* stretch of the imagination." He paused to tap cigarette ash into the ashtray that his wife so magnanimously had provided. "So, what would anyone hope to gain by kidnapping our son? The amount of cash I could raise -- *including* mortgaging our house -- would never justify the risks involved." He shook his head. "No, Honey, I think we can rule out kidnapping…the money just isn't there."

Her eyelids formed slits. "Of course you're right," she said, her lips making a humorless smile, "*if* money were the motive, but what if it's some *nut*?" She paused for effect. "You know as well as I, there's all kinds of crazies out there -- you read about them almost every day."

Paul got up, walked to the sink, and looked out the window at the back yard. So far he had managed to skirt the more sinister aspects of the problem; some, of course, had occurred to him, but he had buried them in the back of his mind, choosing not to mention them, knowing what they would do to Joan. He could feel her eyes boring into his back, waiting for a reply. Trying to think of what to say, he returned to the table and sat down.

He could see the change in her eyes; normally golden hazel, worry and strain had turned them dull, flat. "Naturally, the thought has crossed my mind, but if we allow that kind of speculation to torture us, we'll wind up crazy, too. I wish I could share one of my traits with you. You know me, I just don't let myself borrow trouble, I wait until it comes, then I think of how I'll deal with it."

He stopped then, and the silence that followed was interrupted by an audible growl from his stomach. Joan glanced at the wall clock and got up. She opened the refrigerator, took out the steak and probed it with her finger to test if it had thawed. "You must be starved," she said, cutting away the plastic wrapper. "We did agree on baked potato and corn as a vegetable, didn't we?"

"Yes." He thought to relieve her of having to cook by suggesting they go out to eat, but changed his mind; she was nervous enough now, and eating in a public place would only aggravate the condition.

"I guess I do tend to meet trouble head-on." She turned the broiler on, then wrapped the potatoes in paper napkins for the microwave. "I wish I *could* be more like you. But that's the way I've always been, and it's too late in life to change now."

Paul managed to eat most of his food; Joan left more than half of hers untouched. When they finished, she decided to wash the dishes by hand. He took the editorial section of the newspaper with him into the now darkened living room to see if he could occupy his mind.

Paul had read only half of the first column when the doorbell chimed. He called out to Joan that he would get it, and when he opened the door, an invisible hand yanked that cord in his groin again and roiled the contents of his stomach.

In the doorway stood a stranger holding up a badge in a leather case.

Chapter 6

The man wore a hat, a dark gray suit and an expression that suggested he might be in pain. "I'm Sergeant Joe Finnelli," he said, "are you Paul Becker?"

Paul stepped outside and closed the door behind him. "Yes, I'm Paul Becker."

The sergeant looked at Paul, then the closed door and narrowed his eyes.

"I'd rather not have my wife in on this just yet," Paul explained quickly.

Fennelli nodded knowingly, but his face remained unchanged. "We think we've found your son -- at least, we're pretty sure -- but you'll have to come down with me and make a positive identification."

The phantom hand pulled the cord tighter, and the roiling in his stomach increased until Paul thought he might lose his undigested meal. He leaned against the doorframe for a moment, trying to find his voice. Maybe he misunderstood.

"Does that mean...." The need to swallow cut him off.

"I'm sorry," Fennelli said with a grimace.

It was obvious to Paul that the man was not happy with his job at this moment.

"Was it an accident?"

"No, Mr. Becker, he died of multiple stab wounds."

It took a moment for the words to sink in, then Paul squeezed his eyes shut and moaned. He swayed slightly, and the rhythm of his pulse boomed like kettledrums in his ears while visions of his son's bleeding body filled the eye of his mind with their horror.

"Maybe we should go inside where you can sit down," the sergeant said. "You don't look so good."

Paul managed to open his eyes, shutting off the apparitions. He steadied himself with a labor of will, and the drums gradually slowed to a distant beat.

"I'm okay now," he said, turning to open the door. "I have to break the news to my wife."

Fennelli followed him inside, but remained standing in the entrance hall. Paul heard Joan's voice coming toward him as he walked into the living room. She came into view, drying her hands on a dishtowel.

"Who was that at the door?"

They met in the middle of the room, and Paul felt her body stiffen as he took her in his arms. He knew she must have seen it in his face. He moved her to the couch and made her sit down with him. She looked at him, eyes wide, glassy.

"They found him," Paul said.

Her chin quivered. "He's dead, isn't he?"

Paul lowered his eyes and nodded.

"What happened?"

He searched for a milder word, but there was none. "He was stabbed," he said finally.

No sound came at first, then her shoulders hunched up and sobs broke forth in choking gasps. He held her until the spasms subsided to a soft weeping. When finally she found her voice, the words were broken. "Oh, Paul...." She stopped to wipe away a tear only to have another take its place. “How… how could this…happen?” She buried her face in the towel.

“I don't know,” he said. “You hear about things like this, but you think you're immune; it always happens to someone else, never you.” He shook his head. “I wish I had an answer for you, Honey, but I don't.”

Paul felt another presence near and turned to find Fennelli standing at the end of the hall.

“Joan, I have to go with Sergeant Fennelli and identify the body.”

She looked up at the officer, and her face went blank for a moment, as if her mind needed time to come to terms with this intruder.

“Give me a minute,” she said, getting up to walk away.

Paul grabbed her arm. “You don't have to come with us. You're not up to it.”

She started to speak, but he reached out and gently covered her mouth with his hand. “Stay here, Honey…*please*?”

She pushed his hand away. “What's there to stay here for? He won't be calling any more.” Turning and walking away, her voice trailed behind her. “It's over, Paul,” she said. “It's all over.”

When she was gone, Paul turned to Fennelli with a sigh and a shrug.

They rode in silence the first few miles; Paul and Joan sat in the back seat while Fennelli drove the unmarked car. The nights cooled quickly in May, so they rode with the windows closed and the vent mixing outside air with the heat of the engine to maintain comfort. At Foster Avenue they entered the Kennedy Expressway, and Fennelli maneuvered the car into the inner lane, then picked up speed. He was the first to speak.

"Did your son ever talk about Indian Road Woods, Mr. Becker?"

Paul searched his mind to pinpoint the location. "Isn't that the small piece of land between those two golf courses?"

"That's right. It separates Edgebrook and Caldwells golf clubs -- the north branch of the Chicago River runs through it. I *thought* you'd know where it was; it's not far from where you live."

"Yeah," Paul said, "but I don't recall Kevin ever mentioning it. Why do you ask?"

"That's where he was found. A man walking his dog discovered him sometime this morning -- actually it was the dog that found him -- in a thick bushy area."

Joan sat up straight. "This *morning*?"

Finnelli caught the implication. "I know," he said, quickly, "how come you weren't notified sooner? He didn't have any identification on him. He was just a John Doe to us then. It wasn't until the missing report came out that we made a connection."

"When the officer called about the car this morning, my husband told him Kevin was missing, but he wasn't interested."

"I'm sorry, Ma'am, I don't know anything about that. Lieutenant Burnett and I didn't see the report until early this evening, but we got on it right away."

"Well," Joan said, easing back into the seat, "I'd sure like to give that first one a piece of my mind, just the same."

"How does Lieutenant Burnett fit into this?" Paul asked.

"He's in charge of the investigation. We're both with the Homicide Division. I usually assist him."

Paul felt there was more to Fennelli's original question. "I still don't know why you asked if Kevin was familiar with Indian Road Woods. Did I miss something significant there?"

The sergeant was slow to answer, and when he did, it seemed to Paul that the man took care to choose his words carefully.

"Well," he began slowly, "it's used mostly by joggers during the day, but it's very secluded at night. There's no lights and it's closed to the public. A car parked in there at night is completely hidden from view. A tip came in a while back that it was being used for drug buys. It was staked out and a couple of busts were made."

It was obvious to Paul where the detective's reasoning was leading them, but he checked his resentment. "So, you think Kevin was involved with drugs."

There was another pause. "We can only go by our past experience with cases like this, Mr. Becker. It has all the earmarks of a drug deal gone sour."

When there was no explosion of protest at this from Joan, Paul turned and saw her staring out the window. Her expression held no concern for what was said, and when he looked closer, at her eyes, he got the impression that she was looking out beyond the city lights, as if at some distant, more reasonable world. He reached out to her, but stopped short of contact. He decided that maybe she needed this temporary reprieve from reality.

Leaning forward, Paul lowered his voice. "I hate to burst your bubble, Sergeant, but I assure you my son was not involved with drugs. He was an honor student and a star wide receiver on his high school football team. We made it our business to know all his friends, and he never made any attempt to conceal his activities or his whereabouts." It surprised him that he was using the past tense already. "He had decided what courses he would take in college to insure his plans for what he wanted to be. Does that sound like someone who's involved with drugs?"

Fennelli's head remained cocked for a moment, as if waiting for more information. When he did speak, Paul still could hear residual doubt. "If what you say is actual then we have to look for some other motive. It's just that first appearances naturally led us to that conclusion. We weren't trying to point a finger, or attach any blame. We look at a crime scene and tend to draw our conclusions from past experience."

"Yeah," Paul said, "I guess I can see how it would point you in that direction."

They left the expressway and rode through the city's streets until Fennelli turned into the parking lot of a huge, gray-stone building. Paul's mind had been busy elsewhere during most of the drive, so he had no precise idea where they were, except that this was somewhere in the inner city. Joan awakened from her nether world when Fennelli opened the door and took her arm to help her out. Paul joined them, and, taking command of his wife, they walked to an entrance marked 'Emergency', which told him the building was a hospital.

They rode an elevator to a subbasement that seemed to have an atmosphere separate from the rest of the structure. Fennelli led them through a set of swinging doors, down a corridor, and into a waiting room. He indicated a chrome and plastic couch and told them he would be right back.

In all this time Joan had said nothing. Her silence was out of character and it worried Paul. "Are you okay?"

She closed her eyes. "Yes, I'm all right -- don't worry."

But he did worry. He suspected that she had set up some kind of defense mechanism that was separating her from reality. While the device might shield her from pain, he thought it was unhealthy, maybe even dangerous. Still, his lack of knowledge in the mysteries of psychology made him hesitant to try to break through to her, to tamper.

He was spared making any decision by Fennelli's return, in the company of another man, wearing a knee-length white smock.

"This is Doctor Iwasaki," Fennelli said, "one of our medical examiners."

Paul nodded and the doctor signaled them to follow him. They were led down the original corridor, through another set of swinging doors and into a room that recalled scenes from movies Paul had seen. Along the walls were tiers of drawers, the contents of which he knew without being told.

The doctor went at once to one of the drawers, pulled it out, then motioned for them to come forward, and, watching their faces closely, he drew back the sheet revealing the cadaver's head and part of one shoulder.

Joan gasped and dug her fingers into Paul's upper arm with a power he never would have imagined she had.

CHAPTER 7

Looking down at the face of this familiar stranger on the slab, Paul watched the fragile vessel of hope dissolve before his eyes. There could be no doubt; this white faced, lifeless form was the body of his son. And in this moment that seemed to stretch out beyond reason, he looked into those staring, vacant eyes and found himself searching for the soul that once was his son. Instead he found just the empty dwelling where it had lived. The tenant had fled.

Paul felt Joan's hand relax its grip on his arm, then saw her reach out and pull the sheet back to expose the torso. Her movement had caught both him and the doctor by surprise, and in the moment it took Iwasaki to respond and replace the sheet, the wounds lay open to view.

Paul saw what he thought were five or six gaping slits scattered over the chest and abdomen, and suddenly there came a sinking sensation in his diaphragm, as if he too had suffered a puncture through which air now rushed out of his lungs. He breathed deeply a few times to replace the imaginary loss and help him recover from the shock.

An instant later, he felt the weight of Joan's body as she slumped against him. He managed to stop her fall, and with Fennelli's help, they lowered her gently to the floor. The doctor, who had vanished unnoticed, returned now with a gurney.

"This happens sometimes," he said. "Let me take her head and shoulders. You two lift her middle and her legs." When they had changed positions he said, "Together now, lift." Paul and Fennelli guarded the sides of the cart as the doctor wheeled Joan down the corridor.

"We have a recovery room for this sort of thing," Iwasaki said. "We'll revive her and let her rest for a while."

The room, which contained three beds, was in a hall off the main corridor near the elevators. When they had transferred Joan to one of the beds, Paul was told to wait outside. Fennelli led Paul back to the waiting room with the chrome furniture, then left to make a phone call. Next to one of two mismatched chairs sat a metal stand, topped with a bowl of sand to serve as an ashtray. Paul sat down, fumbled for a cigarette and lit it with unsteady hands.

After twenty-one years of marriage he thought he knew all there was to know about his wife, but her impulsive act back there with the sheet made him wonder. What she did was irrational, as if she had wanted to punish herself. But what for? None of this was her fault. She had helped raise a son that anyone would be proud of. Then why? He shook his head. The answer eluded him now, but he vowed to pursue it. It worried him.

The door swung open and Iwasaki leaned in. "She has come around. You may see her now."

Paul snuffed the cigarette out in the sand and walked back to the recovery room with the doctor.

"We were a little concerned. It took a while to bring her around. Her blood sugar must have dropped -- not an unusual thing, I might add. We got her to drink a can of Coke to bring it up again. She'll be all right, but I want her to rest for half an hour or so before you take her home."

"Yes, of course," Paul agreed. "It took me by surprise. She's never fainted before -- at least, that *I* know of." The elevator doors opened just as they passed by, and Fennelli got out with another man.

"Mr. Becker," he called, "hold up a minute."

Paul stopped, and the two men approached. "This is Lieutenant Burnett," he said, indicating his companion. "Lieutenant, this is Paul Becker, the victim's father."

They exchanged greetings, then Paul said, "I was just going in to see my wife."

"That's okay," Burnett said, "you go ahead. We'll wait for you. We have to talk when you're finished."

"I just want to see how she is…I won't be long."

Joan's eyes were closed when Paul entered. He went to the bedside and noticed that her color still had not returned. She looked so vulnerable. He leaned down to kiss her forehead, and her eyes, minus the gold flecks, fluttered open.

"You okay?" he asked, feeling foolish with the question.

"I'm still a little weak. They've gone to get me some more cola." She shook her head. "Oh, Paul, I'm so embarrassed."

"Don't be," he said. "The doctor said it happens quite often -- why do you think they provide this room if they didn't expect it to happen a lot?" He took her hand; it was like ice. "You had me worried for a while, but you look pretty good now."

"You lie," she said. "I can just imagine what I look like. But I don't care…nothing matters any more." Tears welled up and spilled over onto her cheeks. She closed her eyes and compressed her lips to stifle any sound.

Paul stood mute, helpless. What could he tell her? Why couldn't he find the words?

Iwasaki entered the room with another can of Coke. "Here you go, Ma'am" he said, helping her sit up. "I want you to take these." He held two small pills in his hand. "It's a mild sedative to help you relax."

Joan swallowed the pills and drank half of the cola, then Iwasaki motioned with his head to Paul.

"We'll be back in a little while," he said to Joan, at the same time urging Paul toward the door. Out in the hall he said, "Give your wife a few more minutes. In the meantime you can talk with the lieutenant."

Paul returned to the room where the two detectives were waiting. He took a seat and reached for his cigarettes, but the lieutenant already had his out and was offering one to him. Paul accepted and leaned back in the chair to wait for the other to begin.

"Joe filled me in on some things you told him on the way here," Burnett said, "so we've had to revise our thinking."

He sat down, draped his arm across the back of the couch and drew one bent leg up on the empty space next to him. The casual strength in the man's movements triggered Paul's interest. He made a quick appraisal and figured Burnett's age at about forty, which meant he had to be pretty good to have made lieutenant already. He was tall, perhaps six-two and maybe two hundred pounds, all of it spread evenly over a rangy frame. His hair and eyebrows were black; the eyes -- brown and set deep in a bony face -- had the steady, penetrating stare of a predator. Usually careful of first impressions, this time Paul's instincts prevailed over caution: he had a gut feeling that Burnett was competent.

"We're going to set aside the possibility of drugs and see if we can come up with some other motive," Burnett continued.

Paul interpreted this to mean they were not ruling it out completely, either.

Burnett's eyes narrowed. "I want you to dig deep in your memory now, Mr. Becker, and see if you can think of anyone who might have held a grudge against your son. Did he have any enemies?" He raised a restraining hand. "Take your time."

Images of Kevin's friends flashed across Paul's mind. He went back through high school and several years of elementary, to no avail, then shook his head. "No. I've gone all the way back to grade school -- I remember all his acquaintances -- but I can't come up with anyone that could be considered an enemy. Not that he's never had any squabbles -- maybe even a few fist fights way back when he was eight or ten -- but nothing so serious that would make an out-and-out *enemy*."

"You might think of something later -- right now, you're probably in shock. Any other children? Sometimes a brother or sister would know something you don't"

"No, Kevin was an only child. That's what makes this even harder for us...especially Joan." Paul saw a flicker of surprise in Burnett's face. "I know, you're wondering, 'why only one at our age'? Well, I was twenty-four and Joan was twenty-two when we got married, so naturally we wanted to start a family right away. But it didn't work out that way. She had three miscarriages over a three-year period -- we were just about to give up. Then she managed to carry Kevin full term. She had a hard time of it, and the doctor told us she couldn't have any more." He watched Burnett wince and shake his head. "Do you have children, Lieutenant?"

Burnett held up three fingers. "Two boys and a girl."

"Well, maybe you can understand what Kevin meant to us. *Joan* -- I know -- will never get over this."

"Sure, I could say I know how you feel," Burnett said, "but that wouldn't be true -- I'd have to be in your skin to know that." He paused, then took a new course. "I know it's hard to talk right now, so I'll stop by your house tomorrow. I'd like to get a list of your son's friends and acquaintances."

"Yes, of course. There's an address book in his room -- I'll look for it in the morning."

Burnett gave Paul his card. "If you think of anything in the meantime, give me a call; my home phone is there, too. Don't worry that you'll disturb me...I'm on call all the time."

Fennelli's beeper went off then, and he left to look for a phone. The sound of that personal electronic gadget tripped a switch in Paul's memory. It reminded him of the stereo headsets so popular now. He stood transfixed, holding Burnett's card and staring into space.

Burnett watched him for a moment. "You okay, Mr. Becker?"

Paul's eyes refocused, and he looked at the Lieutenant. "I just remembered…Kevin *did* make an enemy. But..." His nose wrinkled with doubt. "...the guy's in jail. At least, he's supposed to be."

Burnett's eyebrows shot upward. "Tell me about it."

"It's a long story. But, anyway, last year Kevin was directly responsible for the conviction of a man on a burglary charge. The guy was sentenced to three years last August." Paul's expression conveyed his doubt. "He couldn't be out *already*, could he?"

Burnett looked at the ceiling. "Eh, let's see, hmm…yeah, that's about right. If he behaved himself, he could be out about now."

"That's incredible "

"Not today. With the crowded prison system we have now, they're letting a lot of prisoners out on early release."

"Well, that's terrible."

"Tell me about it. We bust our asses trying to put these guys away, and they're back on the street again before their files can be brought up to date." Burnett shrugged. "What's this guy's name? I'll have his file pulled and call Prison Records."

Paul provided the information, including the dates of the trial and sentencing, and Burnett promised to get back to him later.

When he started to leave, Paul grabbed his arm. "When will I be able to make arrangements to...." He stopped, unable to say the words.

"I'm afraid it'll be a while, Mr. Becker. The medical examiner will have to go over the body."

Paul flinched. "An autopsy? "

Burnett raised his hand. "It's not what you think. We already know the cause of death, so there's no need to...ah...disturb the body. The M.E.'ll vacuum it for hairs and fibers, scrape the fingernails, measure the wounds to determine the kind of weapon used...."

"It was a *knife*, wasn't it?"

"Yeah, but there's all kinds of knives, Mr. Becker. We need to be more specific, like what kind of blade was it, how long, was it straight or curved, sharp or dull, the kind of information that tells us what we're looking for. Samples of his blood, saliva, scalp and body hairs will be taken to compare with any found on him that are foreign. His clothing has already gone to the forensic lab. They'll vacuum everything and examine every hair and fiber under a microscope. Believe me, Mr. Becker, they're very thorough, but it takes time."

"I understand," Paul said. "I've read about some of the miracles they perform." He didn't want to seem impatient, but felt he had to press. "Can't you give me some idea?" I have to make arrangements...notify relatives and friends, you know."

Burnett nodded. "Well, now that identification had been made, they can move the body to the lab, and I'll use my influence to get things moving. I have a good relationship with the Chief Medical Examiner. Besides, without something more to go on, there isn't much I can do." He paused and looked at the ceiling. "It's hard to tell. It'll be a few days, at least, but don't worry, you'll be notified as soon as they're finished."

The word 'notified' hit a nerve, and suddenly Paul had a dreadful thought. "Damn." he said.

The lieutenant looked puzzled. "What's wrong?"

"It just occurred to me -- has the news media been in on this?"

"I'm afraid so," Burnett replied. "They don't have a name yet, but they'll keep after us to furnish one. And there's a limit to how long we can stonewall 'em."

"Can you stall until we can call family and friends?"

"*I* can," Burnett said, with a whimsical smile, "but I can't guarantee they won't still get it. By now there's a lot of other people involved, and the press have ways. My advise to you is, as soon as you get home, get on the phone with those you want to know before they read about it in the morning papers. At least you won't have to worry about the late news on TV tonight -- too late for that."

"Thanks," Paul said, getting up. "I should see how my wife is doing."

"Sure, you go ahead, Mr. Becker, and I'll see you tomorrow."

Fennelli came back as Paul was leaving. "Let me know when you're ready," he said, "I'll drive you home."

Paul found Joan sitting on the edge of the bed. "Feeling any better?"

She nodded. "Let's go home."

"You sure you're okay?"

"Yes. I just want to get out of here and go home."

CHAPTER 8

Joan sat huddled against the door on her side, staring out the window. Paul reached out to take her hand, but she pulled away, as if from a stranger. He saw this as a further withdrawal into herself and felt powerless against it. Maybe it was best to let her come out of it on her own, but a nagging doubt told him of the danger in that. He wished he knew what was right.

When they left the Kennedy, Paul lit a cigarette and noticed the pack was half empty. He struck the lighter again and read the dial of his watch: it was ten-thirty-five. When they turned north at Central, he leaned over the front seat.

"There's a convenience store a little ways up the road, Sergeant," he said, "would you mind stopping for a minute? I'm almost out of cigarettes."

"Sure, no problem."

At the store, Paul thought of buying a carton, but changed his mind; there was something about it that spoke of total surrender, and he wanted to think of it as temporary. So he compromised on two packs instead.

Fennelli's attempt at solace when he dropped them off, seemed to echo Paul's ineptitude.

"You two try to get some sleep," he said, then seeing the futility, he added, "I know...that's easy to say."

Paul thanked him, and the sergeant drove away.

A bright moon, still low in the sky, cast dark shadows over the front of their house, and, looking up at it now, Paul felt strangely uneasy. Whenever he viewed it from this distance, the all-brick two-story never failed to radiate solidity, a sense of security, but now it seemed that something was missing, as if in their absence a thief had crept in and kidnapped the sentry. His home looked suddenly vulnerable.

So strong was this feeling as they moved up the walk that he tried turning the doorknob before using his key. He thought he had locked up that afternoon, but so much had happened since then, he doubted his memory. The telephone was ringing as they entered.

"I'll get it," Paul said. He closed the door and headed for the kitchen, turning on lights as he went.

The voice on the phone was soft and young. "Mr. Becker?"

He knew who it was without asking: how many times had he heard this voice ask, "Is Kevin home?"

He thought he would have time to think about how to say it, but here it was, and all he could manage was, "Hello, Kim."

"I've been calling all evening…where's everyone been?"

"We just now walked in the door."

"Is Kevin with you? Can I talk to him?"

He could see her in his mind, holding the phone impatiently, waiting to hear the voice he could not produce. His mind raced. "Is you mother at home?"

"Why?"

"Kim, I just want to be sure you're not alone."

There was a pause. "Something's happened -- tell me -- what is it?"

"Kimberly, *please*, call your mother. I won't say another word until you do."

He could hear her breathing, then the phone being put down. Several moments later he heard Kim's voice coming back toward the phone. "I don't *know* what it's all about, Mom, he just wants to talk to you."

"Hello." The voice was modulated, pleasant.

"Oh, Mrs. Adams, I'm so glad you're home and Kim isn't alone...because I have very bad news. We got word this afternoon that Kevin has been killed, and I was afraid to tell Kim if she was alone."

"I see," she said, no trace of panic in her voice.

Although he had never met her, he felt immediate admiration for this woman. He knew she was a widow and that her pilot husband had been killed in a corporate jet crash when Kim was only thirteen. And now, the way she was handling this situation, he could see how she had managed to continue raising Kim so successfully without the help of a husband.

"How?" she asked, again without divulging anything.

"They found him in Indian Road Woods -- stabbed. We don't know who or why. The police are investigating. They'll no doubt be asking questions of everybody who was with him last night, and Kim was the last one we know of to see him alive so maybe you can prepare her."

"Yes, of course. And I want to thank you for being so considerate of us in this matter. I'd like to call back later to express my feelings, if it's all right with you."

"By all means," Paul agreed.

He heard Kimberly in the background clamoring for information, then the click of the connection break. He went to the dinning room, opened the liquor cabinet and poured two fingers of bourbon, drank it straight and poured again.

There was no doubt in his mind that Kim's mother was the most qualified to break the news to Kim; a stroke of brilliance, considering he had acted on the spur of the moment. One down, and...how many more to go? Good Lord. There was his brother and his sister, Joan's sister -- he remembered Cathy's request that Joan be at the store early tomorrow. He'd have to call her first. Then there was Tommy Reid...or should he let him find out when the story breaks? No, that wouldn't be right; he was Kevin's best friend. Besides, Tommy could notify their whole circle of friends. But first he had better check on Joan. He put his drink aside and went upstairs.

The lights were on in their bedroom and bath, but Joan was not there. Returning to the hall, he saw a sliver of light under Kevin's door and he groaned; that was the worst place for her right now. So far, his concern for her had kept his own grief at bay; now he just had to hang in there until she went to sleep. Surely she must be worn out from the strain.

She was sitting on the bed, holding in her lap the letter Kevin had won at the end of the football season. He took it from her and put it aside.

"Joan," he said, putting his arm around her, "you need to get some rest. Come on, let's get you undressed and into bed; have you got anything to help you sleep?"

She looked up, and for the first time that night, her eyes were focused on him and the vacant stare was gone.

"I'm sorry I've been so distant, Paul. I guess I just couldn't believe something like this could happen -- I refused to accept it. I'm not even sure if I do now. I keep thinking I'll wake up and find it was all a dream."

"I know. I'm not thinking too clearly myself right now. It's been a long, trying day...and tomorrow isn't going to be any better, so you simply must get some sleep."

She frowned. "Oh, Lord, I promised Catherine...."

"Forget it. I'm going to call her, she'll understand. I have to call my brother and sister, too. We can't just let them read about it in the papers."

"Kim! Oh, my God, poor Kimberly...."

"I've already called." A minor distortion. "I gave her mother the message, figuring she'd know how to handle it better than us."

Joan was crying again, and he felt relieved that she was letting it out. Her silence had worried him.

"Oh, that poor little thing...what she must be going through now. She was *so* in love with him."

"Everyone loved Kevin."

She looked at him, eyes brimming. "*Somebody* didn't."

The name Steven Tate jumped into his mind. He remembered the lieutenant saying it was possible Tate could be on the street. If he was, would Burnett be able to tie him to the killing? Paul hoped his early assessment of Burnett was accurate. Usually he was right about first impressions: he felt the lieutenant was competent. But still, he had to admit it was based on nothing more than a gut feeling. Taking her arm, he gently led her out of the room, turning off the light as they went.

While she undressed in the bedroom, Paul opened her medicine cabinet and searched its contents until he found a bottle with a label that read: 'Take two at bedtime to induce sleep'. He remembered it for some dental work Joan had done that included root canal. A combination painkiller and tranquilizer, he saw that it was dated January of that year and figured it was still safe.

She was in her nightgown when he returned with a glass of water and two of the pills.

"Here, Honey, take these -- they'll help you sleep."

She took them without question and got into bed.

"I'm going downstairs to make some phone calls," he said. "I won't be long."

Clutching one of his handkerchiefs, she turned on her side and buried her face in the pillow. For a moment, he watched the involuntary movements of her shoulders, then, knowing she would cry herself to sleep, he turned out the light and went downstairs. He stopped in the dining room to make another drink before going to the phone in the kitchen where his voice would not be heard on the upper level.

He had intended to call Joan's sister first, but now, feeling the need to talk to someone closer, he punched in his brother's number.

"Hello, Ray," he said. "I hope I didn't wake you up...."

They talked for almost an hour, then, because it was getting late and he had more calls to make, his brother volunteered to call their sister for him. Later, after forty-five minutes of explaining everything again to Catherine, Paul felt drained. Tommy Reid would have to wait.

Paul undressed and got into bed where he lay still, quietly listening for any sound from Joan. When none came, he rolled onto his side. The pills must have worked; at least one of them would sleep. He was alone with his thoughts, and now, with the effects of the bourbon gone, the night stretched out endlessly before him. This was the longest day he could remember; not even the worst one in Vietnam could touch it.

Scenes flashed across his mind in quick succession, but the memory of Kevin's ravaged body remained constant in the end. He felt violated by the same evil that had killed his son. It seemed to penetrate the pores of his skin, and, like a dog after an encounter with a skunk, he squirmed and dug into the mattress in an effort to escape the stench of it. The day repeated itself over and over, always ending in the morgue with his wife's hand pulling back the sheet.

Eventually he slept.

CHAPTER 9

The room was bright when Paul awoke, and, glancing at the clock, he saw it was almost nine. Turning to look at Joan, he was relieved to see she was still sleeping. He got up, dressed and went downstairs. As soon as he had the coffee started, he went out for the paper and brought it back to the kitchen table. He scanned through the front section and found no mention of yesterday's discovery, but, on the second page of the local news, there was a column headed: Body of Young Man Found in Woods. He read past the already familiar details, to the last paragraph, the part that he hoped would be delayed. "Late last night, police identified the victim as 18-year-old Kevin Becker of...."

He looked away and shook his head. Well, there it was -- he could forget about breaking the news to their friends personally. The phone would be ringing all day. Maybe he should pull the jacks for a few hours -- at least until they had time to think -- get themselves ready for the onslaught of questions he knew would be asked. Then, just as he was about to go up and disconnect the two phones on the second floor, Joan appeared, looking half-asleep. He poured a cup of coffee for her and began setting the table.

He poured coffee for himself and sat down. "I guess the pills worked, huh?"

She squinted at him. "*Too* good…I feel like I'm in a stupor."

"Drink some coffee."

He saw her looking at the opened newspaper and tried too late to pull it away. She read the column, then looked up.

"They don't waste any time, do they?"

"I managed to reach your sister and Raymond; he said he'd call my sister. It was pretty late."

The telephone rang and Paul answered it.

"Paul, I'm glad I caught you."

He covered the microphone and whispered to Joan, "It's Fred Woodward."

"I read about it this morning and, Paul, I can't tell you how sorry I am."

"Thanks, Fred."

"I won't bother you with questions. I'm sure you have enough on your mind already. I just wanted to tell you to take whatever time you need. Don't worry about this place, just take care of your family. Whenever you feel up to it, give me a call."

Paul remembered the drawing he had brought home on Friday. "Yes, I'll keep in touch. But first, can you send that kid from shipping over here this morning? I have a drawing that I'll mark up, giving you a quick mechanical fix on that problem we talked about. It should be done electronically, but this way might be quicker."

"Hey, I don't want you bothering with things like that now."

"It'll only take a few minutes. The kid can pick it up and have you back in business this afternoon. No arguments; just send him over."

"Well all right, but that's it. I want you to forget work. Just do what you have to do. And, oh, let us know when the…ah…interment is; I want to be there."

"I will. And thanks for your concern, Fred." Paul hung up. "Well, it's started."

"Do you really have to mess with that now, Paul?"

"It's my job. I owe it to him."

In the basement, Paul made two dimensional changes and altered one angle, then rolled up the drawing. He had wanted to let the computer boys sweat. It was their problem, really, but now he didn't have the time to argue the point. He went upstairs, put the drawing on the table in the front hall and rejoined Joan.

He lit a cigarette and poured his third cup of coffee. "I met Lieutenant Burnett at the morgue last night." Paul said. "He asked if Kevin had any enemies, and I mentioned Steve Tate."

"He's in prison," she shot back.

He told her what Burnett had said about crowded prisons and early release. "He's supposed to get back to me today."

Paul saw a scowl form on Joan's face and thought he could see anger swirling somewhere behind her eyes.

"Well," she began, "if he's not in jail, then he *did* it. I saw that man when he was out on bail before his trial. We were in the mall on Central when Kevin pointed him out to me. He saw us too, and I'll never forget the way he looked at Kevin." She closed her eyes and shook her head. "If ever I saw evil in someone's face, it was then. If looks could kill, well...." She hesitated, then opened her eyes. "I knew, right then, it was a mistake for Kevin to have got involved in that thing."

"Hey, let's not jump to conclusions. I seriously doubt he'd be out this soon."

She was glaring at him now. "Of course you'd hope he's still locked up, 'cause if he isn't, then it's your fault Kevin's dead."

Paul winced. "Now wait a minute -- "

"*No*, *you* wait a minute. I begged you to try to get Kevin to change his mind. But you said it was his decision to make."

"Joan, that's not fair. I warned him it might be risky. He did what he thought was right. I was proud of him."

"You let a seventeen-year-old boy make a decision some *adults* would have trouble with, and you're going to have to live with that."

She got up and put her coffee cup in the sink. "I'm going to get dressed."

Paul was stunned. He had no idea Joan still felt resentment toward him for not interfering in Kevin's decision. But what disturbed him most was that she could be right. What if Tate *was* out of prison? What if Tate *was* Kevin's killer?

He poured more coffee and lit another cigarette, while hoping fervently that his son's killer would be caught. If it turned out that it was Tate, then Joan would be right; he'd have to live with that the rest of his life.

CHAPTER 10

Burnett called at two that afternoon to be sure Paul was at home and to say he was on his way over. Joan prepared a side-table with an automatic coffee maker and heat-and-serve sweet rolls that had been in the freezer since her last club meeting. The room contained four easy chairs and a TV.

Fennelli was with the lieutenant, and the sergeant's face lit up when he saw the spread. He turned to Joan. "You're very thoughtful, Ma'am. It's been a long time since lunch."

Burnett gave him a sour look.

Paul sat down in the chair opposite Burnett's. "Help yourselves."

Fennelli took coffee and a roll, Burnett only coffee.

When everyone was seated, Burnett spoke first. "I was right about time off for good behavior -- Tate's on the street -- has been for two months."

He reached for the file Fennelli had been holding, opened it and let a computer printout unfold to the floor. Paul estimated its length at six feet.

Burnett held it up with one hand and looked at Paul. "This guy has quite a history."

"Is that just *Tate's* record? Hell, he can't be more than twenty-five years old, can he?"

"He started early. His first offense was when he was twelve. Mostly petty thefts in the beginning, but it didn't take him long to graduate to burglaries. By the time he was sixteen he was into assaults, muggings, assault and battery, but burglary seems to be his specialty." Burnett began refolding the sheet, stopping at intervals to cite various offenses. "He's what we call a career criminal. For instance, what do you do for a living, Mr. Becker?"

"I'm an engineer."

"Joe here, and I make our living as cops. This guy makes *his* committing crimes -- it's what he does; it's his trade, or profession, if you want to stretch it. And -- "

Joan interrupted. "How can this be? I thought we had habitual criminal laws."

The officers exchanged cynical smiles. Burnett looked at her and the smile disappeared. "Yes, we have…and at one time, they were enforced. But you're going way back now, way back, before I ever joined the Academy." He leaned forward, face intense. "Our job isn't as easy as it was back then. For instance, there was a time when killing a cop was something a crook wouldn't even think about -- when it meant the death penalty -- now you read about it all the time."

He leaned back and raised the 'rap' sheet again. "I'll turn this over to the psyco-boys for a profile study, but I can tell you already what they'll say. This is a violent man. He has no conscience. He's been arrested numerous times, and the charges have been dismissed due to witnesses changing their stories or not showing up at all."

Joan frowned. "Why is that?"

"Because this guy has built himself a reputation for violence -- witnesses know what will happen to them if they testify against him." Burnett turned to Paul again "And the few times he *has* been locked up, he's never had to serve more than a fraction of his sentence. Pretty soon he believes everyone is so afraid of him, that he's become invulnerable. When I see a history like this, I know it's only a matter of time 'till he kills somebody."

He gave the 'rap' sheet back to Fennelli to refold, and the room was quiet while Burnett refilled his coffee cup.

"Well," Paul said, "I can't say I haven't read about these things in the papers, but I guess we never know how serious a problem it really is until it touches us." He raised his eyebrows at the lieutenant. "So, what do you think?"

"Did Tate make any threats to your son, either before, or after the trial?"

"I don't know, for sure. Word kind of filtered back that he said he wouldn't forget who got him into trouble."

"But not an out-and-out threat? That he intended bodily harm to anyone in particular?" Burnett frowned. "How did your boy get involved in the first place?"

"It all started when one of Kevin's friends showed him one of those stereo headsets all the kids seem to have now, and my son recognized a familiar marking scratched into the underside of the metal headband. I don't know what kind of marking it was, but Kevin said it was something that Bob Kowerski, another one of his friends, had a habit of putting on all his valuable possessions. Anyway, it seems that Kowerski's home had been burglarized a while back, and this was one of the items taken." Paul hesitated.

"Go on," Burnett urged, "what happened then?"

"Well, the kid said he bought it from some guy who had a lot of electronic equipment for sale in his garage."

"You mean this guy was selling the stuff in the same neighborhood he *stole* it from?"

"No, no; it's a long story. The kid who bought it heard about some great bargains in electronic gadgets from someone else, who then put him in touch with Tate. Anyway, after the Kowerski kid identified it as the one stolen from his home, the three of them talked about going to the police. But, as it turned out, Kevin was the only one brave enough. A search warrant was issued, and they found more of the Kowerski family's items, and Steve Tate was arrested."

"Wait a minute. Did Kevin testify at the trial?"

"No, not with all the evidence they had. But it was easy for Tate to find out who finally blew the whistle."

When Burnett looked doubtful, Joan told him about her and Kevin's encounter with Tate in the shopping mall, making Tate's ominous stare seem even more evil than she had in the first telling.

When she finished, Burnett nodded sympathetically. "I know, Ma'am, but I'm afraid we still can't consider that a threat. It's just your opinion of his expression."

Joan's face took on a stubborn set. "Well, there's no doubt in *my* mind. He's the one, all right."

"Don't get me wrong, either of you," he said, looking at Joan and Paul in turn. "As far as I'm concerned, I consider Steve Tate a suspect, but we can't do anything about it at this point. I'd pick him up, but we don't have any evidence at this point...no probable cause."

Shaking her head, Joan left the room, mumbling something to herself about criminal rights.

When Burnett turned to him, Paul could read the frustration in the lieutenant's face. He imagined how hard it must be for cops like Burnett. Most citizens tend to see everything in their own black or white logic, making no allowances for the gray areas of the law that the police have to take into account. He wished he could be of more help, then he remembered Kevin's address book and offered it to Burnett, who turned it over to Fennelli.

"Joe'll go over it and get back to you later on specific names. Have you got anything else that might help?"

"No, but I have a few thoughts that bother me."

"Go ahead, what?"

Paul tilted his head and squinted. "Well, I just can't figure out how Kevin could be overpowered and taken to that remote spot without putting up a fight. He was no weakling, and he certainly didn't scare easily. I just can't imagine it."

"I was going to get around to that," Burnett said. "The lab did an analysis on some gauze found near the scene. They said it was once saturated with ethyl ether. We figured the car was forced over to the curb, and the assailant grabbed him fast and covered his face with the gauze. He probably struggled, but that makes it worse, because than he's breathing heavy and it doesn't take long to knock someone out with that stuff."

"*Ether*? I didn't think that was available to just *anyone*."

"It's not just used as an anesthetic; it's a solvent, too…model makers use it a lot. Anyway, your kid didn't have a chance."

"Then," Paul said, hopefully, "maybe he was unconscious during the..." He searched for a less graphic phrase. "...rest of the attack."

Burnett's expression looked pained, as with empathy. "I'm afraid not, Mr. Becker." He seemed to fumble deliberately as he lit a cigarette. "He was bound hand and foot, but the lab found a lot of ground-in dirt on his clothing -- at the elbows, hips and shoulders -- indicating he struggled violently against the rope." He paused and shook his head. "No, it looks like his attacker wanted him conscious…like he wanted him to know who, and why."

Paul shuddered at the mental image Burnett's words created. "I'm glad this didn't come up while my wife was here."

"I know what you mean. We'll watch what we say when she's around." Burnett turned to Fennelli. "Won't we, Joe?"

At the sound of his name, Fennelli looked up from the notes he was making from Kevin's address book. "Yeah, sure."

Paul was disappointed. He thought the scientific group, with all their new equipment and techniques would have found more "Hasn't the lab come up with any clues at all?"

Burnett compressed his lips and squinted, as if debating his answer. "Okay," he said, finally, "yes, they did find a small piece of evidence. It might not seem like much to you, but we have to keep that kind of information under wraps. A leak of any kind could tip off the guilty party to cover his tracks."

"I understand. You have to protect the evidence."

Burnett raised his eyebrows. "That reminds me, has the Press been in touch with you yet?"

Paul caught the implication, remembering TV newscasts he had seen, ones showing witnesses and family members being badgered for statements. "Not yet, thank God."

"Believe me, they'll be in touch. Someone has to do a follow-up on this morning's story. They'll be looking for human interest and anything else they can wheedle out of you. I recommend you say that you and your family need privacy in your time of grief, then hang up the phone, or, if they show up in person, shut the door." Burnett then gave him a sly smile. "But don't tell them I said so. We've found it pays to cooperate with the press, so, if we get them mad, they can get real nasty."

"Thanks for the advice."

"We'll be in touch," Burnett said, getting up. "Thanks for the coffee."

Paul was walking them to the door when the telephone rang.

"You'd better get that. We'll find our way out."

True to Burnett's prophecy, the caller was a reporter doing a follow-up for the Sun-Times. And immediately following, as if on signal, another call came, this one from the Tribune. Paul used Burnett's suggested excuses on each and found that the only way to end the conversations was to hang up.

The phone rang again while he was using the bathroom, but it stopped on the second ring. Thinking it was another reporter, he hurried upstairs to help Joan get rid of whoever it was, but she hung up just as he reached her.

"That was Connie," she said. "She wanted to be sure we were home. She was worried that we wouldn't be eating properly, so she's coming over with food she's prepared. Can you imagine?"

"Knowing Connie? Yes," he replied. "My sister worries about everyone. She's something else. Did you know she even feeds the stray *cats* in her neighborhood?"

"*Paul*, don't make fun of her. Consider yourself lucky to have such a thoughtful woman for a sister."

The phone rang again and Paul answered.

"Mr. Becker?" Tommy Reid's voice was high-pitched with excitement. "I was just talking to Art Herman, a friend of mine, and he said he saw Steve Tate the other day. You remember *him*, don't you?"

"How could I forget? But...."

Tommy interrupted. "He was driving a gray Chevy van. Art said he saw him stopped at a light on Foster Avenue, and he got a good look at him." His voice swelled with self-importance.

"Yes?"

"Well, jeez, I thought you'd be surprised. He could be a suspect, couldn't he?"

"I appreciate your calling me about it, Tom. But I already gave his name to the detective handling the case, and he checked it out. Tate *is* out of jail."

"Oh." Tommy's voice flattened like a punctured balloon. "You already know then."

“Tom, you did the right thing. If I hadn't thought to mention it to the police, your call would have jogged my memory.”

“Anyway, I sure was surprised to hear he's out so soon.”

“We were, too, Tom…thanks for calling.”

“Yeah, okay, 'bye, Mr. Becker.”

Paul hung up, thinking how a van seemed so fitting for Tate; he could picture him loading it with loot. Worse, he could imagine him loading it with Kevin's body.

Chapter 11

Connie arrived at five, her car laden with covered dishes, which could be warmed-up when her husband, Ernie, got there after work. The children, she said, were best left at home; the oldest girl was taking the two younger ones out to McDonald's.

Ernie appeared at six, followed immediately by Paul's brother and his wife, Barbara, who explained that they had already eaten. Paul made drinks, and after the usual offers of sympathy, they spent the next hour discussing the events of the past two days. When he told them about the news the two detectives brought that afternoon, Paul noticed his brother's face getting red, which was no surprise.

"My warehouse was broken into three times in the past two years," Ray said. "The culprits in two of the break-ins were caught, and it turned out they were paroled felons." He paused, then went on. "So, this guy only served *nine* months of a *three year sentence*...with *his record*?" He used his fist to pound his knee. "It's no wonder the crime rate is what it is today; the jails have revolving doors."

"What's your solution?" Ernie put in. "Build more prisons?"

This challenge made Ray's face turn livid. "Hell, yeah, build more prisons."

"You willing to pay the taxes to accomplish that?"

"Damn right I am. We'll never get control if we don't get serious with these guys. Right now it's a joke. I just read about a guy who was sentenced to three hundred years for two torture murders, and the newspaper said he'd be eligible for parole in twenty. What kind of crap is that?"

Seeing where this was leading, Paul raised his hand to intervene, but he was saved the chore when Connie announced from the kitchen that dinner was being served.

By the time everyone got back together, Paul saw that Ray had calmed down, and he attributed that to Barbara's soothing influence on his younger brother's fiery nature.

Catherine and her husband, Bill, came by at eight to offer their sympathy, and, of course, the subject of the bathing suit display came up, so Paul steered Bill toward the other men while his wife discussed it with Joan.

It was almost eleven when the last couple had left, and Paul heard Joan's parting promise to spend some time with Catherine at the store the next day.

"Do you really think you're up to that?" he asked, turning off the outside light.

"I'm not going to spend the whole day there; just a few hours and then maybe go out to lunch with her, that's all." When he gave her a doubtful look, she said, "If I stay home, I know I'll just mope around here all day."

He studied her for a moment. Was she putting on a show for him, or was she actually getting back to normal? She had broken down several times during the evening, but he expected that. Maybe the company, having people around for a few hours, had been therapeutic. Everyone had been tactful; there was no reference made to the specific cause of Kevin's death. No gore.

"Well, maybe it *would* do you good to get out for a while, as long as you don't over do it."

Later, in bed, as they lay still awake, Joan reached out and patted his arm. "I thought sure you'd blow up at Cathy tonight."

"Why?"

"You know, when she said she wished we had taken her advice about moving out of the city."

He felt a twinge deep in his chest. "Oh, that."

"I remember how angry you got the last time she brought up the subject of crime and encroaching minorities, the wisdom of moving to the suburbs, where it's safe."

"I didn't need her to remind me. Don't think I haven't thought about it a few times over the past two days, but I refuse to deal in *what-ifs*."

"*What-ifs*?"

"Yeah, like what if we *had* moved to the suburbs, maybe this wouldn't have happened? You'll drive yourself crazy with that kind of thinking."

Of course he caught Cathy's remark earlier, but he let it pass rather than start an argument defending himself. Still, it was there at the back of his mind, waiting to torment him.

"Besides, I still think this neighborhood's safe. The same people have lived here most of their lives. They're good solid citizens, people who refuse to let fear and panic drive them out. We bought this house when we got married. We both loved it, and I still do. It's the only place we've ever lived. And whether your sister will admit it or not, there's crime in her town, too. There's crime everywhere today."

They spoke no more, and Paul turned onto his side to face the inevitable. His talk of not dealing in 'what-ifs' was, after all, just talk. Even now he tortured himself. If they *had* moved to the suburbs, Kevin would have changed schools; he would have made new friends; they never would have heard of Steven Tate, and none of this would have happened.

Paul got up and went down to the dining room, made a drink and lit a cigarette. He sipped the whiskey and smoked, poured more and lit another, but the thought persisted. He should have sold the house and moved out, like all the others. But no, he had to have this blind faith in the neighborhood and a stubborn attachment to a house that for him was a symbol of security and family unity. And, of course, Joan would never forgive him for letting Kevin get involved in Tate's arrest.

He thought of Kevin then, lying on that slab in the morgue, and all at once the rush of grief rolled over the barrier he had set up through it all. His diaphragm contracted then, driving the air from his lungs in great convulsing sobs. He leaned forward, burying his face in his arms to stifle the sound, and the tears broke their seal at last.

After a while, he went up to bed and finally slept. Along about morning, he awoke from a bad dream to semi-darkness, sweating.

Reaching out for his wife's comforting presence, he found empty space. If she had set the alarm, it would have wakened him. He slipped into a pair of jeans and went looking for her, and out in the hall, he noticed a light in Kevin's room.

Moving quietly, he entered and found her lying across Kevin's bed, asleep; the class yearbook lay on the floor below her outstretched arm. He had a vision of her crying as she leafed through the photographs, and, rather than suffer a repeat of his own breakdown during the night, he turned and went downstairs.

He opened the kitchen curtains to let in the gray light of morning, and later, on the front lawn with the morning paper under his arm, he paused in wonder at the glowing eastern sky. No matter that his personal world had crashed, the sun would rise, as it had on millions of other broken lives since the beginning, on schedule and oblivious to his pain. It reminded him of his insignificance.

As he lingered to watch the tip of the rising orange sphere, his mind cried out his anguish: 'God, where was your mercy? How could you let this happen?' But when the orange arc, unmindful, continued to grow and no answer came, he turned and went into the house.

A brief follow-up halfway through the front section, quoted the police as saying they had an ongoing investigation into the brutal murder Saturday of 18-year-old Kevin Becker on the far northwest side of the city. It said the parents of the victim refused to comment when contacted by reporters.

Paul tore off the top of the pack to get at a cigarette, and seeing only three were left, he decided to quit kidding himself and buy a carton next time. He had scanned through world news, most of the local and was on his third cup of coffee and second cigarette before Joan appeared.

Having dressed and applied make-up, she looked fresh at first glance, but the puffy lids and red-streaked whites of her eyes tarnished the illusion. Paul chose not to notice.

He rubbed his stubble of beard. "You make me look seedy."

She gave him a token smile of gratitude and sipped her coffee. "What are you planning to do?"

"I thought I'd go in and see how the Engineering Department is surviving without me."

"Ah, yes, the indispensable one."

Her impudence lacked the familiar ring he enjoyed so much, but he played along anyway. "And I suppose having to go to the store to help Catherine out doesn't make you feel important?"

"*Touche*." She got up and put her cup in the sink.

"You're not going in this early, are you?"

"If I have to change what she's done, I'd rather do it before she gets there...you know, surprise her without hurting her feelings."

He smiled. "How noble of you."

She swiped at him as she left the room, and he watched her retreating figure, admiring her attempt, though strained, to act as if all was normal.

Later, when he was about to leave for the plant, the coroner's office called to say that he could claim Kevin's body. The call left him drained and confused at first, but then he remembered Kilmer, the mortician his brother and he had used two years before when their mother had died. He placed the call and explained the details of his son's death. After a pause, Paul heard the trained, soothing voice of the undertaker.

"You have my deepest sympathy, Mr. Becker, but because of the delay, the wake can be only one night; the law prohibits anything longer."

"I understand."

"Very well. I'll claim the body for you and begin preparations immediately. Can you come in this afternoon to pick out a casket and discuss the funeral arrangements?"

"Yes, of course. I was going to drop in at work for a while, but that can wait. I'll come see you now if you're free."

"Fine. I'll be in my office when you get here."

Paul called the store and told Joan about the time limitation.

"*One night*?" He caught the edge of hysteria in her voice. "Oh, Paul, that means we can't run a notice in the papers -- nobody will know about it until it's too late."

"Calm down," he said. "We'll just have to stay on the phone this afternoon. My sister and Barbara can help -- they know most of our friends. Whoops, we need two lines; can you use your sister's phone?"

"Yes, but we'll have to decide who's going to call whom. Oh, never mind; we'll work that out later. I want to be with you at the funeral home when you're making arrangements. I'll be finished here in less than an hour and I'll meet you there."

"Okay. I'll call Connie now, and she can get together with Barbara. I'll tell them to just call the ones they know."

The funeral director's office door was open, and, recognizing Paul from previous business, Kilmer came out from behind his desk to offer the usual solicitous greeting. Paul imagined the discipline it must take to commit to memory the faces and names of all the families that must pass through this man's care. Eventually, all of us end up here, or someplace just like it.

Kilmer began the conversation by saying he was pleased that Paul had chosen his establishment again.

"Now, because time is of the essence," Kilmer said, "I set the wheels in motion immediately following our phone conversation; even now, my assistant is collecting your son's remains, and everything should be ready for mourners by this evening."

"That's good," Paul said. "We've got a lot of telephoning to do this afternoon to reach all our friends and relatives."

Kilmer leaned back in his swivel chair and assumed an air of concern. "There is one question, distasteful as it is, that I must ask." He frowned to show his reluctance. "Was your son's face...ahh... damaged in the attack by his assailant?"

Paul shook his head. "No. The wounds are confined to the torso."

"Good. Then there's no problem. We should have him ready by six at the latest."

Joan arrived then, and another hour was spent discussing details. They picked out a bronze casket and ordered a cement box. They already had a family cemetery plot, and Kevin would be placed next to his grandmother. At Paul's request, because they had not attended church services for so long, Kilmer agreed to arrange for the presence of a clergyman at graveside.

CHAPTER 12

At home, they made two lists of friends and relatives. Joan took hers back to the store where she would use the office phone, while Paul used theirs.

Because he postponed his visit to the plant, his first call was to Fred Woodward, who reiterated that Paul should take all the time he needed. The second number was Kimberly's. That it was on his list, surprised him; he thought Joan would have preferred to make that call. Hoping Kim would not break down, he pressed the numbers and held his breath. The phone was picked up on the first ring.

"Hello?"

He breathed again when he heard the soft, intimate tone of her mother's voice, the kind of voice that always made him wonder if the owner's looks would match the vision it evoked. This habit of his usually bred disappointment; he recalled one client's matronly secretary who on the phone sounded like a twenty-year-old sexpot.

"This is Paul Becker...." he began.

"I don't believe it," she said. "It's *uncanny*. I was just now looking up your number. I've been meaning to call, but when I saw the story in the paper, I figured you'd be plagued with intrusions on your grief. This must be excruciating for you."

"Yes. And you're right, we have been kept busy. We just got back from the funeral home, so I thought I'd call and let Kim know that tonight will be the only time for mourners. The medical examiner just released the body, and the law sets a time limit."

"I understand. And I'm grateful you called...we were worried there might not be a viewing at all."

"How is Kim?"

"Devastated. I'm taking some time off to be with her. People have told me, 'She's just a kid', but that simply isn't true. She's a woman, young and vulnerable. And, like you, Kimberly's my only child, and she needs me now in her time of sorrow."

"You're being very wise." Again, Paul was impressed with this woman, then he remembered Kevin mentioning some time back that she was a staff writer for a woman's magazine, the name of which escaped him now. "The funeral is tomorrow. It leaves Kilmer's Funeral Home at eleven, then on to Mt. Carmel Cemetery."

"We'll be there."

An awkward silence followed, then Paul said, "Well, yours was only the second of many calls I still have to make, so I guess I'll see you both tonight."

"Yes, and thank you again for calling, Mr. Becker. You've been very thoughtful."

It was five-fifteen when they arrived at the funeral home. Kilmer led the way to the casket, then, with a flourish of pride, stood back to allow their inspection.

When Joan's grip tightened on his arm, Paul turned and saw her eyes shut tightly with dread. Knowing she was bracing herself, he worried she might faint again. Kilmer also saw it and came around to take her other arm. Compressing her lips she opened her eyes and stared for a moment, then blinked as tears formed and swelled.

Satisfied that she was steady, Paul turned away and looked down at his son's remains, his eyes picking out details. The skin tones were good, the hair was parted as in the photo they had furnished Kilmer. The man's work was good.

But the longer Paul looked, the more he felt as if he were viewing a counterfeit, a skilled reproduction of the masterwork. He could identify the subject, but it lacked the soul the original Creator had brought to it. This was not the beautiful, vibrant being he remembered; some marauding beast had stolen that part.

He thought of Tate then, and the roots of rage stirred in the limbic system of his primitive old-brain, releasing adrenaline to do combat. He felt the need to strike out at something. But what? Then he noticed that his hands were balled up into fists. He forced his hands open, then shook them to release the tension.

Kilmer's voice broke the spell. "Do I have your approval?"

Paul looked at Joan, but she gave no sign that she heard. He turned to Kilmer and nodded. "Yes, you did good."

Apparently Paul and Joan had reached everyone; beginning at six-thirty, a steady stream of people passed through to view the remains and pay their respects. Kevin's teammates arrived, mostly in groups, awkward and ill at ease, especially when offering sympathy; some, unable to find words, merely nodded solemnly. Paul noticed two of them use the backs of their hands to wipe away tears; Tommy Reid found that his handkerchief was necessary.

Many of the young people were strangers to Paul, but then, other than the football team, he knew only a few of Kevin's classmates. And, befitting all Saturday's heroes, there was an impressive number of girls, also in small groups.

An extra wide couch, where Paul and Joan sat, and two upholstered chairs made up the front row. More cushioned chairs along both walls framed the rows of folding chairs in the middle, and by nine o'clock most of them were occupied. Paul could think of no one they had missed; all the available family and friends were there at some time during the evening.

During a break in greeting visitors, Paul's brother signaled with his eyes to join him at the back of the room.

"Time for a cigarette," Ray suggested. "Do we have to go outside?"

"No," Paul answered, directing him to a small room set aside for smokers.

Ray drew heavily on his cigarette, then sat back, frowning. Paul recognized his brother's discomfort. Although their personalities were dissimilar in most everything else, in this they agreed: both hated functions of this nature.

"How's Joan holding up?"

"I don't know how to describe it, Ray...she seems numb, like she's in a daze most of the time. Sometimes I get the impression she's built a wall around herself, shutting everything out -- including me."

"Barbara and I talked about that. She says it's going to take a long time for Joan to get over this. It might have been easier if he weren't an only child, but...." He shook his head.

"He was *my* only child, too."

Raymond smiled crookedly. "Yeah, but I've never worried about you -- you've always been a rock."

Paul remembered when they were growing up, the periods of instability he helped Ray get through. Even now, at forty-two, Ray still had a tendency to flare up like a young bull, with no thought of caution. It surprised him that Ray had managed to reach the level of success he enjoyed today.

"Have you heard anything more from the cops? Are they getting anywhere at all?"

"No, but it's still pretty early in the investigation."

Ray's face twisted. "*Bullshit.* What in *hell* are they waiting for? Why don't they pick up that bastard? What's his name? Oh, yeah, Tate."

"There's no evidence. You can't convict a man without some evidence."

Ray glowered and mashed out his cigarette. "Oh, I know. It's just that when I think there's some guy out there, walking around free -- after what he did to Kevin -- I get so mad I want to go after him myself."

"Take it easy, Ray. We don't know he did it. It might look like it to us, but you can't resort to vigilante justice. We have to let the police do their job. We have to believe the system works."

He was saying all the right words, but Paul knew they were meant mainly to calm Ray down; they had a false ring, even to his own ears. Only hours earlier, his own brain was sending messages of rage to his nervous system, demanding blood reserves for strength to do the very same thing for which he now criticized his brother. He watched Ray cock one eyebrow and sneer.

"The *system*? Come on, Paul. You read the papers and watch the news the same as I do. You know it fails more often than it works."

"Okay, so it *isn't* perfect...we still have to wait and hope it does."

When they went back to rejoin the others, Paul saw two women sitting with Joan. He recognized Kimberly in profile, dabbing at her eyes with a handkerchief while the other, whose back was to him, seemed to be talking earnestly to Joan.

Catching Kim's eye as he approached, he reached out and greeted her softly. "Hello, Kim."

At the sound of his voice, she was up and in his arms, weeping anew. "Oh, Mr. Becker -- " Her voice cracked.

"I know," he whispered, holding her and patting her back as he would were she his own.

After a moment, she drew back, looking embarrassed. "I'm sorry, I --"

"It's okay," he said quickly, "I understand…really."

She glanced toward the two women, then back at him. "Oh, you've never met my mother," she said, turning away again. "Mom, this is Mr. Becker."

Paul nodded. "Mrs. Adams, it's a pleasure."

"Diane…" she prompted, "...your wife and I are on a first name basis already. We were just saying, what a pity we have to meet, finally, under such circumstances."

"Yes," he said, "I guess we've allowed ourselves to get so busy we neglect the chance to make new friends."

He thought her eyes fascinating. The lightgray irises, with just a trace of jade undertone and accented by jet black haloes, lent a sense of mystery to her ancestry. He had seen eyes like hers only once before -- in a beautiful Eurasian woman.

They were interrupted then, by another couple paying their respects, and Paul became involved in conversation. But when he saw Kim and her mother preparing to leave, he broke away and walked them to the door.

"Kim," he said, "I hope you'll still visit us. I'd hate to think you'd stay away because of…well, you know. Joan and I think a great deal of you."

"I like both of you, too; you've always been nice to me." She gave him a weak smile. "It might take a while, but I'll come by to see you, I promise."

He turned to look at Diane.

"I told Joan I'd call her," she said. "We agreed to have lunch when she feels she's ready."

They said goodbye, and he watched them walk to the parking area. There was no doubt in his mind where Kim's beauty came from. While her blonde hair and light skin differed from her mother's darker tones, their facial bone structure was the same. But when it came to beautiful eyes, Kim's paled when compared with Diane's. This time, he was not disappointed; Diane surpassed the image suggested by her voice on the phone. He let the door close and walked back to the others. But on the way, he felt a stab of guilt. He had no right to his recent thoughts. And at a time like this. What kind of man was he?

It was after ten when the last of the visitors departed, and Paul convinced Joan that it was also time for them to leave. When he spoke to her on the drive home, she answered in monotones. She looked exhausted, and he thought she would go right to sleep, but, long after they had gone to bed, her breathing told him she still was awake. When he tried to hold her she moved away, drawing further into herself. He lay for a long time, wondering at his inability to reach her. Maybe she'd return to normal once the funeral was behind them. If not, he would insist she see their doctor.

But when he thought about that again, he wondered if an M.D. was what she really needed.

Chapter 13

Paul winced when he opened the drapes and looked out at the mud-gray morning sky. He had hoped the weather would hold, but now the threat of rain promised to make the day's grim proceedings even more depressing.

He was dressed and waiting when Joan came downstairs wearing a simple black dress that did nothing but heighten her pallor. When he hinted that her pearl necklace would look good with it, she said any adornment would be in poor taste. But then his frustration was blunted somewhat when she offered no resistance to his suggestion that they have breakfast at a restaurant on the way.

By the time they reached the funeral home, a light, steady rain had begun to fall and promised to continue throughout the afternoon. Kilmer, always prepared, furnished them with umbrellas and also made arrangements with the cemetery to have a canopy erected over the gravesite.

The number of people attending -- though not so great as the previous night's turnout -- was impressive. Other than the two limousines furnished for the immediate family, Paul guessed there were at least twenty private cars in the procession. At least half the football team was there, as were many of Kevin's classmates. Standing discretely at the fringe of the mourners was Fred Woodward, accompanied by three of the engineers who worked directly for Paul.

The voice of The Reverend Michael Bonn was barely audible over the steady drum of rain on the canvas canopy. He had been given a brief history of Kevin's life, and, as Paul listened, he heard him speak of our inability to comprehend the reasons behind the taking of our loved ones, especially at a time when their lives seem to be just beginning.

Age-old phrases of God's will and the mysterious wisdom behind it did little to ease Paul's pain. How could he be expected to accept the loss of his only child as part of a grand plan that was 'meant only for our good'? He remembered reading something by a psychologist some years back, to the effect that our grief at the loss of a loved one was actually a manifestation of our own selfishness, that, instead of rejoicing at the other's release from the burden of mortality, we were bereft over the loss of a possession.

Well, he didn't buy any of it: not what the Reverend said, nor the psychologist's theory. Kevin was a happy person, eager for life, and Paul knew in his heart that he grieved just as much for Kevin's loss at a chance for that life as he did for his own loss. He had serious trouble understanding God's will, and he believed his grief was not just selfish.

The silence following the Reverend's words was interrupted by the faint whir of a motor turning the reel that paid out the belts supporting the casket. As he watched the gleaming metal box being lowered into the grave, Paul felt his stomach tighten, and tears ran down his cheeks. From the moment Kevin was born, Paul had seen him as an extension of himself, the propagation of his genes, and now his chance at immortality lay dead at the bottom of this cold, black hole. He felt cheated.

The rain fell without interruption, and when Joan dropped a long-stemmed rose into the grave signaling the end of the ceremony, most of the mourners moved quickly to their cars. Ray had used his own instead of the limousine because Barbara had invited the family and close friends to their house for a buffet and refreshments.

Barbara came over now and touched Paul's arm. "You *are* coming as soon as you pick up your car, aren't you?"

"Yes. We'll ride back in the 'limo' to the funeral home, then drive our car from there."

Barbara leaned closer and indicated with her eyes a spot on the other side of the grave. "Paul, isn't that the girl Kevin was going with?"

He looked up. "Yes, that's Kimberly Adams."

Barbara raised her eyebrows. "Who's the beauty with her?"

"That's her mother."

"Kimberly looks so forlorn. Why don't you ask them to join us?"

"Oh, Paul, yes," Joan said, "Barbara's right, you should invite them."

"Okay. Come on, Barb, I'll introduce you."

Paul caught Kim's eye just as they were about to leave and motioned with his arm for them to wait. They both looked puzzled when he approached with Barbara in tow.

"Diane -- Kim, I'd like you to meet my sister-in-law Barbara. The family's meeting at her house for refreshments and we'd like very much for you to join us."

Diane looked at Kim, then back to Paul. "It's very kind of you, but…I don't know…I -- "

"Joan insisted I ask you. She'd be disappointed. We have to pick up our car, but you can follow Barb and Ray in yours."

When she turned to Kim again and got a shy shrug in response, she said, "All right, Paul."

"Good. I'll leave you and Barb to work it out. See you later."

Paul and Joan met briefly with Kilmer in his office to pick up their bill and copies of the death certificate, then drove on to Ray's home in Des Plaines. They were the last to arrive and had to park down the street from the house and walk, but, fortunately, the rain had slowed to a fine mist.

The house, a three-bedroom ranch surrounded by trees, sat on a lot three times the size of Paul's. He had to admit, there were some advantages to suburban living, like wider spacing between the homes and the extra room for trees; he had only one stately old elm in the parkway at the front and none in the back. Out here, they brought their garbage to the curb for pickup once a week while he had to watch out for rats when he took his out daily to the huge can in the alley, where it was collected once a week. Also, having the driveway off the street would be much easier than backing his car into a garage in the alley. Of course property taxes were much higher than in the city, but then again 'you get what you pay for', they say. Maybe if he *had* made the move, maybe all this wouldn't....

He was at it *again*, after telling himself that kind of thinking was useless, that it wouldn't bring Kevin back. But who was he trying to fool? He knew there was no getting away from it. The guilt would follow him the rest of his days.

Ray met them at the door, carrying two cans of beer. "Barb and Connie are getting the food ready. The rest of the women are in the living room, Joan." He grabbed Paul's arm. "We're all in the den."

Seeing Catherine coming to Joan's rescue, Paul allowed himself to be pulled toward the den. Good old take-charge Ray, always rushing, never quite willing to shed his college linebacker days.

Ray gave the beers to Bill. "The other one's for Ernie," he said. Then turning to Paul, "What are you having?"

“I could use a bourbon and water, but you'd better let me make it.”

“Yeah, well, you know where the bar is.”

With his back to the others, Paul poured an inch of whiskey and drank it straight, then made another drink in a highball glass with water before joining the others. Almost immediately, he could feel the spring in his stomach begin to uncoil. The conversation had been about baseball: new line-ups, trades, pitchers, but it trailed off when he approached. An awkward silence fell until Cathy's husband, Bill Woods, spoke up:

“Cathy and I were wondering about the lack of news on the investigation...have the police come up with anything new, Paul?”

“Yeah,” Ernie said, “I haven't seen a thing in the papers, and Connie watches all the newscasts. They seem to have dropped the story completely.”

Paul watched his brother look at the ceiling and roll his eyes, the corners of his mouth pulled down with cynicism.

“No,” Paul said, “I haven't heard a word. But that doesn't mean they aren't working on it. I have confidence in Lieutenant Burnett. Somehow I get the impression he's pretty sharp.”

Ray shook his head. “I swear, I don't know how you can be so calm -- ”

“What the hell makes you think that?” Paul cut in. “Just because I'm not frothing at the mouth doesn't mean I'm not angry. I'm mad as *hell.* I just don't show my feelings the way you do. Besides, I still believe the system works, if you give it a chance.”

“So do I,” Ernie agreed.

Paul saw Ray's eyes shift to their sister's husband and knew it meant trouble: those two never agreed on anything. He was about to intervene when Connie herself appeared.

“Come on, you guys, lunch is ready.” Connie looked at Ray, and, knowing her brother, sensed the tension. “Leave your drinks sit 'till later. Come on.”

Paul got up. “Yeah, let's go,” he said, grounding out the static charge in the air.

The buffet looked inviting: cold roast beef, potato salad, olives and celery sticks. Paul took a little of everything and looked around for Joan. When he saw her at the dining room table with Kim and Diane, he pulled a chair up and joined them.

“Have you two met everyone?”

“How could they,” Joan said, “with all you men holed up in the den?”

“Allow me,” he said, scanning the room and nodding his head toward each man as he identified him. He managed to get a laugh when he said it was safer at this distance.

When everyone was finished eating, Paul noticed that the food on Kim's plate was untouched.

“Kim, what's wrong? You haven't eaten a thing.”

“I'm sorry, Mr. Becker,” she apologized, “I guess I'm just not hungry.”

Paul thought the blue of her eyes seemed faded. The spark he was accustomed to seeing was gone. He reached over and squeezed her hand.

Chapter 14

It was half past nine when they got home. Joan went directly upstairs. She had been quiet again on the way home, speaking only in answer to Paul's attempts to draw her out. He went to the liquor cabinet for a nightcap, and, as he mixed his usual bourbon and water, he noticed the vodka bottle was almost empty. To be sure, he held it up to the light and had to tilt it to see the level. The last time he had fixed a drink was two nights before, and he remembered it being at least three-quarters full.

He sat down, lit a cigarette and went back over the events of the past two days. There were visitors, yes, but he had served none of them drinks. He frowned and bit his lip. So, that left only Joan. But she was such a moderate drinker he had trouble with that. Still there were just the two of them, so it had to be her. He finished his drink, turned off the lights and went upstairs.

She was already in bed, so he undressed in the bathroom. He got in next to her and stretched to loosen his tense muscles, but he knew his troubling discovery would keep him awake. They needed to talk, but how should he start? Certainly he would not accuse her. He turned onto his side, facing her, wanting to reach out, but not daring. He tried preparing the words, then gave it up. Why not just say what he felt?

"Joan," he said, finally, "we should be comforting each other at a time like this. I've tried to reach out to you, but you keep pulling away. Why?"

He waited. Then when no response came, he went on. "This isn't good, Honey. There's just the two of us now, and we need each other more than ever. Can't you see that?"

She lay on her left side, her back to him. He hesitated, then put his hand gently on her shoulder; his first impulse was to encircle her waist, but he felt she would think it suggestive.

"Building a wall around yourself is not the way to handle this. I wish you'd open up to me -- I want to help you."

Again he waited. Then, just when he was about to give up, she rolled onto her back.

"I can't explain it, Paul; I just can't seem to accept what's happened. It takes me forever to fall asleep, and then I wake up in the middle of the night and drive myself crazy thinking. Then I can't lay still, and I get up so I don't disturb you"

She paused, but he made no comment, hoping she would lay it all out so they could look at it together.

"And I've been drinking at night, trying to find sleep that way. It works eventually."

He stroked her shoulder and arm. "That worries me. I love you, and I don't like to see what's happening to you. Honey, you're drinking for the wrong reason. Don't get me wrong; I like a drink, too, it helps me relax, but drinking to escape reality is dangerous."

She turned to him, sobbing. "I...I know."

He drew her into his arms. Her tears fell to his chest and collected in the depression of his breastbone.

"I keep thinking we failed him," she said.

He winced and clenched his teeth. What she really meant was *he* failed. She blamed *him*. First, for his stubborn refusal to move out of the city, and again now that she was convinced Tate killed their son. And the worst part was that he believed Tate did it, too.

"I've heard of support groups that can help people get through the grief that comes with the loss of a loved one."

"I don't know," she said. "How can a group of strangers help you?"

"I guess because they've been through it themselves." He could feel her shaking her head. "Look, we'll go together. I could use some help myself -- especially with the anger."

She lifted her head. "You're angry?"

"Of *course* I am."

"I'm just numb with the loss...I guess I haven't got to the anger yet."

"I'll see what I can find out about a group in our area. Will you go with me?"

"Maybe. Give me some time to get used to the idea first."

"Well, don't take too long; you need help *now*. In the meantime, I want you to call Dr. Gordon and make an appointment. Maybe he can give you something to help you sleep."

"*Okay*, okay, I'll call him tomorrow." She turned away from him, shaking the bed with the finality of the move.

After a moment of silence, she said, "When are you planning to go back to work?"

"I thought I'd go in tomorrow. The sooner the better. It'll help get my mind on something else."

"Maybe I will, too...good night."

The last time they were this close was Kevin's prom night. So much had happened since then it was hard to believe it was only a matter of days. He remembered Joan suggesting they help Kevin celebrate and how he had teased her about using any excuse to satisfy her lust. She retaliated with a mock attack upon his body, her fists pummeling him ineffectually until they both collapsed in laughter. And then the wildly passionate act of love that followed.

The memory of it started a rustle of need down below his pelvis. It shocked him that he was capable of desire at a time like this, and the hardness that had started, wilted now under a spotlight of guilt.

He wrestled with these mixed feelings until he was able to look at the paradox rationally, then he decided he'd been too critical of himself. Why should he feel guilty for a natural, instinctive reaction? And what of the guilt he already carried by his stubborn refusal to leave the city for the suburbs? Did he really need more of that?

He fell asleep wondering how long it would take for Joan to feel the same stirrings he just had.

Chapter 15

The weather cleared during the night, bringing a bright, mid-May morning. Paul ate and dressed while Joan still slept. He wrote a note reminding her to call the doctor, then left for work.

Avoiding the engineering department, he went directly to Woodward's office. The secretary was at an open file drawer when he approached.

"Morning, Jan," he said, pointing to the inner office. "Is Fred in?"

The woman looked up. "*Paul.* I didn't expect to see you so soon." She looked flustered for a moment. "Yes, go right in."

He tapped on the door before entering.

Woodward got up and came around from behind his desk. He shook Paul's hand. "I thought I told you to take it easy."

"You should know me by now, Fred. I can't just sit around moping; I need to get my mind on something else."

"Okay, but if something comes up -- I mean, of a personal nature -- that requires your attention, feel free to tend to it."

"Thanks, Fred."

Woodward returned to his swivel chair and leaned back. “Sit down a minute, Paul. How's Joan doing?”

Paul sat in one of the guest chairs in front of the desk and gave Woodward his version of his wife's depression. “I'm more than a little worried about her. Last night I suggested we try to find a support group.”

“That's a good idea. Have you got one in mind”

“No. I don't even know where to inquire.”

Woodward pressed a lever on his intercom. “Janice?”

“Yes.”

“Dig out that file on that grief support group in the employee help file, and give it to Paul on his way out.”

“Yes, sir.”

“That'll save me some time,” Paul said. “I really didn’t know *where* to look.”

“My wife heard about this group through our church, and I thought it would come in handy some day.”

Paul nodded. “Anything new come up that I should know about?”

“Yes, there is. We just received a sample of a subassembly and component parts from Turner Electronics. Your men have it laid out on the analysis table, and they're studying the process sheets that go with it.”

“Oh, yeah…I remember seeing the labor cost figures on their present assembly method. We shouldn't have much trouble cutting those down. What kind of time frame are we committed to?”

“Don't worry about it. They've been living with those figures for a long time, and we're the first ones they've come to for help. I told them how long it would take to make a study to estimate the tooling costs, and they'll want to know those to see if they can come up with the kind of money it'll take to go with automation. And if they'll need a loan…well, you know how tight money is today.”

Paul smiled. "Yeah, but if they want to stay competitive in the market, they *have* to cut their manufacturing costs. They don't have much choice, as I see it." He stood up. "Well, I'd better get to work."

"Okay, Paul. Take your time, but get back to me when you've had a chance to look at it."

After acknowledging condolences from employees who had not attended the services, Paul went to the analysis table to look at the new project.

A quick glance told him the sequence of events. Beginning with the basic chassis, each step of the operation was laid-out. By lunchtime, he had gone through all of the steps, reading the process sheets and studying the configuration of each part and its destination on the chassis. At several of the steps he was quick to visualize a rough idea for an automated handling method, but most of them, he knew, would take many days of brainstorming by him and his group.

His crew consisted of three mechanical engineers and a design draftsman, and they had a three-day head start on him, so he called them together for a meeting after lunch to get a feel for where they were in their thinking. They were still at it when Woodward joined them just before quitting time. Paul adjourned the meeting, but stayed a while to brief Fred on a few ideas he had developed so far.

"It sure is good to have you back, Paul. It gives me a feeling of security."

"It's good to *be* back."

"Yeah, but that's enough for the first day -- time you went home to your wife. By the way, we didn't have to make that change you sent us." Fred smiled and winked. "They found a glitch in the computer program."

Paul resisted the temptation to gloat; the message -- from one mechanical engineer to another -- was sufficient satisfaction.

In the days that followed, the new project became an opiate, insulating Paul from his pain, and he embraced it like a sinner at a revival meeting. Time spent pouring over sketches of rough designs, which later were fed into computers for analysis during progress meetings ate up the daylight hours with the voracity of a shredding machine.

While more than a third of his waking time was consumed in the bliss of this creative stew, the nights were something quite different. Joan still was distant. Her indifference to his attempts at rebuilding their former relationship left him feeling abandoned, as if she had fled to some distant place of her invention that denied him entrance.

He told her about the support group, and after several false starts, Joan finally agreed to attend the meetings, at least on a trial basis. During the first session, Paul and Joan just listened. The meetings were conducted informally by the two most senior members, both of whom had at least some formal training in psychology. Their approach was as Paul had expected.

They were told that keeping their grief locked up inside made their grief harder to bear, that expressing it, talking about it with others, especially those who had been through similar experiences, would help relieve the pain. They were urged to just listen until they became comfortable enough to want to contribute.

It made sense to Paul, and near the middle of the second session, he found that he had loosened up enough to speak. Joan took longer to open up. The third meeting was more than half over before she found her voice, and even then it came haltingly. But once she started, the words spilled forth in a rush of feelings that, except for her sobbing, left the room hushed.

Paul came away from it with a new understanding of the gulf separating their common grief. He knew a mother's feelings at the loss of a child would be different from the father's, but he was unprepared for the enormity of the gap. He thought about what she had said and he began to see her view.

Her bonding began earlier, with the embryo, and grew stronger in the tender years of childhood. She still saw the infant Kevin, and the toddler, still felt her first sense of separation on his first day of school, the bittersweet cleaving when he moved from elementary school to Jr. High. How could he know her loss when she was closer to Kevin during that time of early development than he was.

Paul knew he had delegated that period of Kevin's life to Joan, that he had shirked the responsibilities of those early years. Oh, sure, he had derived pleasure in seeing those stages of development, but he really didn't share in them the way Joan did. It wasn't until he noticed Kevin searching for models to emulate that he stepped into the role. Some of the best times for Paul were when Kevin would abandon his own plans to watch him work on one of the cars.

Back when automobiles were simpler, Paul enjoyed repairing and maintaining theirs. That was before the proliferation of technology made the engine compartment so crowded it took special tools and hours of preliminary work just to get at the problem; now he let the dealer's service department do it.

He still remembered the look of fascination on Kevin's face when he tackled jobs like replacing worn brakes or a leaking water pump. He began by letting Kevin set the gap for the spark plugs, then replacement of the rotor and distributor cap, taking care to explain the firing order and the correct method for every procedure until he was able to do a complete tune-up without Paul's help. Kevin's interest in everything mechanical was a source of pride for Paul. His genes were at work.

That Joan grieved differently, was clear to Paul. In his mind, Joan was the mother whose 'baby' had died; he was the father who had been robbed of his genetic heir. She was having trouble accepting the reality of the loss, while he was feeling anger at the theft of reproduction. For Paul, it was as if the killer had used his knife to emasculate him. He felt that violated.

Paul's anger continued to grow, and Tate became the symbol of all that had been taken from him: his son, his happy marriage, his sense of accomplishment and security. His anger loomed heaviest at night, when the project at work no longer insulated him. It was during these lonely times that he began inventing fantasies of revenge. Plotting different ways to kill Tate became a game that seemed to promise relief in some indefinite future. It helped him fall asleep.

CHAPTER 16

A prescription to help Joan sleep ended her nocturnal drinking, and an improvement in communication between them in the week following their fourth therapy session made Paul believe their lives were getting back to normal.

So convinced was he of this, that after an evening of easy conversation and banter reminiscent of better times, he thought it was time to test her response to physical love-making. In the past, she was as likely to initiate an overture as he, but the possibility of that happening now was too uncertain, so he would have to make the first move.

Instead of the considerate kiss on the cheek -- the pattern of late before saying good night -- he ran his hand down the valley of her waist and up along the curve of hip and thigh. When no movement of protest came, he reversed direction and began the journey again, this time moving to the soft, warm inner thigh where he stopped and waited.

His desire, built on weeks of denial, struggled against the haste that could spoil the moment. Softly, he kissed her shoulder while his hand moved to the triangle of hair and down under the rise of pelvis. Ordinarily at this point, she would have moaned with pleasure, now he heard only the sound of his own breathing. After a period of delicate maneuvers with his fingers, she finally turned toward him, but the motion lacked her usual enthusiasm. Actually, he thought he heard a faint sigh of resignation.

Then, when he began probing, and the absence of lubrication made her gasp with pain, he knew she had surrendered only out of her sense of duty. The joy of mutual participation was missing, and normally he would have stopped in deference to her feelings, but any thought for her comfort now was dulled by his present need.

He had found out early in life that a healthy, happy sexual relationship depended upon mutual satisfaction, and he learned ways to discipline his timing so that his mate was not left unfulfilled. Not that he was perfect in this ability -- sometimes he got carried away, too -- but when it did happen, he usually managed to bring his partner to completion by other means. Tonight could be one of the exceptions; Joan was completely unresponsive.

Sure, her legs were spread and her arms were around him, but other than that, it was like making love to an inflatable doll. He knew he had to fulfill his need, but the lack of Joan's customary enthusiasm threatened to take the edge off his desire. Even now, he could feel his virility wilting with each thrust of his hips.

He resorted to fantasy, and although it took much longer than usual, it carried him through to ejaculation. Then he lay still for a moment while disappointment washed over him. He tried to remember the last time he had used mental images while making love to Joan. Everyone indulged in fantasies at one time or other, but Joan's role in their lovemaking was usually so active he almost never felt the need of a substitute for stimulation.

Until now.

A droplet of sweat rolled down his neck, hung briefly to his throat, then dropped onto his wife below. He rolled onto his back and stared at the ceiling.

"I'm sorry," she said, so softly he barely heard. "I guess I'm not ready yet."

He found her hand and squeezed it gently. "No, I'm the one who should be sorry. I should have known..."

"Paul, don't...don't blame yourself." She turned to him and put her hand on his shoulder. "I know how it must be for you...I understand."

They were silent for a while, thinking their own thoughts, than he heard her get up.

"Where ya goin'? You okay?"

"I have to take a pill if I hope to get to sleep. Maybe I'll read for a while -- downstairs. Don't worry, I'll be all right."

When she was gone, he smoked half a cigarette and put it out. Eventually he slept.

The following night, Paul brought home a set of drawings on one stage of the new project that had a particularly tough problem. Rather than delay their progress, he told everyone else to go around it while he worked on a solution.

He retired to the basement after dinner and had just spread the sketches out on the drafting table when Joan called down to him.

"Paul, Lieutenant Burnett is here -- he wants to talk to you."

He sighed and shook his head. "Okay, I'm coming."

Joan was sitting on the couch in the living room; Burnett was in one of the chairs. He was alone.

"Sorry to interrupt you, Mr. Becker, but I was in the neighborhood, and I have some news I just *knew* you'd want to hear."

"It's okay, Lieutenant. The problem I'm working on isn't going anywhere. So what's up?"

"We got a tip that Tate was selling hot television sets--expensive consoles -- and when we went to his house with a search warrant, one of the officers found a knife that fit the description of the murder weapon."

Suddenly Paul felt a little heady. He moved to the couch and sat down heavily next to Joan.

"How could he tell…was this knife so unusual?"

Burnett's face took on that look of the hunter Paul had thought he saw on their first meeting at the morgue.

"Remember when I was here before, and I said we had one small piece of evidence?"

Paul saw a smile playing at the corners of Burnett's mouth. It was obvious the detective enjoyed his control of the moment.

"I recall your saying you couldn't divulge what was found because it would jeopardize the investigation."

"That's right. Well, they found a small piece of metal in the waistband of your son's trousers. It looked like it could have broken off the crossbar of the knife..."

"Crossbar?"

"Yeah, that metal bar at the hilt -- some call it a hand guard."

Paul frowned. "That's hard to believe, it's a pretty sturdy part."

Burnett's smile widened. "On a *good* knife, yeah, but this was a piece of junk, a cheap knife with an imitation bone handle, the kind you'd find in a discount store. The crossbar was die cast, and the lab people said there was evidence of an old crack line. They think it got snagged in the belt buckle and broke off when he yanked it loose -- the attack was pretty savage, you know, and this guy's strong as a bull."

Paul felt Joan's hand tighten on his arm.

"Anyway, the knife had part of the guard broken off and the piece the lab found matched perfectly." Burnett shook his head. "You know, this guy isn't very smart. Anyone with an ounce of brains would have ditched the knife -- and not only that, but he didn't do a very good job of cleaning it either. The lab found a trace of dried blood and a strand of body hair in the space between the blade and the handle. The results of a DNA genetic coding comparison proves it's the knife used in the murder."

Joan leaned back and crossed her arms over her chest. Her lips formed a tight line and her nostrils flared as she took in a deep breath. "I knew it! I just *knew* it." Her head bobbed down at the end of each phrase, as if to punctuate the words with her fervor. "I'll never forget the look on that man's face when he saw us in the mall."

She turned to Paul, eyes blazing, and he wondered how much of her anger was against Tate and how much was directed at him.

He turned to Burnett. "So, where does that leave things now?"

"The D.A. submitted the evidence to the grand jury, and they voted to indict. The arraignment is scheduled for this Thursday."

"I hope Tate's not out on bond again, is he?"

"*No way*. At his hearing on the dealing-in-stolen-goods charge, the prosecutor convinced the judge that Tate was a high risk, so bail was set high enough to keep him locked up. We needed time for the lab tests. Fortunately, the grand jury was in session and the D.A. was able to slip the request for a murder indictment into their agenda." Burnett hunched forward. "And now the best part...." He was the predator again, about to spring. "...the prosecution served notice they will seek the death penalty." He leaned back, draping his arm over the back of the chair, a big grin of satisfaction lighting up his face.

Paul felt a glow begin somewhere in his chest and radiate outward to the banjo strings that weeks of frustration had made of his nerves. He slumped against the back of the couch with a blissful sigh. The system really did work. His faith was restored.

Burnett frowned. "Hey, I thought you'd be happy."

Paul managed a weak smile. “Give me a chance to come down, Lieutenant.” He looked at the ceiling. “I'm still floating around up there somewhere.”

When he turned to Joan and saw a smile mixed with tears, he reached out, but she moved away.

“Well,” Burnett said, getting up, “I have to be going.”

Paul rose and shook Burnett's hand. “Thanks for coming. We really appreciate it.”

“I wanted you to hear it from me before you saw it in the papers or on the news. I'll keep you informed.” He started for the door.

“Lieutenant, can we attend this hearing, Thursday?”

Burnett stopped and turned. “Well, sure you can. In fact, I think it's a good idea for you to be there.”

“What time is it going to be and where?”

“You'd better get there at nine...sometimes they actually start on time. It'll be in Judge Stoltz’s Court Room, in the Criminal Courts Building.” He took out his note pad. “I'll write down the information for you.”

Chapter 17

Paul thought he had allowed enough time, but it was quarter past nine when they got off the elevator at the second floor and hurried down the hall to the courtroom. He saw groups of people gathered along two benches outside the double doors and was relieved to see Burnett among them, talking with two uniformed officers. When he saw Paul and Joan approaching, he broke away and came to greet them.

"Let's go inside and find you a place to sit," he said, taking Joan's free arm and leading the way.

"I tried to get here early," Paul said, but the traffic was something else."

"I can imagine. You came half way across the city in the morning rush hour." He stopped at a spectator bench three rows from the front. "You should be able to hear everything from here. I have to sit with the arresting officers over there." His head bobbed, indicating chairs along the wall.

A door opened at the front of the room, and the clerk jumped to attention. "All rise. The Superior Court of Cook County is now in session. The Honorable Herman Stoltz presiding."

The announcement brought a flurry of activity as the crowd from the hall rushed in to find seats. Paul watched the judge settle into his high-backed swivel chair and nod his head at the clerk, who then called out the case number. Another door opened on the left, and all heads turned to watch a bailiff lead a scowling Steven Tate to the defense table and then return to a position against the wall.

Before taking his place beside his lawyer, Tate took a moment to search the faces of the audience. Joan gripped Paul's arm and pressed closer, as if to avoid recognition. Paul saw Tate's act as a deliberate intimidation of possible witnesses; certainly it had worked on Joan. But this was not her first encounter with their son's killer; there was that time in the mall with Kevin.

As Paul's eyes swept over the man, he estimated Tate's height at about five-ten, shorter than he had imagined. But the lack of height was compensated for in mass. He was big-boned, with exceptionally wide shoulders, and the cheap, ill-fitting suit he wore did little to hide the girth of his arms and chest. Burnett had it right when he said the guy was strong as a bull.

His features might be considered ruggedly handsome by some, but his eyes spoiled the effect; they had a dark, brooding menace in them that, to Paul, suggested an unstable personality. When Paul finished his study of Tate, he had a mental image that he could recall later. Now, the phantom of his rage had a face.

"Counsel will please identify themselves for the record."

Both attorneys rose.

"Your Honor, I am Michael Sloan, on behalf of the people of the State of Illinois." He turned and pointed. "Also, seated, is Chief Deputy District Attorney, Richard Polk."

The judge nodded. "So noted."

Paul's immediate impression was that the prosecutor looked too young for the job. But who could tell; maybe that was a sign he was exceptionally sharp.

"Benjamin Bass, Your Honor, on behalf of the defendant, Steven Tate. I request leave to file our appearance."

“Motion is allowed.”

As Paul eyed the attorney's suit and the diamond ring on his little finger, he tried to estimate the income of a burglar. It had to be good to afford a lawyer as expensive-looking as this guy.

“Your Honor,” Bass continued, “the defendant is present and we acknowledge receipt of the indictment. We waive formal reading, Your Honor, and on behalf of Mr. Tate, we enter a plea of not guilty to the charge.”

“Defense plea of not guilty to the indictment. So noted.” The judge made a note. “Bail will remain as previously set.”

Paul was shocked. He had expected plea bargaining. As far he was concerned, the case was open and shut. So what the hell was going on?

“Your Honor,” Bass said, holding up a legal document, “this is the list of the evidence which was submitted to me by the prosecution, showing what they intend to present at the trial. But I specifically asked that I be allowed to examine the warrant issued.” The judge looked at the list. “You will notice, Your Honor, that the warrant is not included.”

The judge scanned the list, then looked at Sloan. “Counsel?”

Sloan winced and turned to the chief deputy, who was fumbling through a sheaf of papers on the table. A murmur came from the press section, and the judge directed a scowl in that direction. Finally, Polk found the document and brought it to Bass.

“Your Honor, I beg the court's indulgence to allow time for me to examine the evidence and consult with my client.”

“There will be a ten minute recess.” The judge rapped the bench with his gavel.

Joan tugged at Paul's sleeve. “There's something wrong, isn't there?”

He tried not to let her see the doubt that had yanked his stomach muscles into a tight ball. "I don't know…I hope not."

He glanced in Burnett's direction, but the detective was turned the other way, talking to one of the uniformed officers. When he looked back and saw Joan's questioning eyes, he felt the need to reassure her.

"Don't worry, it's probably just some legal formality. You'd have to be a lawyer to figure out the mysteries of court procedure." His words did not erase her frown.

"That lawyer representing Tate worries me, Paul."

"I got the same impression, but I don't see how the DA can lose this one -- not with the evidence they have."

The clerk called the court to order again, and Judge Stoltz settled into his chair.

"Before we discuss a trial date..." He stopped to look at the attorneys over the top of his glasses. "…pretrial motions, Counsel?"

Sloan declined.

Stoltz's head swiveled, turretlike, to Bass.

"Your Honor, we move to exclude item four as evidence against my client."

Sloan exploded. "Your Honor!"

The judge consulted the list of evidence again.

"Your Honor," Sloan reiterated, "that's the *murder weapon*."

Stoltz looked up from the list. "I *see* that." His head swiveled toward Bass again, eyebrows raised. "Grounds?"

Bass came forward with a document and placed it before the judge. "As Your Honor can see, the warrant specifies console television receivers as the items to be seized. Nowhere in its wording is there mention of a weapon. The purpose of the warrant was to search for illegally obtained TV sets, not a murder investigation."

"Your Honor," Sloan protested, "the defendant was a suspect in the case before the court today, and we maintain the officers acted in good faith."

Bass was about to speak again, but Stoltz raised a restraining hand. He turned to the clerk. "Call the arresting officer."

One of the uniformed officers came forward.

Stoltz squinted at him as if in recognition. "Where was the knife when it was discovered?"

The officer cleared his throat nervously. "It was in a drawer, Your Honor."

"A drawer? Elaborate."

"A dresser drawer, Your Honor."

Stoltz leaned back and looked at the ceiling. "What were you doing in a dresser drawer, Officer, rummaging?"

"No, sir -- I mean, Your Honor. The drawer was partially open when we entered the suspect's bedroom, and I became suspicious when he moved so quick to get around us and slam it shut."

Again Bass tried to interrupt, and again Stoltz's hand stopped him.

"You'll have your chance, Counsel." He turned to the officer. "Continue."

"Well, I could see he was trying to hide something, so I pushed him aside and opened it, and there was the knife, Your Honor."

Sloan bowed his head, and squeezed his eyes shut, as if in pain. A murmur arose from the press again.

Stoltz reached for his gavel. "Order!"

The Chief Deputy DA came forward. "Your Honor, is this proper procedure at this time?"

Stoltz swung around and glared. "Let me remind you, Mr. Polk, this is *my* courtroom, and *I* will decide what is proper."

A hush fell over the courtroom while Stoltz reread the warrant. Gone was the rustle of shifting, impatient bodies, the clearing of throats, the occasional sharp bark of a nervous cough. Paul listened to the silence roaring in his ears as he waited for the judge's next move.

Finally, Stoltz raised his head and looked at the prosecutor. "It is my decision that the knife was seized in violation of The Fourth Amendment and, therefore, cannot be entered as evidence against the defendant in this indictment."

Polk's hand came up. "Your Honor, the search was made in good faith -- "

"Let me remind you, Mr. Chief Deputy, the wording of the amendment clearly states that the particular things to be seized shall be named in the warrant. I see no mention of a weapon anywhere in this warrant." Stoltz raised a restraining hand against interruption. "Before you say anything more, let me offer you something to ponder." He leaned back and made a steeple of his fingers over his chest. "Suppose...instead of the knife...the defendant's diary was discovered in the dresser drawer. Would that justify its seizure in the hope of finding evidence of some crime other than the one for which the search warrant was issued?" He paused, and when no answer to his question came, he continued. "Of course not. The intent of the Fourth Amendment is to *protect* against unreasonable search and seizure -- the right of the people to be secure in their person's, houses, papers and *effects*."

The courtroom buzzed and Stoltz banged his gavel for order.

"No, Mr. Prosecutor," Stoltz continued, "clearly, the evidence in question was seized illegally. Now, before you answer my next question, I want you to consider the time and expense of the trial court." He paused, looking down over his glasses. "Do you wish to proceed with this case without item four in the list of evidence?"

Polk was on his feet now. "Your Honor, the state maintains that the knife posed a danger to the officers doing the search, and its seizure was proper in order to ensure their safety."

Stoltz smiled and shook his head. "Didn't you hear the officer's testimony, Mr. Chief Deputy? I can have the stenographer read it back for you. But, as I recall, the officer stated that the defendant slammed the drawer shut in an attempt to *hide* the weapon. Hardly a threatening move. Also, I assume the defendant's apartment had a kitchen, where carving knives were stored. Were these knives -- weapons -- also seized?"

Polk looked at Sloan, who shrugged and made a face to show the hopelessness of their position.

"Your Honor," Sloan said, "the state withdraws the charges."

It was Bass's turn now. "Request a continuance pending formal withdrawal, Your Honor. Also, defense moves that bail be reduced to personal recognizance until such time."

"Motion granted."

The judge turned to the chief deputy DA and sighed. "I hope that you and everyone concerned with this case has learned something today about the proper procedures in gathering evidence." He reached for his gavel. "The court will recess for one half-hour before calling the next case."

Paul heard a rumble of running feet as members of the press bolted for the corridor, and he watched in disbelief as Bass pumped Tate's hand and clapped his shoulder.

Joan tugged at his sleeve. "Paul?"

He forced himself to look at her. "I watched the whole thing," he said, "but I still don't understand what happened. All I know is it looks like this bastard got away with it."

He turned away in time to see Tate and Bass come down the center isle. With head held high, Tate swaggered like a conquering hero and, as he drew abreast of them, he made a point of sneering as if to show his contempt.

With a rush of hate-born adrenaline, Paul lunged at the man, but already Burnett was behind him, gripping both his arms. At the same moment, near the hall door, a camera flashed.

For the first time in his life, he felt the urge to reach out and, with his bare hands, tear another human apart. It frightened him. Not even combat in Nam had done this. Still, watching Tate's retreating figure disappear through the courtroom doors, he felt the need to vent his rage and frustration. "You won't get away with it!" he yelled.

"Take it ease, Mr. Becker."

Paul pulled loose from Burnett's grip and turned to face him. "God dammit, what happened?"

Burnett winced, then, taking both by the arm, he urged Joan and Paul toward the door. "Come on, there's a coffee shop across the street...we can talk better there. I'm buying."

It was still too early for the lunch crowd, so they had their pick of booths. Burnett led them to one near the kitchen, away from everyone else. He ordered a hamburger and coffee; Paul and Joan had just coffee.

"Okay, Lieutenant, you want to explain to us how that killer was able to walk out of that courtroom?"

"Like the judge said, seizing the weapon was improper; it violated Tate's rights under the Fourth Amendment."

"His *rights*." Paul's rage returned. "Since when do habitual criminals have rights?"

"I know what you're saying, and believe me, we're just as disappointed as you are."

"Disappointed? Hell, we're *outraged.*"

"We're long past outrage," Burnett offered, "this is something we have to live with all the time...and, like you, we get frustrated."

"I just don't understand"

"I don't either," Joan said.

The waitress brought his food, but Burnett ignored it.

"Have either of you read The Fourth Amendment?"

"Of course," Paul said, "but that was back in high school civics; I know what it's about, but I don't remember the exact words."

"That's the key, the exact words. Hardly anyone reads them and really gets the whole implication. Let me recite it. I know it by heart -- I have to." He sipped his coffee, then closed his eyes. "'The right of the people to be secure in their houses....'" He shook his head. "Wait, that's wrong. It's 'persons, houses, papers and effects against unreasonable searches and seizures, shall not be violated, and no warrants shall issue, but upon probable cause, supported by oath or affirmation, and particularly..." He opened his eyes and studied their faces. "...describing the place to be searched, and the persons or *things* to be seized.'" He took a bite of his sandwich.

"Yes, but..."

Burnett raised his hand while he washed the food down with coffee. "Not only that, but the courts added another kicker: "The Exclusionary Rule". With that, our warrant for stolen television sets made looking in that dresser drawer illegal, so the knife had to be excluded as evidence."

Joan leaned forward, frowning. "Then why didn't the officers get another warrant that would include the knife?"

Burnett smiled sadly and shook his head. "That wouldn't have done any good, either. The defense would argue that the evidence was discovered previously, by the act of rummaging -- again the exclusionary rule. So, you see what we're up against? Our only choice was to seize the knife and hope a green, court-appointed lawyer might not be sharp enough to catch it." Burnett shook his head again. "We thought Tate wouldn't have the kind of money it takes to hire an experienced lawyer. We gambled...and lost."

"But he walked out a free man," Joan said. "What about the other charge?"

"We couldn't tie the serial numbers to any stolen TV's, and besides that, our witness disappeared." Burnett caught the waitress's eye and pointed to his coffee cup. "This guy has worked hard to scare the hell out of everyone who comes in contact with him. He's built a reputation. For example, the news stories pointed out his motive when they said Kevin was instrumental in one of Tate's burglary convictions, and the fact that Kevin is now dead shows everyone what happens if you cross him. We think that's what happened with our witness. Tate's a dangerous man, and he wants everyone to know it."

Paul's eyes narrowed. "The guy's a punk. He may scare a lot of people, Lieutenant, but not *everyone*."

Burnett studied Paul's face, as if to read the mind behind the last statement. "Mr. Becker, I spent hours studying a profile our shrinks did on Tate, and the one word that impressed me the most was 'Sociopath', a person who has no conscience."

Paul smiled. "I *know* what sociopath means, Lieutenant."

Burnett looked sheepish. "I'm sorry, I should have know. Anyway, when I said Tate is a dangerous man, I also meant he's dangerous to himself. He's got to that point now, where he thinks he can do anything and get away with it." He held Paul's eyes while he sipped his coffee. "He'll keep right on doing what he does until he makes a fatal mistake. And that's what I'm counting on. *Believe* me, Mr. Becker, he *will* make that mistake, and I'll *be* there when he does."

Paul sighed and shook his head. "In the meantime, a killer is free to walk the streets." He looked at Burnett and saw in the detective's eyes a reflection of his own frustration. "I guess my interpretation of The Fourth Amendment is wrong. I thought it was meant to protect law-abiding citizens from a police state. Now I see it protects the habitual criminal, too."

"Equal rights under the law."

"As I recall, when The Fourth Amendment was written, our government was still new, and they wanted to guarantee our right against a general warrant -- there was another name for it -- "

"It was called a 'writ of assistance'. It gave arbitrary power to officers of the Crown when conducting a search. They could use anything they found in court against a defendant."

"Yeah, they could do anything they wanted in the name of the King." Paul used his hand to make a gesture of dismissal. "But that was a long time ago. With today's crime rate, people are more concerned with protection against the criminal. They're not worried about government trampling on their rights. The average, law-abiding citizen has nothing to fear from the cop on the beat. The ones worried about searches are those with something to hide. I don't see anything wrong with the prosecution being able to use evidence uncovered accidentally in an otherwise lawful search. I know we have nothing to hide in *our* house."

"If everyone were like you, I wouldn't have a job." Burnett's smile was bittersweet. "But you're oversimplifying…the court doesn't consider the discovery of the knife as accidental. It says we were 'rummaging' and that violates his rights."

"Well, I don't think habitual criminals should have the same rights as honest citizens. What about the basic question of guilt or innocence? Surely, that judge knows he turned a murderer loose."

"Hey, I'm on your side. Today a cop has to have a law book in his pocket. Even with that, who would have guessed he still had the murder weapon in his possession? We'd have needed a crystal ball to include it in the warrant as items to be seized."

"I don't blame the officers who made the search," Paul said, "or you either. I blame the laws for letting the guilty go free."

The silence that fell between them told Paul there was nothing left to be said. "Well, Lieutenant, I just want to say we appreciate the personal concern you've shown us. I know you went out of your way to keep us informed."

Burnett stood and extended his hand. "I wish I could have made things turn out better."

Paul shook Burnett's hand. "We know you did everything you could."

Burnett gave him a crooked smile, then picked up the check and walked to the cashier.

With a sigh of resignation, Paul turned to Joan. "Let's go home," he said.

Driving east into the sun that morning, Paul had needed his sunglasses; now it was overcast, promising rain and relief from the July heat. Traffic on the expressway was thin, and now, as they approached the northwest side, Paul turned to Joan.

"You've been awfully quiet -- you okay?"

She started as from a trance. "What?"

"Are you okay?"

"Oh, I was just thinking. I just can't believe what happened in that courtroom. I keep seeing that man walking away...free as a bird. And I keep thinking, 'What can I say to Kevin?' How can I explain to him that his killer won't be punished for what he did?"

Paul felt his stomach quiver. What the hell was she talking about?

“Paul, would you mind....” she said, touching his arm, “I mean, as long as we have this afternoon free, would you mind stopping at the cemetery?”

His hand tightened on the steering wheel. She knew he hated cemeteries. “It looks like it's going to rain any minute.”

“We won't stay long…just a few minutes. Please?”

How could he refuse? They hadn't been there since the funeral, and this was the first time she had asked. “Okay.”

He eased over to the right and took the next exit ramp.

Some of the dread Paul was feeling lifted when they pulled up to the graveside and he saw the first warning drops of rain on the windshield; they held promise the ordeal would be short.

Young grass was already growing over the faint mound that marked the disturbed earth, and as they approached, Paul noticed a small bouquet of flowers at the foot of the headstone. They were wilted only slightly, which suggested to him that they had been placed there as recently as yesterday. He looked at Joan and pointed to the flowers. “Who do you suppose was here?”

After a moment's hesitation, she said, “Me.”

“What? You mean you were here yesterday?”

“I've been coming almost every day after work since the week after the funeral.”

He had to grit his teeth to control the flash of anger her words ignited. He wanted to shake her and shout, 'For God's sake, why?' But he knew the futility of it; the past two months had revealed too many serious splits in their thinking already.

“I come here to be near him,” she said, as if reading his mind.

When he saw how vulnerable she looked, he felt a burning, as from tears, start behind his eyes. To hide from her, he looked up at the sky and swallowed hard several times. Then he put his arm around her and, together, they looked down at the grave until the rain forced them back to the car.

The cemetery exited onto Roosevelt Road and forty-five-mile-per-hour traffic. Mixed in with the cars, were trucks that serviced a nearby industrial complex. It made blending into traffic from a standing stop an adventure. But the squeal of the Buick's tires as he made his break was a reassuring sound.

Joan gasped. "Paul, why don't you wait until it's safe?"

"Is that what you do?"

"Of course."

"Good."

"You!"

He had to lower his arm to fend off the blow she directed to his ribs.

"Hey, that's more like the girl I used to know."

"Is it?" She looked away. "I don't know, Paul. It seems to me that person became a casualty, too. I'm not sure she'll ever return...at least not the one you remember."

Paul reached out and gently squeezed her hand. "Of course she will." He made his voice sound cheerful, but silent gloom persisted for the balance of the drive home.

The rain was coming down in sheets when they pulled into the garage, and they both got wet running to the house. After changing to dry clothes, Joan went downstairs to start dinner.

Paul was slower getting changed; his mind was preoccupied with thoughts of her cemetery visits.

He wandered out of the bedroom and down the hall to Kevin's room, to the door that, by some unspoken agreement, was kept closed now. After a moment of hesitation, he opened it, went in, and memories jumped at him from all directions. Shelves with Kevin's books and trophies, pictures on the walls of his favorite sports figures and rock stars, the desk where he did his homework, all of it proclaiming the territory that he defended as his right to privacy.

To Paul, these were the mementos of a person who once clenched life with joyous vigor, and as his eyes swept over the room, his thoughts turned to Joan. If their son's spirit were to be found anywhere, it was here. This was where he'd return, if it were possible, which Paul doubted. If she wanted to talk to him, this was where he'd be, not some cold impersonal cemetery. He wished he could make her see it his way.

He went to the desk and stared at the photograph of Kevin in his football uniform. Taken after he had scored the winning touchdown in the last six seconds of a game, Kevin was holding a football over his head in a gesture of victory, his smiling face flushed with excitement and pride. Paul remembered clipping the story from the local paper for Kevin's scrapbook. He blinked away the mist starting in his eyes and shook his head.

"Sorry, son," he said, "the opposition won this one -- the referee's decision went against you. And the officials backed him up."

The photo was in a hinged double frame; the other half held one of Kimberly, her blue eyes matching the background sky, hair the color of August wheat. Paul smiled at the pair staring out at him. They made a beautiful couple.

When he felt the muscles in his throat contract, he turned quickly and left the room.

Chapter 18

The project at work filled Paul's days with consuming activity. He came home tired, to nights of frustration and bad dreams. Joan moved into a gray world of mechanical duties: days with her sister at the store; evenings cooking dinner; the laundry and cleaning on Saturdays. The spontaneity that he valued so much in her was gone.

He remembered the nights when she would undress with deliberate slowness, then linger at the closet, striking seductive poses in her high-heeled slippers and bikini panties while she chose and rejected outfits for the next day. She knew how to play 'the game', and when he could stand it no longer, he would jump up, scoop her into his arms and carry her to bed.

Then, as if to deny her complicity, she would feign a look of wide-eyed innocence before collapsing with laughter. The charade was her invention; it provided a hint of the illicit that seemed to excite and prepare her for the lovemaking.

But that was then.

Now *he* initiated the sexual overtures, and then only when abstinence became unbearable. Even on those widely spaced occasions, what should have been lovemaking became, instead, an act of copulating by obligation. At times she would pretend participation, but her performance was insincere, reminding him of heroines in the few pornographic films he had seen.

In an effort to sustain the pleasure during these sessions, he indulged in trysts with imaginary partners. These dreamy excursions always brought the desired result, but they left him with a lingering feeling of guilt. When it was over, he would roll away to his side of the bed and fall into a restless sleep filled with disturbing dreams.

To counter the effects of his empty nights, he buried himself in his work, pushing himself and others around him, sometimes to the extent that brought grumbling from his subordinates. But the results paid off one Friday in late August. After an exceptionally good progress meeting, a pleased Fred Woodward suggested they take the afternoon off and have lunch downtown at the Engineer's Club to celebrate. Paul welcomed the break; he also was a member, but seldom availed himself of the club's benefits.

The club offered a modest businessman's lunch during the week. It was served in a section partitioned off by accordion-panels from the large banquet hall that could be rented for special occasions.

Paul and Fred identified themselves at the front desk, then headed for the dining area where they had their pick of tables. They ordered drinks and made their selections from the menu.

"I can't remember when I was here last," Paul said.

Fred smiled. "I wish I could say the same."

"Why's that?"

"I was here a couple of months ago and ran into an old engineer friend of mine who bent my ear all during lunch. Seems he'd been at the bar a little too long and was more than half in the bag."

"That must have been a pain."

"Yeah," Fred continued, "he was ticked-off because someone ripped off the stereo in his new car. The damn fool left it unlocked."

"What did he expect? "

"Well, this guy just got back from eight years in Saudi Arabia. He was on a contract, designing a couple of desalinization plants, and wasn't used to locking his car. He didn't have to worry about thieves over there because crime is almost nonexistent."

"Okay, I'll bite..." Paul said, grinning, "...why is that?"

"Now remember he's had too much to drink, so I quote him. He said, 'They don't fuck around with criminals over there'. Then he tells me how depressed he is by what he reads in the newspapers, and he can't believe the shit that's going on here at home."

"Hey, he's right. I've read about some of the things they do to people who break the law over there."

"I have, too. But he had to tell me anyway -- like the guy who stole his stereo would get a finger cut off if it was his first offense. His hand, if it were a second."

"Yeah, rapists and murderers are beheaded, and the executions are carried out in public." Paul was thinking of Steven Tate.

Fred nodded. "That's when we got into a disagreement. I said I had to admit that maybe we're too lenient sometimes, but, hell...Paul, you and I both know, the American people would never permit the drastic measures used in some foreign countries. We have a completely different concept of justice here."

The food arrived and he broke off. They ate in silence for a few minutes, but Paul felt the need to know more.

"So, is that where it ended?"

"No, there was no stopping him. He went on about how the Saudi people were perfectly happy with their form of justice. That they felt secure in their homes and on their streets. They can come and go without fear of being mugged or murdered. Then he asked, 'How many people do you know can say that?'"

"He scored a point there," Paul said.

Fred shrugged. "Well, our system may not be perfect, but I still think it's the best one anyone's come up with so far."

Paul winced. Fred's words were almost the same ones he used with his brother when Ray had criticized the system the night of Kevin's wake.

A light rain had fallen while they were inside the club, just enough to make the oily streets slick, and traffic already was heavy with commuters when they started back to the office. It took fifteen minutes just to get out of the Loop and onto the expressway. Paul glanced at his watch.

"I think I should have used my car."

"You can't plan for everything."

"You know, Fred, I was just thinking about what your friend said... that the Saudi people were happy with their kind of justice. He used the term, 'they feel secure in their houses'. I knew it sounded familiar, but I couldn't place it then. Now I remember…Lieutenant Burnett quoted The Fourth Amendment to me, and the opening phrase is almost word for word."

"Refresh my memory, Paul."

"It goes: 'The right of the people to be secure in their persons, houses, papers and so forth, blah, blah, blah....'" Paul hesitated. "I guess what alerted me was the way he used the word 'secure' instead of 'safe', like most people would."

"I'm not sure I follow you."

"It's kinda mixed up in my mind, but it seems ironic to me that The Fourth Amendment was written to protect us -- like he said, to make us feel secure -- and yet, this very document protected Kevin's killer instead."

Fred's silence led Paul to think he failed to convey his feelings clearly.

"I used to feel secure in my home -- which, of course, includes my family -- now I don't any more. I know Steven Tate didn't actually invade my home, but when he killed my son, he tore it apart. I guess what I'm trying to say is there's something wrong with our system when its laws start protecting the habitual criminals instead of the law-abiding citizens."

"Are you saying we should do what they're doing over there?"

"No, no. I just want to know why the courts aren't looking for the truth. *The question of guilt.* I think the main responsibility of our courts should be to search for the truth. But they don't do that. How can they get at the truth when vital evidence can be excluded or suppressed under the exclusionary rule?"

"Paul, you know as well as I do, the politicians aren't about to fiddle around with The Bill of Rights. It would stir up a storm like you wouldn't believe. Besides, most people believe the Founding Fathers had the right idea."

"Yes, but I think we have a problem with the way the courts are interpreting the law today. They're stacking the deck in favor of the criminal. The law is getting liberal to a point that defies *reason.* And that's *wrong, dammit.* What about the victims?"

Paul stopped talking and turned to blink at the crawling traffic ahead. He looked down at his hands gripping his knees, the white knuckles.

Damn. Why had he let himself get so worked up? The last thing he wanted was to get into an argument with Fred. Usually, they saw eye to eye on most issues. He wondered what Fred was thinking.

When Fred spoke, it was slowly, as if from deep deliberation. "When I think about what you've been through, it's easy to understand your anger and frustration. Lord knows, I sure don't know how *I'd* react *myself* if I were in your shoes."

He shrugged and smiled. “And who knows, you may be right. Maybe someone should be looking at where we are concerning justice today.”

Paul thought Fred made a vital point; nobody could say how they would react unless they had lost a loved one to a killer the way he had.

“That guy who killed Kevin is a career criminal. He's been in trouble a couple of times since the court let him off. Every time I see his name in the paper, I clip out the story and save it. I'm building a file on this killer.”

“What are you going to do with it?” Fred asked.

“I don't really know. Let's just call it morbid curiosity.”

It was well after five when they pulled into the company parking lot, and Paul pointed to one of two remaining vehicles.

“Isn't that your secretary's car?”

“That's funny…what's she still doing here?”

As they were getting out of the car, the front entrance door to the office opened, and Janice called out to them.

“Paul, wait -- don't leave -- there was an emergency phone call for you.”

The secretary held the door open for them.

“Use the phone at my desk,” she said. “The number's on my memo pad.”

Paul hurried through the Accounting Department, to the desk outside Fred's private office. He found the number and was making the call just as Fred and Janice caught up with him. They stopped a short distance away and waited, while he listened to the ringer signal. He could read in their faces the universal apprehension that always accompanied emergency calls.

A woman's voice came on the line. “Oak Park Hospital, Emergency Room.”

He felt every muscle in his body contract. His lips moved several times before any sound would come out, and then he stumbled with the words.

"Aah, yes…ah, I was told to call this number? My name is Paul Becker."

"Your wife is Joan Becker?"

"Yes."

"She's been injured in an automobile accident, Mr. Becker. Can you come here? Now?"

He gripped the phone to still the sudden trembling in his hand. "Yes. Yes, of course. How bad is it?"

"I don't know her condition, sir…she's in surgery."

"Oh, no...." For a moment, it was all he could say.

"Mr. Becker? Are you still there?"

He took a breath and let it out. "I…I'll be right there."

He lowered his hand to chest level and stared at the phone, as if trying to decide what to do with it. Fred came forward and hung it up for him.

"Are you all right?"

Paul saw him through eyes slightly out of focus.

"There's been a car wreck. Joan's in surgery. I have to get over there right away."

"Anything we can do to help?"

"I'll be okay." Paul turned to go, then stopped. "Maybe you and Jan can make a few calls for me. Her sister should be told. And my brother -- he can get the accident information while I tend to Joan."

Janice picked up her notebook and took down the numbers Paul gave her.

"Call me at home..." Fred said, as Paul headed for the door, "…I mean, when you get a chance."

The drive to the hospital was a blur to Paul. Then the nurse in Emergency was directing him to a waiting room where she said the attending surgeon would meet with him. He tried pressing her for details, but when she told him that only the doctor could furnish such information, he turned and walked down the hall to the waiting room.

He was relieved to find it was unoccupied; the thought of forced conversation with strangers right now was inconceivable. It held the usual furnishings: a padded couch and chairs, vending machines for coffee, soft drinks and snacks. He sat down in one of the chairs and looked around. A television set, tuned to a popular talk show, sat on a shelf suspended from the ceiling; and hanging on the wall, above the magazine rack, was the inevitable 'No Smoking' sign.

Leaning his head against the backrest, he closed his eyes and tried to quell his imagination. He thought about others who had sat here, waiting for news of loved ones. Were their fears as terrifying as his? He opened his eyes and sat up to blot out the frightening visions forming in his mind. His hand reached instinctively for a cigarette, then fell back when he remembered the sign. He got up and began to pace.

Finally the door opened and Paul saw a man, dressed all in green, enter, a facemask still hanging from his neck.

"Mr. Becker?"

"Yes. How is she, Doctor?"

The resident sank wearily into a chair and motioned with his hand to another.

"Please, sit down, Mr. Becker."

A shiver ran down Paul's neck and back, then to his legs where it threatened the stability of his knees. He preferred to remain standing, but the doctor's expression was insistent. Knowing there'd be no discussion until he obeyed, Paul frowned and sat down.

"Your wife suffered massive head injuries. We knew from the X-rays that her chances were slim...we tried everything possible." The surgeon paused and winced. "I'm sorry."

Paul had been holding his breath, and when he let it out now, it seemed that part of him went with it. He sat for a moment in stunned silence. Only moments before, he had waited, imagining the worst. Now it had come to pass.

He forced himself to get up. "I'd like to see her."

"Of course."

They walked past the emergency facilities and down to the end of the hall where the doctor opened the door to a room and turned on the lights.

Paul stared at the gurney, and the form under the sheet struck him as being childlike in size. There must be some mistake. Can this really be Joan? His *wife*? She looked so small and alone.

He could feel the doctor's presence. "I'd like to be alone with her for a while."

"I understand," The doctor turned to leave. "Stop at the nurses station, and give her the name of your mortician before you leave -- she'll call and make the arrangements for you."

When Paul heard the door close behind him, he went over and pulled back the top half of the sheet. Except for the chin and right cheek, Joan's head was covered with temporary bandages. But what he saw, he recognized. His eyes moved down her left side and stopped at the wedding band...the final confirmation.

That it was Joan, there could be no doubt. Still, he was filled with the same sense of detachment he felt when he had looked at Kevin's lifeless body: the feeling that he was looking at just the shell, the temporary form used by the soul during life. The warm, vital being he knew as his wife was gone.

He wanted to say good-bye. But it was too late. How do you say good-bye to someone when she can't hear the words? His hand closed on her arm with an urgent need to let her know, somehow, that he was there. That she was not alone. He squeezed gently and was shocked to feel how cool she was to the touch. And all at once, he realized she was already getting cold.

After a while, he pulled the sheet up over the body and walked out to the hall.

CHAPTER 19

Paul stopped at the desk to give the nurse the phone number of Kilmer's funeral home.

"He'll recognize the name," he said, "-- tell him I'll call later about arrangements."

She thanked him and then, on a signal from her, a uniformed policeman came over.

"Mr. Becker? Here's the address of the garage your car was towed to." He gave Paul a business card. "Your insurance adjuster can look at it there."

Paul put the card into his pocket without looking at it. "The hell with the car," he said, "tell me what happened."

"I'm not allowed to discuss the accident. You'll have to request a copy of the accident report."

The words had that impersonal ring to them, but still, Paul thought he saw a soft spot in the man's eyes.

"Come on, Officer, there's just the two of us -- you can always deny it later. Gimme a break, huh?"

The cop winced and shook his head. Then, glancing at the nurse, he moved away, signaling with his head for Paul to follow, and as they moved toward the exit, he spoke quickly, in a whisper that Paul had to strain to hear.

"We've got a statement from two witnesses, and their version matches the one the driver of the truck gave. Apparently, he braked to avoid a fender-bender on the road ahead of him, but the trailer jackknifed on the wet road, and the whole rig tipped over on your wife's car. The Fire Department had to use the 'Jaws of Life' to get her out."

Paul winced at the vision the words evoked. "How fast was he *going*, for crissake?"

"The speed limit there is forty-five," the cop said, with a shrug, "so the traffic was probably moving at about that speed."

"*Forty-five*?" Paul was stunned. He knew the route Joan took coming home from the store and the speed limits were nowhere near that high. "Where did this happen?"

"On Roosevelt Road, at Mount Carmel Cemetery."

Paul closed his eyes and bowed his head. "Oh, shit."

"What's the matter?"

Paul looked up. "Oh...never mind -- it's a long story."

The officer shrugged, gave Paul the address of the station where he could pick up the accident report, then left.

Tense with futility and anger, Paul walked blindly through the parking lot to his car. He thought the therapy sessions had helped her let go. He tried to make her see that visiting the grave as often as she did was morbid, and, for a while, it appeared he had succeeded. Apparently not.

A sharp drop in temperature and an increase in wind speed, following the afternoon's drizzle, made the air damp and raw. Paul started the car and turned on the defroster to keep the windshield clear. It was still a week until the first day of autumn, but he felt like it was here already. He felt empty and cold.

Where had the summer gone? He remembered it vaguely, as if in some dream or trance. The whole beautiful season had passed in a fog of grief and frustration. He felt robbed of his favorite time of year -- stolen from him, like his son...

And now his wife, too. And all by the same thief.

Sudden anger rose from somewhere in his stomach and, like bile, it burned his throat. That son-of-a-bitch, Tate. He might just as well have been driving that truck. If not for him, she would have had no reason to visit the cemetery.

Behind him, a horn blared, bringing him back to the present, and the reality that he had missed his turn. At the next stoplight, he turned north and got back on course.

The phone was ringing as he opened the back door. It was Catherine.

"Paul!" Her voice was sharp with indignation. "I went all the way to the hospital and they wouldn't let me see her."

"They did the right thing."

"But I'm her sister -- don't I have the right?"

He closed his eyes and sighed. "Cathy, believe me, it's better you didn't see her."

She was silent for a moment, then, "They said she died of head injuries."

"Yes," he replied. "Massive. You could only see a little of her face…most of it was covered in bandages."

There was silence again. Then when she spoke, her tone changed. "I was *shocked* when I didn't find you there."

"Why?"

"*Well*, I would think you'd want to spend some time with her."

He sighed, knowing any attempt to explain his feelings was futile. Still, he was compelled to try.

"How do you spend time with someone who isn't there?"

"What?"

"That body in the hospital isn't Joan -- she's gone." He sighed. "I know, you're thinking I'm callous, but I can't help that; it's the way I feel."

"My God, I can't believe I'm hearing this."

"Cathy, I'm sorry, but I'd rather remember her the way she was: the warm, wonderful person and loving mother that I knew as my wife -- not that broken shell under a sheet in the hospital."

He heard Catherine sniffle and knew she was crying.

"Oh, yes," she said, her voice cracking. "She was a wonderful person. Everybody loved her." She stopped for a moment, then went on. "I'm trying to understand. I've always thought of you as being…well…different, Paul. I heard Joan say many times, it was one of the things that attracted her to you. I don't know. Maybe you have the right idea...if it helps you get through your grief. Lord knows, Joan still had problems with hers."

She was silent for a moment, then continued, "That reminds me, did Joan happen to phone you this afternoon?"

"No, why?"

"Oh, *darn*. Now I may never know."

"What are you talking about?"

"Joan had an appointment with someone for lunch today, and when she came back -- well, all I can say is she was like a different person."

"How do you mean?"

"She was smiling, absolutely radiant. I haven't seen her like that since…well, you know. Anyway, I tried to find out what happened, but all I could get out of her was that she had wonderful news, but that I'd have to wait until she could tell you first. Now you say she didn't get in touch with you, so how are we going to find out?"

Paul heard the doorbell.

"Someone's at the door, Cathy. I'll get back to you, okay?"

"Oh. All right. Paul, listen, if you need anything, or maybe someone to talk to, Bill and I can come over…."

"Thanks, Cath, but I'd really prefer to be alone right now. I appreciate your offer, though."

The doorbell rang again, followed by pounding.

"Cathy…"

"I heard. Call me...'bye."

Paul heard his brother's voice shout his name. He flipped the living room light switch on and opened the door.

"Jesus! What took you so long? What were you doin', sitting in the *dark*, for crissake?"

"Take it easy, Ray -- the phone was ringing when I let myself in -- didn't have time to turn on the light. It was Catherine, complaining that they wouldn't let her in to see Joan at the hospital."

Ray let out an audible sigh. "Oh yeah, I was there, too. They told me you left already, so I hurried right over -- then I see the house all dark, and you don't answer the bell…well, *hell*, I got worried, you know?"

Paul led the way to the bar in the dining room. "I suppose it would look bad, under the circumstances." He poured bourbon for himself. "You want a beer? It's in the refrigerator."

Ray considered the whiskey bottle. "No, I think I'll have what you're having."

"Help yourself."

Paul sat down and watched Ray sip his bourbon and make a face.

"I need ice with this," he said, moving toward the kitchen.

"Take the bucket with you…I'll want some for my second one."

Paul drained his drink, and when Ray returned, he added ice, poured another and let it sit on the table while he waited for the buzz he knew would come from the first one. Ray sat down, leaned back and sipped his bourbon.

"I can't believe this happened to you again," he said. "I mean, it's only been...what, four months? Yeah, twice in four months."

Paul stared at his glass in silence, relishing the effect of the alcohol, already in his bloodstream and circulating through his brain. The tension that had built up during the past several hours began to fade.

When Ray mentioned that he was unable to get any information at the hospital about the accident, Paul filled in the details for him.

"By the way," he said, digging into his pocket, "I'd appreciate it if you'd pick up a copy of the report for me."

"Will do." Ray glanced at the address on the slip of paper and put it into his wallet. He finished his drink and shuddered. "I've gotta have a beer," he said, getting up. "I don't know how you can drink that shit."

He came back, beer in hand, talking. "You know, Paul, I was just thinking how different we are -- I mean, about visiting the cemetery. Some people go all the time, even put flowers on the graves of their loved ones. I can only remember going to see Pop's grave once with Ma. And, after her funeral, I haven't been to either of their graves, have you?"

Paul drank half of his bourbon and shook his head.

"Is there something wrong with us?"

"I don't think so. *Different*, yes, but that doesn't mean there's something *wrong* with us. I think it's a matter of family custom more than anything. It's just something we never did. That time you went with Ma, I must have been in Nam."

"Yeah, come to think of it, you were. As I recall, she was worried because she hadn't heard from you for a while...probably thought Pop's spirit might give her strength."

"Could be. Anyway, we're just different, that's all. As a matter of fact, I tried to discourage Joan from going." He sighed and shook his head. "But, I see now, it did no good."

Ray finished his beer and went for another can. Again, he came back talking: "Too bad she didn't listen to you -- she wouldn't have been there, and...." He sat down and shook his head. "*Damn it*, she shouldn't have been there at all. That *bastard* did it to you again."

"What bastard?"

Ray threw his head back and looked at the ceiling. "Don't give me that. You know what bastard – *Tate*! Steve Tate, *dammit*! It all started with him."

"Okay, okay." Paul sighed. "Yeah, I've thought about it. That's about *all* I've been thinking about."

"Well?"

"Well, what?"

Ray looked at Paul and rolled his eyes. "Look, everyone knows he's guilty -- I know it, you know it -- even the judge knew it. The verdict is in. The next step in the process is sentencing -- the punishment phase." His face twisted, exposing his teeth. "But the system failed."

"So, *I* should take over? I should execute him, is that what you're saying?" Paul frowned. "You amaze me. Everything is so simple to you. What good would that do? It won't bring either of them back...and I sure as hell don't want to spend the rest of my life in prison." He didn't feel comfortable telling his brother about the games he played with himself, trying to come up with a way to kill Tate and get away with it. The problem he kept running into was the need of an alibi. After that newspaper account of his threat to Tate in the courtroom and the photo of him being restrained by Lieutenant Burnett, he would be a prime suspect.

"Come on, no jury would ever convict you of murder -- manslaughter, maybe. And the way things are today, you'd probably be out in a couple of years."

Paul could see where their conversation was taking them and knew the alcohol was motivating it. Ray never could handle whiskey, and chasing it down with beer was even worse.

"By the way, did you let Barbara know you were coming here"

"That's right, change the subject."

"Well, did you?"

"*Yes*, I *did*." Ray frowned. "Come to think of it, she said she'd delay dinner...and I should make you join us."

Paul smiled. "I accept. Call her and tell her we're coming"

"Okay, okay, but you're not getting off the hook that easy."

CHAPTER 20

For the next three days, Paul was never alone. Connie and Ray, it seemed, had formed a conspiracy of protection, and with Ernie and Barbara aiding and abetting, the couples managed to keep Paul at one or the other of their homes every night. Except for a few quick trips to pick up personal items and a change of clothing, he spent almost no time at his house, and even then, someone always was available to go along for the ride. They conceded to him the responsibility of notifying the car and life insurance companies, but Ray took over the driving and legwork required to obtain copies of the death certificate and accident report.

At Kilmer's suggestion, Paul agreed to a one night, closed casket wake. Catherine produced a photograph of Joan, taken on the occasion of a recent fashion line promotion campaign, and Kilmer had it mounted in a tasteful display on the lid of the casket. Accounts of the accident had run in both Chicago newspapers, making explanations to mourners unnecessary, and the next day, in a simple ceremony of family and friends, Joan was laid to rest next to Kevin's grave.

At nine o'clock that night, Paul was relieved to see the last of the guests depart the post-funeral gathering at his sister's home. He declined her offer that he spend another night there, but Connie persisted.

"*Ray*," she said, looking at her brother for an ally, "help me convince him. It's too soon to go home to that empty house."

"Yeah," Ray said, "what's the hurry?"

Paul smiled and shook his head. "Look, you two, I'm grateful for all you've done -- I don't know where I'd be without your help -- but it's time I broke out of this circle of family concern. You both have responsibilities to your families, and I have to get on with my life." He could see Connie's protest coming and raised his hand. "One more night isn't going to make that much difference."

He put his arm around Connie's shoulder and held out his hand to Ray.

"Don't worry" he said, pulling them together, "I'll be okay."

Connie blinked away a tear and tried to smile. "Promise you'll call if you need us?"

"I promise."

He left them watching from the doorway and walked to his car.

Traffic going toward the city was light at this time of night, so, in less than half an hour, he was in the alley behind his garage. He activated the remote control that lifted the door and turned on the interior light, then, when he saw he had the whole garage to himself, the first pang of reality hit him. He was struck by how empty it looked, and suddenly the thought of entering the house filled him with dread.

It took a moment for acceptance to come, then he pulled up, spun the wheel, and backed the car into the center of the garage. The extra space provided by the missing second car made the interior seem huge; even the click of metal when he shut the door sounded like an explosion.

The sensation of amplified space and sound followed him into the house, where his footsteps on the kitchen floor seemed to echo as if he were walking in a huge, empty hall. He went to the bar in the dining room, where he downed one bourbon and poured another. Then, carrying it with him, he turned out the lights on the first floor and went upstairs.

He stripped down to his shorts and went into the bathroom to use the toilet. As he washed his hands, his eyes strayed to the row of cologne, perfume and nail polish bottles, lipstick tubes and make-up brushes on Joan's side of the vanity. The sight of the intensely personal items made the muscles of his diaphragm contract. He stared at the feminine paraphernalia, teeth clenched, water running, for almost a minute -- remembering.

Then, using his arm, he swept the whole collection of toiletries into the plastic waste can liner, stuffed the bag into one of the cabinets under the vanity, and returned to his drink in the bedroom. He smoked a cigarette while he finished the bourbon, then turned out the light and went to bed.

It took some time, but a restless sleep finally came. And with it, a dream that he was driving home from work. Word had reached him through his sister-in-law that Joan had left the store with wonderful news for him, and he was in a hurry.

Just as he changed lanes to get around a slow moving car, the one now ahead of him signaled for a left turn. Meanwhile, the slower moving car passed through the intersection and the traffic light turned red.

A huge tractor-trailer pulled up on his right side and stopped. He heard the hiss of air brakes and the chatter of gears as it shifted down. The noise diminished to the characteristic rattle of a diesel engine at idle, then, as if to demonstrate the power at his control, the driver revved the powerful engine repeatedly.

His curiosity aroused, Paul leaned forward and looked up at the window of the cab. Expecting to see the typical trucker, Paul froze when he recognized the maniacally leering face looking down at him. He pulled his head back and tried to gather his thoughts. As he remembered it, Tate was a burglar, since when did he become a truck driver? It didn't make sense. Did he steal that rig?

Hoping maybe his eyes had tricked him, Paul looked again. The face was laughing now, taunting, and there was no mistake, no trick...it was Steve Tate.

Cold fear flashed through Paul's chest when he saw the light turn green and the truck lurch forward and roar through the intersection; for, somehow he knew, in the traffic up ahead, Joan's car lay in its path. He had to get to her first, but the car ahead of him was waiting for a break in traffic to make a left turn. He thought to back up and go around, but the car behind was on his bumper.

His path opened just as the light changed from yellow to red, but panic drove him on, horns blaring at either side of him at this infraction of the law. The accelerator was on the floor, but the car seemed sluggish. He pushed his foot down harder and rocked back and forth in his seat, as if by the momentum of his body he would increase his speed, but the engine failed to respond.

Hopelessly outdistanced now, Paul pounded the steering wheel in frustration as he watched the truck bear down on the familiar shape of his wife's Caprice. And, like some mammoth machine of the future, it seemed to devour the tiny car. Then, as if nourished by this repast, it spit the digested wreckage out its hulking rear end and roared off again, belching exhaust into the sky.

He moaned aloud and the sound of his voice woke him. He was sitting up in bed, disoriented. Then, in the faint moonlight from the window, he recognized his bedroom. Moist with perspiration and shaken by the dream, he reached to the night table for his cigarettes.

Knowing sleep would not come easily again, he got up and looked out the window at the moonlit yard below, and for a moment, memories of summer barbecues filled his thoughts, happy days spent with Joan and Kevin, family and friends. Would he ever know that kind of blissful existence again? He shook his head and turned away.

The air felt cold against his damp body, but he was reluctant to get dressed again. He turned the closet light on and stared at the robe. The birthday gift. After trying it on once for size, it had hung in the closet unused. She never asked why, but he knew she must have been hurt. He wondered at this rare manifestation of insensitivity. Why couldn't he have worn it at least once in a while to please her? With a sigh of regret that she was not there to see, he put it on and went downstairs. In the dining room, he made a drink and carried it with him to the basement.

When the walls were paneled, he had the space under the stairs enclosed to make a small storage area for odds and ends. He opened the access door, pulled out his old footlocker containing his war souvenirs and dragged it over to his worktable. Then, reaching under several layers of mementos, he removed a leather pouch, opened the zipper closure and slid his hand inside.

The gun felt cold to the touch.

He pushed the pouch aside and held the weapon up to the overhead light, where the metal glimmered darkly under a thin coating of oil. It was a Government Issue, forty-five caliber, Colt semiautomatic pistol. Actually, it was not one of the souvenirs.

Five years before, while attending a machine tool display in the convention center at Arlington Park, he had wandered into a gun show on another floor. Struck by the diversity of the weapons being offered, he made a tour of the booths. It was curiosity only that motivated him; he had no intention of buying. But when he started for the exit, a roving peddler approached him, one of many with so few weapons to sell that renting a booth was an unjustified expense.

The man appeared to be at least sixty-five, and when he introduced himself as a WW II veteran, Paul was inclined to believe him. Paul told him that he was not interested in buying, but then the man thrust the Colt into Paul's hand, saying, "There aren't many of these around anymore in this condition."

A quick inspection verified the claim, and after some haggling about price and the man's offer of two extra clips, Paul wrote a check. He knew, from the moment he held it, he would buy. This model always had been a favorite of his. At just over two pounds, there was a feel and look about it that left no doubt as to its purpose, and its stopping power was legendary.

Also in the pouch was a rolled-up T-shirt, which he used now to wipe away the oil. He pressed the magazine catch and removed the empty clip, then went through the takedown procedure. Although he had done this at least a dozen times, his engineer mind never failed to admire the genius that went into its design. It was little wonder to him that it remained for so many years the standard sidearm of the military.

Satisfied with the condition of the gun, he took a rod from the pouch, wrapped the T-shirt around it and removed the excess oil from the inside of the barrel. Then, working slowly, he reassembled the parts, pulled back the slide and raised the gun to eye level.

Suddenly, on the wall across the room, in line with the sights, an image took shape. Like an unbidden memory, there was Tate, dressed the same as that day in court when the charges against him were dropped.

Paul could hear his brother's voice echoing in his mind: 'The verdict is in! Go on to the next step...the punishment phase!' Moving instinctively, Paul trained the sights on a spot directly between Tate's cold, mocking eyes, then squeezed the trigger and the hammer fell with a metallic snap.

The sound broke the spell, and the image was gone. He stared at the blank wall and blinked his eyes. At this distance, it should be covered with blood and brains. He put the gun on the bench and sighed.

After a while, he put everything back and went up to bed, but no amount of punching made the pillow right, nor did turning and tossing make the mattress yield. Churning with anger and hate, his mind developed plan after plan, all with the same flaw. When last he looked at the clock, it was after one, and he still had not come up with one that eliminated him as a suspect. To kill Tate, he needed an alibi.

Several times, with his mind on the brink of sleep, he thought he heard noises.

The first of these was footsteps and the sound of a door closing in the hall, and in his semiconscious state, he imagined it was Kevin coming home late. He was halfway out of bed, intent on investigating, when he realized his mind was playing tricks. The second was a moan that seemed to come from the chair near the window, and when he turned to look, he thought he saw the shadow of Joan's head at the top of the backrest.

This he thought to be real. Joan was sitting up in that chair! He jumped out of bed and went to what he was sure was her, but what he found, instead, was the robe, bunched up over the top of the chair where he had thrown it earlier. It had looked so real. The robe had formed a mound over the top of the chair that, in the dark, resembled the top of her head. As he stood staring, he heard the moan again and realized it was the wind in the big, old elm tree outside.

Suddenly, he felt weak and dropped into the chair, where reality took over. Joan would never sit in this chair again. She was dead. And then his diaphragm convulsed in the agony of this truth, and he was shaken with wrenching spasms of weeping.

After what seemed hours, and when he was all cried-out, he returned to bed where sleep finally came.

The next morning, Paul was again grateful for the robe; it was late, and he did not have time to get dressed and out for the morning paper before his neighbor disposed of it for him.

Then, when he had to use Joan's powered creamer in his coffee because his cream was sour, it struck him that he could feel her presence...still helping him. It was uncanny: first the robe, then this.

He made breakfast, of sorts, but when he piled the dishes into the sink, it came to him that he was on his own now. Joan would not be there to wash them. For that matter, many things would not get done any more.

Joan's role as mother diminished about the time Kevin entered high school, and she bristled at the term 'house wife'. 'Demeaning', is what she called it. 'I need something that will help me express myself', she had said. Catherine solved the problem by urging Joan to join her in the business.

She worked only part time, and Paul volunteered to help with a few of the household chores. He did some of the laundry and helped with food preparation and weekend cleaning. But when it came to jobs like washing dishes and vacuuming, he drew the line. Thinking about it now, he remembered another one: there was no way he could iron his shirts -- handkerchiefs, maybe, but that was it. He would have to think about hiring someone. But where do you go to get reliable help?

As he finished the last cup of coffee, he had the feeling that the house was growing; it seemed to loom threateningly around him. He left the kitchen, and on his way upstairs, the dining room, den and living room, all looked bigger than usual. Even in the hall on the upper level, the two extra bedrooms and bath added to the illusion of growth. The whole place seemed empty and outsized without another body occupying space. At this moment, he was unsure of his own physical presence.

Actually, this house was too big for just him. Maybe he should start thinking about selling and going into a condo. He had always loved this house…but did he still? Hell, he didn't know. He'd have to think about it some more. Right now, he just wanted to get out of there.

It was still early, so he decided it was time to go back to work.

He noticed a few raised eyebrows when he came in; it seemed no one expected him so soon. To everyone commenting on his early return, he gave the same answer: 'The empty house was getting on my nerves.'

The last time Paul saw Woodward's secretary was the day of the accident, and now, as he approached her desk, she looked up at him in wide-eyed surprise.

"Hello, Janice." He smiled and nodded his head toward the inner office. "Is he alone?"

"*Paul*," she said, finally finding her voice, "how nice to see you."

"Same here." Still smiling, he raised his eyebrows and nodded again at the closed door.

"Oh, yes, he's alone…go right in."

He tapped on the door.

"Come in!"

Woodward was on the phone, but seeing Paul, he cut the conversation short, and in one quick motion, was up and moving toward him. He put an arm around Paul's shoulder, guided him to the guest chair, then stepped back and half-sat on the edge of his desk.

"This is just a *visit*, I hope."

Paul's silence produced a scowl from Woodward. "You aren't thinking of returning *already*, are you?"

Paul answered with a shrug.

"Come on, Paul, it's too soon. You haven't given yourself a chance to grieve."

Paul looked away for a moment while he searched for the right words. How could he explain his feelings without sounding callous? No matter what he said, it would come out sounding as though he didn't really love his wife at all. He wasn't even sure himself just what it was he was feeling. Most people, faced with his loss, would be overcome with grief.

"It's hard to explain," he said, facing Woodward's questioning stare. "I didn't just *now* lose Joan. I feel like I've been grieving a long time. When Kevin died, it was like she went with him...the life we had together was gone. We were never able to get close again." He hesitated, wondering if Fred could understand, then went on. "You see what I'm getting at? This grief isn't something new to me. What I'm really feeling now is -- I don't know -- loneliness, I guess. I find myself lost in my own house, Fred. Everything in there reminds me of them."

"I had no idea, Paul -- I guess I just assumed that you and Joan had picked up the loose ends by now and had gone back to something like a normal life. It's hard to imagine what it must be like for a woman to lose an only child."

An awkward silence fell between them, then Paul spoke up. "I need to get back to work."

CHAPTER 21

A contract for a new project that Woodward had been negotiating for months finally was signed. The client company extended the completion date to compensate for some of the time eaten up in the haggling stage, but the time frame still was unrealistic.

The overtime everyone knew this would entail was welcomed by the hourly employees, but the engineers were salaried, and Paul foresaw the grumbling he knew would come. To offset this inequity, Fred and Paul worked out a bonus system based on a set of target dates that placated almost everyone.

Paul hired a part-time housekeeper to do the cleaning, laundry, and some of the shopping and food preparation, which left him free to stay late at the plant and bring work home.

He worked with this heavy schedule from the beginning of September through all of November, but it shaved weeks off the anticipated time overrun, and by Friday of the first week in December the basic stages of the system were delivered to the client's manufacturing site.

It would take another month to get the equipment in place and operating, but the pressure was off for Paul and his group of engineers. Woodward called a one o'clock project status meeting, and when it was over, he asked Paul to join him in his office.

He told Janice to hold his calls, and Paul eased his weary body into the guest chair.

Fred leaned back in his swivel chair and smiled. "Well, you can finally take a breather, Paul."

"I can use it."

"How have things been going for you?"

"I've put my house on the market, and I'm toying with the idea of maybe buying a condo. I've always loved that house, but now…it's just too damn big and…full of ghosts."

Fred tilted forward in his chair and leaned across the desk, pointing his finger at Paul. "You haven't taken a vacation this year. You need to get away from there for a while -- two weeks minimum."

"Yeah? Where? My sister -- and brother -- both asked me to stay with them for a while, but I don't like living in someone else's house. I always feel in the way."

"No, no, I didn't mean anything like that. You need to get away completely…out of town."

Paul wondered where Fred was going with this.

"Listen, when you mentioned condominium, I got this great idea. Nobody's using my Florida condo now -- "

"Wait a minute, Fred -- "

"No!" Woodward raised a restraining hand. "We never go down there until late January, so it's just sitting there, gathering dust. The weather is getting nasty here already, and this place is right on the beach. It would be great for you. Just what you need. Take a couple of weeks…at least."

"Fred, I can't accept that --"

"Look, Paul, you've been with me twenty-one years. You're not just an employee to me; you're a long-term friend. And I'd like to do something for you…besides, you earned it after what you did in the last three months."

“Okay, okay, I'll tell my housekeeper. She'll probably welcome the time off to get ready for Christmas.”

“Good! Let me know when you're ready, and I'll call the building manager to let her know you're coming. I'll have her get someone to clean up the place.”

“You told me about the condo, but I don't remember where you said it was.”

“Ormond Beach. It's just north of Daytona.” Fred produced a manila envelope from the file drawer of his desk, took out a glossy brochure and spread it open. “You're gonna love it, Paul. When we're down there, we turn the air off at night and open the windows to hear the surf.”

Paul leaned forward and followed Fred's moving finger.

“We're on the third floor,” Fred said, pointing to a unit facing the ocean. He turned the brochure over, to a display of floor plans. “This is our layout. We picked one with three bedrooms for when the kids decide to come down.”

“It looks great,” Paul said, sitting back in his chair.

Fred emptied the folder onto the desk “Here's a local map, with directions from the airport, and here's the key.” He put everything back into the envelope and gave it to Paul.

“This will give you a chance to see if you'd be satisfied with just a condo. You've been living in that big house of yours a long time.”

Fred rose, signaling the end of the discussion. He came around the desk and put his arm around Paul's shoulder.

“Okay, now you *get*. I'll break the news to your men.”

Ten minutes later, Paul was in his car with the key in the ignition, but he made no move to start the engine. He leaned back and closed his eyes, then his mind went back to a night three months before, when he first had tried to form a plan. He remembered dreaming up one strategy after another and discarding them all because he could not come up with an alibi.

Well now, good old Fred had just solved the problem.

He turned the key, and when the engine jumped to life, he drove away. It occurred to him that his departure depended on the airline schedules.

He remembered a travel agency in a small shopping center that he passed every day, and when he saw it come into view, he switched lanes and pulled into the parking lot.

A middle-aged woman with heavy eye make-up beckoned him to a chair at her terminal as soon as he came in. He was their only customer, and she flashed an eager smile.

"My name is Verna, how may I help you?"

"When is the next available, nonstop flight to Daytona Beach?"

She began searching the commuter. "Will this be round trip?"

"Yes."

"We have one leaving at eleven-fifteen tomorrow morning. Is that too soon for you?"

He blinked at her, suddenly realizing how unprepared he was.

"Yeah. When's the next one?"

She consulted the computer again. "Monday morning...nine-fifty?"

"That would be fine," he said.

"When do you want to return?"

"I'm not really sure. I thought maybe two weeks, but that could change either way. How flexible are they about schedule changes?"

"They're pretty reasonable, but of course a lot depends on available seats. You'll have to take what they offer."

He thought about that for a moment, then shrugged. "I don't have any deadlines -- so I guess I'm flexible, too."

She gave him one of her cards. “I'll set it up for two weeks. If you want to change the time, give me a call. Would you like me to arrange for a car rental?”

“Yes.” He took out his wallet and gave her his credit card.

The woman finished feeding information into the terminal, then left for the printer. The presence of an ashtray on her desk was Paul's signal to light a cigarette. He leaned back and thought about the schedule. Two weeks should give him enough time. It *had* to be enough -- he wouldn't get another opportunity like *this* again.

The woman returned with the tickets and went through the itinerary with him; the car rental was Avis. He signed for the credit, retrieved his card and left.

Chapter 22

It was a pleasant December day, with crisp air and a sunny sky, but Paul drove toward home without a thought to it. With his airline tickets tucked into his inner jacket pocket, his mood had changed. The yoke that had bound him to his leaden anchor of frustration was lifting; he was moving forward again, and suddenly his life seemed full of purpose. His mind was busy at his mental drawing board, sketching plans, laying out each stage of the operation. When finished, he hoped to have it worked out like an assembly line, every step timed with computer accuracy...*his* computer, the one in his engineer mind.

Using generous estimates, he came up with a cost figure. In cash. Credit cards left trails. A glance at his watch told him he still had time, and at the next intersection, he made a detour for the bank.

The teller read the withdrawal slip and turned to her computer terminal to verify the account.

"How would you like this, Mr. Becker? "

"Forty fifties and fifty twenties," Paul answered, "in new bills if possible."

She counted the bills in each banded packet and entered the amount into a calculator, which then issued a printed receipt. Paul totaled the amounts stamped on the bands and frowned at the bulky stack.

"Would you like me to get you an envelope for that?"

He looked up at the teller and saw the amusement in her eyes. "No thanks, I'll manage." Splitting the packets equally, he stuffed them into the pockets of his suit jacket and hurried away.

He would be using the car again later, so he parked at the curb in front of his house. The usual empty feeling greeted him when he opened the door, but he buried it under the list of things he had to do between then and Monday morning.

In the dining room, he fixed himself a drink and carried it to his desk in the study, where he used the phone to call Woodward. As usual, Janice answered and connected him with Fred.

"I thought I'd better call you right away, Fred -- I got lucky at the travel agency."

"How lucky?"

"I got a flight leaving Monday."

"That's great. I'll call the building manager and have her get the telephone connected."

They were silent for a moment, then Paul spoke. "I still feel guilty about this."

"Nonsense! You need the break. But if it'll make you feel any better, the pressure will be waiting for you when you get back."

Paul laughed.

"You call me if you run into a problem with anything down there."

He made two more calls: one to the newspaper carrier, stopping delivery until further notice, and then his neighbor, to relieve her of the responsibility of disposing of it for him.

When she assured him that her family would keep an eye on the house during his absence, he thought to tell her that he would set timers on two lamps, one on the first floor to go on at dusk and off at eleven, the other in the upper bedroom, to go on at ten and off at midnight.

With those items out of the way, he leaned back, lit a cigarette and sipped his drink. If his memory was correct, that old money belt he had bought for a vacation years ago should be somewhere in the desk. He reached down to the bottom drawer, pulled it out all the way, and there it was, at the back, all rolled up. It was made of skin-tone cloth and was designed to be worn under the shirt.

Stretching the belt out across the top of the desk, he emptied his coat pockets and broke open the packets of money. Then, keeping the fifties separate from the twenties, he distributed the bills evenly throughout the compartments. He was pleased with the results. He had asked for new bills knowing they would add the least bulk to the belt and would not be obvious under his shirt.

He went upstairs to the closet in the guestroom, where he chose two, thirty-inch Pullman-size bags and took them to the bed in the master bedroom. One bag would hold mild weather apparel for Florida, the other, winter clothing for up here in Chicago. He would use a small, zippered bag for toiletries.

It took much longer than he had figured. In the past, when they traveled, Joan had always done the packing. He lost time on simple things, like learning that a shirt should be buttoned first then folded so the front lies flat. It was almost five when he finished packing.

He went out to a nearby restaurant for dinner, then returned home instead of going to see his brother, as originally planned. It would be easier just to call him.

"That boss of yours is one hell of a nice guy," Ray said, when Paul told him of his trip.

"He's more than that," Paul said, "he's a good friend."

"How long are you gonna be away?"

"I really don't know. I wouldn't think I could stand it for more than a week -- maybe two."

"*Stand it.* Jesus, Paul, you make it sound like a sentence."

"Okay, bad choice of words, I guess. It's just that I can't help feeling guilty."

"Come on, that's a bunch of crap. He knows you've made a pile of money for him -- he owes you. Take it and run."

Paul laughed. "Sometimes I envy you, Ray...you never complicate things. Like you say, 'take it and run'. And you're right. I don't know why it takes me so long to see it."

"Listen, Paul," Ray said, his voice suddenly serious, "you've been through hell." He hesitated, then went on. "Look, you may not like this, but I got the impression that things weren't all that great between you and Joan for quite a while...probably since Kevin's death." He paused. "You don't have to answer if it makes you uncomfortable. But now you have some time to get away and maybe put it behind you."

The silence seemed to hum in Paul's ears. He had never talked to anyone about the deterioration of his marriage, the damping of the fire he and Joan had shared…her withdrawal. Actually, he thought he had done a good job of hiding it. Now he wondered who else had noticed.

"It must have been painfully obvious for *you* to suspect something was wrong."

"*See*? There you go again…you never gave me any credit for being perceptive. You think I'm just a big ox who thinks with his balls. Well, you're *wrong*, Paul. Hell, I could see you hurting a mile away. For a while, I thought you might open up -- you know, unload on me. But no, not *you*. You're the *rock*."

Paul saw the old resentment rising. "Okay, okay, you' re right. I *do* tend to keep things bottled up inside. And I know what you're thinking. Brothers should be able to share, and you think I don't have the confidence in you to understand. But that's not it. It's me…it's just the way I am."

Silence fell between then, and Paul let it stretch, hoping Ray would calm down.

"Yeah, well…I don't care if you *do* get mad, I'm going to ask anyway." Ray hesitated.

"What?"

"How long has it been since you got laid?"

Paul laughed, and the tension was broken. "You mean, *really* laid?"

Ray made a hissing noise through his teeth. "It's been that bad, huh?"

"Yeah, it's been one hell of a long time. Oh, I had a couple of bad experiences -- well-meaning friends trying to fix me up. Both times, the women were all messed up emotionally. You know, divorcee's, still not reconciled to the failure of their marriages, blaming men in general for their unhappiness."

"Well, you won't have to wait much longer. Those beaches down there are just crawling with beautiful things. And with whatever that thing is you have, you shouldn't have any trouble at all."

"Whoa! Wait a minute. What's this, *whatever it is I have* thing."

"Hey, come on, Paul, we've been out together -- I've seen the way women look at you. As a matter of fact, Barbara mentioned that Joan used to get a little upset about it. And that time after Kevin's funeral, at my house, I saw the way Kim's mother…eh, what's her name?"

"Diane, Diane Adams."

"Yeah, Diane Adams...anyway, her eyes were on you all night. I remember thinking, 'What a beautiful woman', and she never even glanced at me once. Every time I looked her way she was looking at you. And, as usual, I was envious."

Paul was glad they were on the phone; if he had gone there instead, Ray would have seen the flush of heat that burned his face now. He remembered that night and how many times his eyes had met Diane's. And the guilt.

"I can't believe you aren't aware of this effect you have on some women; you can't be that blind."

"All right, *there* you have it -- *some* women. Maybe. But the way you tell it, every woman I meet want's to jump into bed with me. You've always had a tendency to exaggerate."

"No I don't...but that's beside the point. All I'm saying is you shouldn't have any trouble getting lucky down there. So, for chrissake, enjoy yourself, okay?"

"I'm gonna do some sightseeing. I've been on the Gulf side -- Tampa, St. Petersburg -- so I'll probably enjoy exploring the Atlantic side."

"Have you got someone to pick up your mail? I can stop by if you don't."

"I've got a mail-slot in the front door, but thanks."

"Okay, call me when you get back."

"Woodward called ahead to have the phone turned on, so I'll be in touch."

When Paul hung up, he leaned back and smiled. Oh, he'd be in touch with Ray, all right...Connie, too. It was part of the plan.

His last call was to his housekeeper to let her know he would be out of town and would call her when he returned.

Then, with all the calls out of the way, he removed a folder from his file drawer and spread out the newspaper clippings he had accumulated on Tate's criminal career. Tate had been arrested and released twice and the subject of three other investigations involving burglary, assault, and a threat to do bodily harm.

Paul had watched for follow-up stories, and when some did not appear, he called Burnett. In every instance the results were the same; the victims refused to testify, and witnesses either disappeared or developed memory loss. The lieutenant always empathized with him, while stressing the value of patience. 'We'll get this guy,' Burnett would say, followed by the inevitable qualifier, 'eventually'.

Well, Paul's patience had run out.

He skimmed through the stories, looking for the one he remembered that mentioned where Tate lived. Halfway through the clippings, he found W. Diversey Avenue, and the city block it referred to was west of Cicero Avenue, but east of Elmwood Park, an area Paul could visualize in his mind.

Although the location covered an entire city block, it was narrowed down by a remark Burnett once had made about Tate living in an apartment above a video store. Satisfied that he could find it, Paul dumped the newspaper clippings into the wastebasket and took it outside to the garbage can in the alley.

The phone was ringing when he returned to the house. He took the call in the kitchen and heard the voice of his real estate agent.

"Mr. Becker," she said, "I've got an offer on your house. Are you willing to come down five thousand?"

"You mean they've offered a hundred and forty-five?"

"Yes, and these people have no problem getting mortgage money."

"I'll take it."

"Okay. I'll call the buyers and tell them they can get their mortgage application started. Can I bring the offer for your signature tomorrow morning."

"Sure, I'm usually up early."

To celebrate the occasion, Paul made a drink and took it with him down to the basement, where he pulled out the footlocker and removed the pouch containing the Colt. He checked the action once more, then loaded one cartridge clip and reached for another. But he stopped when an old saying came back to him: 'If the job ain't done in seven shots, you're in serious trouble'. Shaking his head, he put the gun and clip, separately, into the pouch and closed the zipper.

He went upstairs and put the pouch in the suitcase with the winter clothing.

For a change sleep came easily. A rehash of the phone conversation with his brother was the last thing Paul remembered; he wondered if Ray's account of that evening was just his brother's way of making him feel good. Maybe. If it was, it worked. Still, Paul took pleasure in the possibility that Diane might find him attractive.

He knew the thought had carried over into sleep when he awoke from a dream of her and a sticky mess, forcing him to get up for a change of shorts. Later, reviewing the dream, it surprised him that her image had been so real while they made love. Apparently she had made a powerful impression on his subconscious.

Chapter 23

The real estate agent arrived at ten the next morning, and Paul signed the papers, then went out to a restaurant for a leisurely breakfast. It was almost noon when he returned home and let himself in to the silence he had come to dread. He closed the door and stood for a moment with his back against it, wondering how he was going to pass the time until Monday.

It would have been better to pack and prepare today, when he had plenty of time. But his excitement of the previous day, when Fred opened the door of opportunity, had pushed him into activity. Of course it wouldn't hurt to go over everything again to be sure he hadn't missed some detail.

The telephone rang then, and he pushed himself away from the door and headed for the den.

"Hello?" he said.

"Hello, Paul."

His pulse quickened when he recognized the voice, and suddenly the room seemed to get brighter. "*Diane*?"

"I called earlier, but didn't get an answer."

"I went out for breakfast. Just now walked in the door."

"I know your wondering why I'm calling. I've wanted to for some time, but didn't want to intrude on your grief."

"You wouldn't have been intruding." he said. "I'd have loved to hear from you." Then he quickly added, "And Kim."

"Well, I wanted to give you some time. You've been through so much in the past six months."

Paul went silent. He made it a point not to burden other people with his suffering.

"Paul..." Diane began, then hesitated before going on, "if you're feeling up to it, we need to have a long talk."

"What?"

"I know how strange this must sound, but it's too involved to discuss over the phone."

Another silence fell, then he said, "Okay. How about letting me take you to dinner?"

"I'd like that."

"What time should I come by for you?"

"I could be ready by seven."

"Seven it is then."

"I have a new address. I sold the old place and bought a townhouse. Do you have a pen and paper handy? It isn't easy to find."

He wrote down the directions she gave him.

"I see you've abandoned the city. That's quite a ways to commute, isn't it?"

"In distance, yes, but not in time. I'm close to the toll road and that connects me with the Kennedy. Besides, it's worth it; no congestion, countrylike surroundings. It's quite pretty out here."

"Yes, I'm familiar with the area."

"Paul, thank you."

"*Thank* you? For asking you out to dinner?"

"No, of course not. I meant, thank you for not pressing me with a lot of questions."

"I'm saving them 'till seven -- see you then."

Paul tried to keep himself busy going over his preparations, but the afternoon dragged on endlessly. His mind was full of questions, but nothing he imagined could explain her need to talk. Was his brother right? Had Diane concocted some bogus excuse to get together with him? He dismissed the idea at once; it didn't fit the opinion he had formed of her. He simply could not imagine Diane as a 'designing' woman.

Later, while shaving away the shadow of an early evening beard, Paul made a critical study of his reflection in the bathroom mirror. The hair at his temples was almost all gray, and the lines at the corners of his eyes and mouth had deepened, but his skin was still tight, no signs of sagging anywhere that he could see. He was blessed with sound teeth, and regular checkups kept them bright. At six feet even and a hundred-eighty pounds he still looked lean.

The inspection complete, he decided he didn't look bad at forty-five. Not handsome, but not too bad either. He saw nothing to warrant Ray's contention that women were drawn to him.

It was six-fifty when he found Thornton Lane, a two-lane blacktop that circled a small lake. Even in the dark, he could see why Diane had chosen the area. The developer had been careful not to disturb the natural beauty; the lots were large and tree-shaded. Her unit was in a white brick structure with a view of the lake.

He got out of the car and took a few moments to look out over the water, glistening softly in the light of an early moon. A lake this size would freeze solid by midwinter, and he imagined how it would look with snow piled along the shore and children skating and sledding.

At the sound of a door closing behind him, he turned and saw Diane coming down the walk.

"I saw you admiring the view and thought I'd join you." She made a sweeping gesture with her arm as she approached. "What do you think of my neighborhood?"

"I'm impressed. I was just thinking I'd like to see it in daylight."

"Come on a weekend so I can show you around."

Taking her arm, he led her back to the car and she got in.

"Times sure have changed," he said as they drove off.

"How do you mean?"

"As I remember it, a man could expect to be kept waiting at least half an hour while the woman put the finishing touches on."

She laughed. "Haven't you heard? Today's liberated woman doesn't do things like that."

He looked at her, eyebrows raised. "Is that what you are?"

She laughed again, and to him it sounded bubbly, almost musical.

"Yes," she said, "but not hard-core. I don't even like the term *liberated.* I prefer *new* woman; it's less militant. Besides, making a man wait was a silly custom I've never liked."

To change the subject he asked about Kimberly, but Diane's response left him wondering. After a vague reference to Kim's need of time for adjustment, she ended by asking where they were going.

"I made reservations at the Satellite. I've heard a lot about it, but I've never eaten there; have you?"

"No, but it sounds interesting."

"I saw a picture of it in the paper when it opened for business. Rotating on top of that nineteen story office tower, it's supposed to create the illusion that you're the center of the universe and everything's revolving around you." He laughed. "I know some people who'd be right at home up there."

"So do I. Our magazine's research editor and the art director, to name just a few."

"Our chief computer engineer for another. I'm sure every company has at least one."

Access to the restaurant was an elevator that ran up a transparent tube attached to the outside of the building. When compared with elevators in most office buildings, this one rose at a snail's pace. Paul figured it was deliberate, to give people a chance to enjoy the experience.

They were the only occupants on their trip up.

"An elevator with a view," he said.

She was looking up at the stars. "Makes me feel like I'm levitating."

"You're right, it does."

The restaurant was circular in design, and a circular bar at the center served as the hub, with tables arranged in the same pattern, fanning out in ever-growing circles to the glass wall at the periphery.

Paul checked their coats and gave his name to the headwaiter, who showed them to a table in the outermost ring along the glass wall. The waiter asked if they cared to order anything from the bar.

Diane gave her order to Paul. "I'd like a Manhattan."

"Two Manhattans," Paul said and the waiter left.

Diane looked at her reflection in the window. "I should have worn a scarf -- my hair's a mess. Would you excuse me while I go fix it?"

Except for a few errant wisps, Paul thought her hair looked great. Just short of shoulder-length, it was all soft waves, swept back from her face.

Half rising in his chair as she got up, he then sat down again to watch her walk away. She wore a black, fitted dress that allowed a view of her shapely legs. And from the hollows behind the knee where tendons joined, his eyes moved over the gentle swell of calf and down to the delicate ankle, then up again over the curving contours of a deceptively youthful body.

His brief inspection gave rise to wonder. How young could she be? Even if she married at eighteen and became pregnant with Kim immediately, she'd have to be thirty-seven, and that wouldn't include college time. Her position at the magazine demanded at least that much education, so he added another four years. That would make her forty-one, which still cut the timing of events unrealistically close. Although it was hard for him to imagine, he decided she was probably a year or two older than that.

CHAPTER 24

When Diane returned, Paul was facing the windows, sighting down his index finger at a light on the ground below.

"What are you doing?" she asked.

"I'm proving to myself that we're moving. Try it. Pick out a stationary object below and point to it, then don't move your finger."

With an indulgent smile, she obeyed.

He studied the delicate line of her profile. "Can you see the target moving away from your finger?"

"Yes. It's slow, but I do see it." She lowered her hand and turned to him. "That's clever."

"I figure we'll make a few revolutions by the time we finish dinner."

She looked at him, and he saw only her eyes, those light gray irises, made translucent by the black, contrasting coronas, and, for a moment, he imagined them lovers again, the way they were in the mist of his recent dream.

"Diana," he said, considering the name itself. "Goddess of the moon. Protectress of women."

She smiled, eyebrows arching. "Roman deity? From an engineer?"

"It wasn't all math and design...I managed to squeeze in some liberal arts, too."

"I got that impression just talking to you on the phone." Her expression turned quizzical. "But where did you pick up the *Diana*?"

He grinned. "From your magazine's masthead."

"*You*? I can't believe you read a woman's magazine."

He tried, but could not suppress a laugh. "Just the masthead. I saw the magazine one day while looking for another one and couldn't resist looking for your name."

"Well!"

The one word was all she seemed able to manage, but he thought he saw her eyes glow before she looked away.

She took a sip of her drink, then put it down.

"I didn't hear about your loss until after the funeral."

The change of subject caught him by surprise.

"I was out of town on assignment." she said. "In fact, I left the same day the accident happened."

He saw her eyes search his face, as if she were expecting something more than just a simple 'I see' from him.

"Paul, I had *lunch* with her that day."

He stared at her, and his mind began switching memory circuits, leading him back to the telephone conversation with Catherine.

"So, *you're* the one she was with. My sister-in-law told me Joan had lunch with someone. I remember Catherine saying Joan came back to the store a changed woman...happy, animated. When she tried to find out what caused the mood swing, all Joan would say was that she had good news, but she'd have to tell *me* first."

"Then she never got the chance to tell you, did she?"

"No, and it's been bugging the hell out of me ever since."

Diane looked out at the sky for a moment, then turned back and leaned toward him.

"Earlier -- when you inquired about Kim -- I'm sure you noticed how evasive I was. But, again, you didn't press -- it seems you never do." She smiled. "You have a rare quality, Paul."

"Maybe." He smiled. "But I feel you're about to open up *now*, aren't you?"

Her bosom swelled as she took in air, and then the words came in a rush, like prisoners held captive beyond their term. "That was the day I told Joan that Kimberly was pregnant with Kevin's baby. That was the news Joan wouldn't share with anyone but you."

Paul,at a loss for words, could only stare at her.

"She was three months pregnant the night of their prom. They planned to tell us the next day."

The memory of the gathering at Ray's house after Kevin's funeral popped into Paul's mind, and suddenly he understood the real reason Kim wasn't hungry. He had attributed it solely to grief. But it also could have been early pregnancy nausea.

"She was overcome with grief...and deprived of Kevin's support, it was several days before she gathered the strength to tell me. Naturally, I was shocked...disappointed. But I knew, with Kevin gone, she needed me desperately."

The waiter came to the table to inquire if they were ready to order. When Paul saw Diane shake her head, he pointed to her empty glass. She nodded, and he told the waiter to bring two more Manhattans.

"My first thought," Diane continued, "was that I'd failed her somehow. I needed to hear it from her. I had to hear how this could happen despite all my guidance. We've always been close, never had a problem communicating. So, when I asked, she told me." She stopped and shook her head. "It seems, no matter what we do to educate them about the risks, a time comes when opportunity and overwhelming passions join to conspire against us. She swears it only happened once, but, of course, we know that's all it takes."

The waiter brought their drinks and moved away again.

Paul watched her take a sip. "You shouldn't have had to face this alone."

"Kim and I discussed it and decided you needed time to grieve."

"That was unfortunate."

She frowned. "Why?"

"You had no way of knowing, of course, but it might have saved our marriage."

When he saw her surprise, he went on to explain.

"Kevin's death was too much for her -- she couldn't handle it. She withdrew. And, no matter what I did, I couldn't reach her. I found a support group, but that didn't work -- she went with me to a couple of meetings, then quit." He sighed and looked out at the night. "Our marriage just dried up and died."

He imagined how things might have been different had they been told of the pregnancy, but left his thoughts unsaid. What end would be served by saying that a change in timing could have prevented Joan's death? Who could say that she wouldn't have gone to the cemetery that day?

Diane reached out and squeezed his hand. "Oh, Paul, I'm so *sorry*. If only we had known...."

He knew it was merely a gesture of compassion, but her touch electrified him. Previous contact had been through layers of clothing when she linked her arm with his as they walked from the car to the elevator. This was more intimate, a joining of flesh.

He maneuvered her hand into his. "Hey, don't start thinking *if*. *If* only you had known...there was no way you could have. *If* leads to guilt -- I found that out when I caught myself thinking that maybe if I had sold our house and moved out to the suburbs, Kevin would still be alive. Thoughts like that make you feel as if everything's your fault -- when it isn't."

He felt a twinge of conscience. How good he was at giving advice that he couldn't follow himself.

She looked at him and smiled. "You're something else, Paul. I've never met anyone like you."

"Well, *good*. Now you have." He turned and caught the waiter's eye. "I think we should order, don't you?"

Reading the menu required that he release her hand and he did so, reluctantly. When Diane heard Paul's selection, she agreed that his choice sounded good and ordered the same. After a brief silence when the waiter left, Paul steered the conversation in another direction.

"Tell me about Kim. How was the decision made to have the baby?"

"Kevin and she already had decided to end the pregnancy -- both knew what it would do to their futures -- but they didn't know a doctor or how to go about finding one. They needed our advice -- and financial help, I imagine."

"But she changed her mind."

Diane took a deep breath, then sighed. "Yes. We talked about it -- and argued. But her mind was made up."

"And you went along with that."

Paul watched her turn away to look out at the night sky, and seeing her in profile -- the high, smooth forehead, frowning now in thought, the straight Nordic nose, sensuous lips -- he wondered that such a woman could be unattached for almost five years. But then he thought of how presumptuous that was. Really, he knew nothing about this woman's private life. It occurred to him suddenly that she could have a lover, and the rush of panic he felt at this likelihood surprised him.

She turned towards him again. "Kevin was Kimberly's first love, something a woman never quite forgets. Then fate took Kevin from her -- and there was nothing she could do about *that*. But their *baby*...well, that was something else. *She* still had control. Kevin was gone, but her love for him would live on forever in this wonderful new life growing inside her. This baby was an extension of their love, the result of their only sexual union...."

"Were these your feelings, or Kim's?"

"Kimberly's...but I could understand them. The thought of abortion was unthinkable. For her, it would be like killing a part of Kevin."

The waiter brought their food, and, as they ate, Diane explained that Kimberly's education would be delayed until next term.

"Who's going to look after the baby with Kim in school?"

"We decided on a local college so she can be home every night. And I have a younger sister who's complaining that she has too much time on her hands during the day now that her youngest has started first grade, so she said she'd love to take care of him."

"Him? "

"Oh, I'm sorry," she said, looking contrite, "I got ahead of myself. You have a grandson, Paul. Kim gave birth last month to an eight pound, ten ounce baby boy."

"A *boy*? My God, that's *wonderful.* "

"When I heard about Joan, I knew how lonely you must be. With Kevin -- and now your wife gone -- well...."

"My God," he said again, "a *son*." Then he caught himself. "I mean, grandson. You were right -- it's the best possible news."

“Kim’s just been dying to show him to you. Would you like to see him...tonight?”

“How about as soon as we finish eating? Unless you had something special *you’d* like to do.”

He heard the music of her laughter again. “I'll pretend you didn't ask.”

Declining both dessert and an after-dinner drink as a waste of time, they left the restaurant and started back to Diane's place.

CHAPTER 25

Before and during dinner, with the news of the baby dominating the conversation, talk had come easily, but now as they reached the expressway, Paul noticed that Diane had grown pensive. He let the silence between them linger for several miles, then glanced her way.

"Hey, where did you slip off to?"

"I'm still here. Now that you've had time to digest the news I dumped on you, I guess I've been waiting for what I thought would be the typical male reaction -- the usual questions." She made a face. "The suspicion."

He gave her a puzzled smile. "I'm not following…what typical male reaction, what questions?"

She winced, as if she had just lifted the lid from a container of food left in the refrigerator too long.

"I shouldn't have said that, so let's just forget it, okay?"

With his eyes on the road again, he said, "No, Diane, it's not okay. I'd like to think I was right when I decided you were someone I could rely on to be candid."

He looked her way, then back to the road and waited. When finally she spoke, the words came slowly, measured:

"A while back, I said I'd never met anyone like you, and that's true. So, I should have known better. It's just that -- well, you know -- there are a lot of men who'd say, 'How do I know it's his? She could have been seeing other guys. It's too late now to ask *him*....'"

He glanced at her, and frowned.

"I *said*, 'I should have known better'. I'm sorry. It's just that I'm not accustomed to sensitivity in men, at least not in the ones I've met in the last couple of years."

Her words started him speculating again. Did they mean she might in fact be unattached? From the negative tone of her last comment, he easily could imagine some of the men a woman as beautiful as she would attract. He knew the type. He had seen and heard them everywhere -- in college, the army, the work place: immature brutes, disguising their insecurities in male virility, the macho image, exploiting feminine vulnerability then denying responsibility.

"Those questions never entered my mind, Diane. I remember all the times Kimberly was a guest in our house, and I can't think of a single thing she did or said that would lead me to believe she was anything but a well-bred, lovely young woman. And it was *obvious* how she felt about my son."

She reached out and squeezed his arm.

"Thank you, Paul."

Kimberly met them at the door, hands behind her back, lips compressed with anxiety.

Paul held his arms out to her. "Ah, Kimberly," he said, smiling, "beautiful as ever, I see."

A look of relief passed over her face as she came to him. "Oh, Mr. Becker."

He hugged her, then held her at arm's length to inspect for changes that pregnancy might have wrought. Her face he could see was untouched by the ordeal, and the loose-fitting smock she was wearing concealed the possibility of damage to her waistline curve.

She endured his appraisal with a brave smile, though he could see in her eyes a glistening where tears tried to form. He wondered about the emotion that triggered them. Did the sight of him rekindle her grief? He hoped not. Better they be tears of relief, knowing his being here meant acceptance of her decision, that perhaps he, unlike some, believed her.

"Motherhood becomes you."

She made a face. "You wouldn't think so if you saw what this smock is hiding. But the bulges are only temporary -- I bought an exercise video tape that I plan to start using when the doctor says it's okay."

"You worry too much," he said. "Young bodies are like rubber -- stretch 'em 'till you think they'll burst and they spring right back."

"I was so sorry to hear about your wife. I can only imagine how lonely you must feel."

"Yeah, well…I *was* feeling pretty empty." Suppressing a wave of gloom that threatened his mood, he forced a smile. "But that was before your mother dropped the bundle of news about the baby tonight. I'm still trying to get used to it."

Brightening at the change of subject, Kimberly seized his arm and urged him forward. "He's sleeping, but it's almost time for his feeding, so it won't hurt if he should wake up."

Kimberly led him down the hall, to a large bedroom, which he knew at once had to be hers. Half of it was decorated in a nursery design. His eyes found the crib along the far wall, but the occupant was hidden from view by padding attached to the bars.

When the women deserted him and took positions around the crib, Kim behind the headboard and Diane at the side-rail, he thought they must have rehearsed the scene. Then, like the conspirators he knew them to be, they exchanged satisfied smiles, and Diane signaled that he approach. To show his tolerance of their charade, he flashed an indulgent smile and took his place at the rail, next to Diane.

He looked down at the sleeping child, and his mind jumped back over the years, to the day he and Joan had brought Kevin home from the maternity ward. Even the room reminded him of Kevin's when it, too, had served as a nursery. As he studied the baby's features, the illusion that he was viewing his own newborn son for the first time grew stronger. He saw Kevin's dark brown hair and sooty-black eyelashes, fanned out now in sleep, against the white of cheek, his nose and firm jaw-line.

Diane's voice broke the magic trance.

"Well?"

He looked up at her, then at Kim, and smiled. "I had the strangest feeling," he said, turning back to Diane. "It like going back and seeing Kevin as a baby again."

"Oh, Mr. Becker," Kimberly said, "you see the resemblance, too?"

"It's uncanny," he said. "But enough of this *Mister* thing -- we need something less formal."

He frowned, as though in deep thought, then brightening, he said, "How about 'Paul'?"

She shook her head. "I think it's lacking in respect." Her lips stretched into a mischievous smile. "How about 'Dad'?"

She paused, then glanced suggestively toward Diane. "You know, you could make me your daughter."

Paul turned instantly to Diane, a reflexive movement so fast he was not conscious of making it. Their eyes met for a second, then as quickly, hers broke contact and followed something on the ceiling visible only to her. He watched her face twist with an unsuccessful effort to suppress a smile. Kimberly's face, when he turned back to her, was a mask of wide-eyed innocence, as if he alone had read the implications in her suggestion.

"Kim," Diane said, "I think you may have embarrassed Paul."

He chose to ignore the mock censure in her voice. "On the contrary, I think 'Dad' is a good idea…at least, she didn't suggest 'Grandpa'."

"*Heaven forbid.*" Diane exclaimed, laughing.

Whether purposely or not, Paul felt he had been put in an awkward, if humorous position, and the need to retaliate was instinctive. "Now," he said to Kimberly, "if you meant the word 'Dad' to imply something more than just a respectful term of address…."

He paused for effect, then shifted his gaze to Diane, and he knew satisfaction when he saw the astonished look on her face, the realization she had been ambushed.

In a surprising show of resilience, Diane recovered her poise. "This conversation had got out of hand," she said, starting for the door. "I'm going to make some coffee."

He turned to Kimberly, who was smiling at her mother's obvious embarrassment, then he pointed to the baby. "He's a sound sleeper."

"*So* far…and I just hope he stays that way."

"What have you named him?"

"Michael, Paul."

He raised his eyebrows.

"The 'Paul' is for you," she said quickly, "the 'Michael' is for Mom's father."

"I'm flattered…and grateful." He tried to hide the question that popped into his head, but her next words told him he was unsuccessful.

"Kevin's name was out because I don't like the 'Junior' part of it, and my father's name is too painful."

"I understand. "

"I don't think you do. You see, my father hurt my mother -- deeply."

Paul frowned, but remained silent, somehow knowing more would come.

"He was a *womanizer*."

His frown changed to a wince, and he shook his head. "With a wife like *Diane*?"

"You have to understand the image...the dashing, blond, ex-fighter pilot, zipping all over the country flying corporate jets. Women just naturally gravitate to the glamour of if all. And he knew it." She paused. "My mother heard of his affairs. Usually phone calls from women who didn't know he was married. One poor girl, nineteen years old, came to our house looking for him. She was pregnant." Kim shook her head. "Of course, he denied having anything to do with it." She paused again and bowed her head. "My mother filed for divorce; it was pending when he was killed."

The story explained a few undercurrents he had picked up in some of Diane's comments, but the way Kimberly told it -- words tumbling out, the raw hostility of her tone -- stunned him. He didn't know what to say, or if she even expected a response.

She moved to the dresser, looked at her reflection and poked at her hair.

He remembered her description of her father: 'dashing, blond', and now he knew why her coloring differed so sharply from her mother's.

"So...what do you think of my mother?"

He was unprepared for the change of subject; it seemed to him she had a switch in her head that she could trip at will.

"I'm having trouble trying to imagine a man chasing other women while married to Diane. What in the *hell* was he looking for?"

"Should I take that as favorable?"

Her conversational agility surprised him. For someone so young, she was exceptionally quick to see the artful dodge in his answer. And he could see she wasn't about to let him off the hook; she was pressing for something more specific. He smiled and shook his head.

"Okay, I think she's beautiful, intelligent and caring."

She gave him a look as of someone suffering the response of a mentally handicapped student. "You left out something vital…do you think she's sexy?"

He thought how typical she was of the young today; how direct they were in boiling everything down to the one word they felt said it all. "Very sexy," he said. He felt uncomfortable saying the words, as if he were confessing to this girl that he had made love to her mother in one of his dreams. But then he recovered when her smile of approval told him he had chosen exactly the words she wanted to hear.

"She thinks you're special."

"Oh? How do you know that? Until tonight, we've met only twice, and then very briefly."

"I talked about you lots of times when Kevin and I were dating. I used to say how great it would be to have a father like you."

He remembered what she had said about her father and understood how she might feel this way.

"And she was very impressed when you called that night to tell me what happened to Kevin. She said you were..." Kim stopped and bit her lip. "*...compassionate*, that's the word she used. She was impressed when you were worried that I was alone, and you insisted on speaking with her because you thought she'd know how to tell me better than you could. And she thought it was very kind of you to invite us to join the family get-together after the funeral."

Paul found himself at a loss for a reply, but was rescued when Diane appeared in the doorway and announced that coffee was ready.

Chapter 26

On their way to the dining room, Paul became interested in the surroundings and asked them for a tour of the town-house. He explained his sudden aversion to his own house and his thoughts of selling it and buying a condominium.

"My place is too big," he said. "I'd never find the time to keep it looking decent. And, besides, it holds too many memories." He mentioned that he had just got word of its sale.

"There's not much to show," Diane said, leading him through the rooms. "We have two bedrooms, living room, dining room and kitchen with pantry."

She took him through a utility room and into the garage, which served also as storage area. The tour ended in the large kitchen.

"I like this room," he said. "It's bright and homey, so why don't we have coffee in here instead of the dining area."

"You're like us," Diane said. "We eat in here all the time. The only use I get out of the dining room table is when I bring work home and need space to spread out…or, on rare occasions, when we have guests."

"One thing this place has that a condo doesn't," Paul said, "is a private entrance. I'm not comfortable with elevators and hallways -- too much like an apartment building." He paused while Diane set out cups and poured coffee. "I'd really like something like this."

He saw Kimberly's face light up.

She turned to her mother and, after exchanging knowing looks, Diane said, "Oh, Kim, I don't know...."

Paul frowned. "*What*?"

"I don't care, Mom," Kimberly said, "if *you* don't tell him, I *will*."

"*What*? Tell me what?"

"*All right*," Diane said, "*I'll* tell him." She turned to Paul and sighed. "She wants you to know there's a unit next to ours that's for sale, or rent with option to buy."

He took a moment to let this news sink in. "How do you mean, it's next to this one?"

Diane pointed in the general direction of the living room. "We're separated by the entrance hall."

"Wouldn't it be *great*?" Kim's eyes sparkled with enthusiasm. "You could see Michael anytime...every day if you wanted. I could come in on Saturdays and help you with laundry and cleaning. With us here, you'd never be lonely."

"Kimberly! *Slow down*. I know you think you're being helpful, but you're pushing Paul into a corner. What makes you think he'd be all that eager to have *us* as neighbors? He seems like a man who values his privacy."

"Seems to me, turning down a chance to live next door to you is a pretty high price to pay for privacy, Mom."

"That's enough, Kim."

Paul raised a restraining hand. "Whoa, you two, there's no cause for an argument." He smiled and turned to Diane. "You think Kim is pushing? Well...maybe, just a little. But her suggestion has some good points."

Still looking at Paul, Diane tilted her head toward Kim. “Don't you see what 'Dolly Levi' here, is doing?”

Knowing Diane was serious did little to contain his laughter.

“*Matchmaking*?” He tried looking incredulous and turned to Kim. “Is that what you're doing?”

Kim's eyes opened wide. “Who, me?”

Satisfied that they had turned confrontation into comic relief, Paul and Kim broke into peals of laughter. A moment later, caught up in the contagion, Diane abandoned her scowl of disapproval and joined them.

Composure returned, and in the silence that followed, Kim jumped up and went to the refrigerator.

“I almost forgot,” she said, glancing back at Paul, “I baked a cake today -- in your honor--*dad*.”

Diane rolled her eyes. “What sin did I commit that I should be given such a daughter as penance?”

“I'm sure it was venial,” he said, watching her set out dishes and silverware.

He tasted the cake and looked at Kim in surprise.

“I heard you mention once when I was at your house that lemon was your favorite.”

“And you *remembered* such a little thing?”

“You wouldn't think it little if you had known I planned to become your daughter-in-law some day.”

Diane took a gulp of her coffee and swallowed hard. “You still think my sin was venial?”

“Well, whatever it was you did, you got a reward, not penance. I think Kim's a jewel.”

“That's because you don't live with her.”

He finished the last bite of his cake and leaned back. “Speaking of where I might decide to live -- who do I call to ask about seeing the empty unit next door?”

"*Mom*, you still have the agent's card, don't you? You didn't throw it *away*, I *hope*."

"Paul," Diane said, ignoring Kim's plea, "are you sure? Maybe you should give it more thought."

Paul saw uncertainty in Diane's expression. Had he presumed wrong? Was Kim -- in her need for a father image -- alone in her desire to have him live so close? Was the frown he saw now on Diane's forehead a sign of reluctance, or merely concern for his well-being? Maybe he had read the signs wrong. Maybe she didn't share the chemistry between them that he felt so strongly.

Suddenly he felt as though he were inching his way along a mountain precipice, blindly testing the ledge for a firm footing. "You may be right," he finally said. "Perhaps it needs a little more thought."

"*Mother*! *You're driving him away*."

Diane looked confused. She blinked several times, looked at her daughter, then back to Paul. "Is that what it sounded like to you?"

"Well, what *else would* he think, Mom?"

Paul was about to protest, then changed his mind. It would be better to find out now, rather than delude himself into thinking something existed that really didn't.

"Oh, Paul," Diane said, "I'm sorry. I didn't mean to sound like I was against the idea. It's just that…well, I didn't want you to think we had conspired to trap you. Kim can get quite brash at times..." She glanced at Kim. "…especially tonight, it seems."

Kim hung her head, but the smile that played at the corners of her mouth mocked her contrition.

"Actually," Diane went on, "I think your being here would be beneficial to Michael. Babies develop so fast, he'll be noticing his surroundings in no time. And the population of his big new world shouldn't be just female. He needs to feel a *man's* presence."

Kim looked up. “He's not the only one.”

Diane turned with a warning look, but before she could speak, Kim cut another piece of cake and grabbed Paul's plate.

“You can't just have one piece of my lemon cake; you'll hurt my feelings.”

“I was afraid you'd never ask,” Paul said, winking.

Diane shook her head at them, then got up and went to a counter in a corner of the room, where she rummaged through the contents of a small box. When she returned, she placed a business card on the table in front of Paul.

“She's the agent for the complex. Give her a call; she'll be happy to show the unit to you.”

He glanced at the card before slipping it into his wallet and noticed the Realtor symbol after the woman's name. It was comforting to know she was a professional, qualified to discuss the terms of a contract with option to buy.

“He's *awake*.”

Paul saw Kim's head tilted, listening to something only mothers seem to hear.

“I'll bring him in here before I feed him so you can see him while he's awake.”

When she was gone, Paul turned to Diane. “Does she nurse him?”

“Oh, yes. She thinks that a boy without a father needs every advantage he can get.”

“She's a smart girl. I'm impressed by her ability at verbal sparring, and she's very assertive.”

“Sometimes to a fault. I have to remind her now and then that people can take offense at some of the things she says.”

“Too bad about them. I think it's a sign of a healthy, agile mind.”

Kim returned with the baby, and Paul got up to peer at the tiny, struggling bundle, legs kicking, arms waving.

"His eyes sure are blue," he said, "but I understand they could change."

"The nurses said no," Kim said. "They said there's no sign of any underlying pigment."

"They're probably right. Kevin's were blue and so are yours."

He watched as the baby strained his neck to reach his mother, mouth open, hands groping, but when these efforts brought no reward, Paul saw the tiny face wrinkle and redden with rage, then heard a powerful voice fill the kitchen with howls of indignation.

"I have to feed him," Kim said, heading for the bedroom.

Paul looked at Diane. "Nothing wrong with *his* lungs."

"Fortunately, my bedroom is down the hall from Kim's, so I don't usually hear him during the night."

He looked at his watch and saw it was almost midnight. "I can't believe it's this late. I guess I'd better go."

She got his coat from the closet and walked him to the door. They stood facing each other for a moment in awkward silence, then Diane spoke: "Thank you, Paul…for everything."

He opened his mouth to protest, but she interrupted. "You're the most understanding man I've ever met."

He took both of her hands. "It's been wonderful seeing you…and Kim, again," he added hastily.

Looking up at him, her eyes seemed enormous. The light-gray irises appeared transparent, and he wished he could see through them into her mind, where he would know what she really felt for him.

Then, abandoning the fantasy, he resorted to the only other way he knew to find out. He released her hands and encircled her waist, then drew her to him. Sensing no resistance, he moved his hands up her back and lowered his face to hers, and in the second before their lips met, he saw her eyes close in consent.

He kissed her softly at first, but the feel of her hands pulling him closer released the flood of repressed emotions that told him he had been too long without a woman. A restless stirring began somewhere deep down, sending electric like ripples through his body. Heart pounding, he probed gently with his tongue, and when her lips parted in acceptance, the erection he felt was almost painful. There was no doubt in his mind that she could feel him, but she clung for one more moment before pulling away.

She kept him at elbow length and smiled wistfully. "This isn't doing either of us any good," she said. "For one thing, the timing is terrible. And second, I have to know it's something more than just sex."

"I know…and I don't blame you. It's easy to imagine the long line of guys who must have come on to you with nothing but lust in their veins."

She made a face and kept nodding, as if to confirm their numbers.

"I'd like to see you when I come back. I mean, on a regular basis."

"When you come *back*? "

"I'm sorry," He said, launching into a lie he had concocted earlier, "I forgot to mention…my boss asked me to look at a problem a company down in Florida is having with a system we sold them. I fly down Monday, but I'm pretty sure I know what it is, so it shouldn't take long at all to fix it. No more than a week or two, at most. I'll call you soon as I get back."

He hated having to lie to her, but what else could he do? Certainly, he couldn't tell her he intended to kill Steven Tate and was setting up an alibi in Florida.

Looking at her now, he definitely read disappointment in her face. Then suddenly she smiled.

"What are you going to be doing tomorrow?"

"Well, now that my house is sold, I have to decide what to get rid of. And I've got seven rooms of furniture."

She grinned and shook her head. "*You* can't make decisions like that."

"Why not?"

"Because you're a *man*."

"Will you help me?"

"Love to. What time should I be there?"

"Get there early; I'll take you out for breakfast."

"Sounds good."

She opened the door, gave him a quick kiss, then pushed him gently on his way.

Paul was on the toll road before it occurred to him that he had not smoked the whole time he was with Diane. He wondered why he hadn't felt the need for a cigarette. Did he abstain in deference to her because she didn't smoke? That didn't add up; Joan didn't smoke, but it didn't stop him from starting again. It must have been the evening; he couldn't remember when he had enjoyed one as much.

He recalled the three of them grouped around the crib, the feeling he had watching the sleeping child. Then the scene changed, and he was at the door saying goodnight to Diane, the kiss, her warm response. His life could begin again.

But what about the underlying hate, the gnawing anger that had become part of his life? To come to her with this load of baggage weighing him down was unthinkable. He must deal with that first.

His son's killer had to be brought to justice.

Chapter 27

Diane arrived at nine-thirty, carrying a large insulated bag designed primarily for picnics. Paul helped her out of her coat, and his eyes moved over her quickly, noting the contrast from the previous night. She was dressed casually in a denim knee-length skirt and blue and white print blouse.

"We're not going out for breakfast," she said. "I decided to cook for you instead."

He gave her a wide-eyed smile. "Sounds great." He pointed to the bag. "What's in there?"

"Everything but my kitchen sink. I figured, being a man, you probably don't have much food in the house, so I brought the makings for just about anything, including my Belgian waffle iron."

"How domestic you are," he said, moving toward her, arms outstretched, "and...beautiful."

She smiled and raised a restraining hand.

"I'm here because you asked for *help*, remember?"

He made a face, then grinned, grabbed the bag and led the way to the kitchen.

She found an empty counter and started unloading the bag.

"So, what would you like? I've got eggs, bacon, sausage, pancake mix...."

"You mentioned waffles; I haven't had them in years."

"I *knew* it. I made a bet with Kim -- even thawed strawberries to go over them."

He watched her arrange the items she would need.

"What do you want with them, bacon or sausage?"

"Doesn't matter to me. What's your preference?"

"I like bacon."

"Okay, fine."

He washed out the coffee maker and started it brewing again.

"What else can I do to help?"

"Nothing. Just sit and relax."

It amazed him that she could find her way around a strange kitchen without having to ask where anything was. Then he decided it must be something instinctive in women.

After his second helping of waffles, he pushed his plate away and tried to remember when he had enjoyed a breakfast as much.

"You make me feel like a pig," he said. "You had only one waffle and half a strip of bacon."

"I'm a light eater."

"So *that's* how you keep that world-class figure."

Her face lit up. "Oh, you *are* charming. *World-class*?"

"*I* think so."

After they finished their coffee and loaded the dishwasher, he made another attempt at intimacy, but again she sidestepped his advance.

"Time to show me the rest of the house. We have work to do."

As they moved through the first floor, Diane took time to study the size of each of the rooms.

"It looks like you can keep most to the furniture you have on this level -- the rooms are about the same size as mine. What you have in your study, you can put in the spare bedroom."

"Okay," he said, "let's go upstairs."

He started with the one room he thought would be the most difficult, and as they entered it, Diane stopped and grabbed his arm. She took only a moment to look around at Kevin's belongings, then turned away.

"Oh, Paul," she said, closing her eyes, "I can't help you here."

"I guess you're right. It 's something *I'll* have to decide."

They moved on to the master bedroom, where he made a sweeping gesture with his arm. "I've decided not to keep most of this. I don't need a king size bed, and the furniture in the guest room will do fine for my needs."

He moved to the closet that took up one whole wall.

"But in here," he said, shaking his head, "I do need help."

His hand moved over Joan's clothing, which was more than half of all the hanging garments. Then he pointed to the floor where her shoes were lined up in rows.

Diane looked at him and frowned.

"I could ask my sister-in-law, but knowing her, it would be an emotional ordeal. I thought your magazine might know of a worthy charitable organization."

"Oh," she said, looking relieved. "As a matter of fact, I know of one myself. It's run by a group of wealthy matrons on Sheridan Road. They donate their time, so all of the proceeds go to charity."

She picked out several dresses, examined them, read the labels, then put them back. "They'll have no trouble selling these…Joan had excellent taste. They hold two bazaars a year, and one of them is right before Christmas. I'll give the organizer a call tonight, and they'll have someone pick up, so you'll have to be home."

"Good," he agreed. "Her winter coats are in the guest room closet -- that's the only room you haven't seen."

They moved across the hall to the third bedroom.

"This is the furniture I plan to use."

She pointed to the bed. "That's king size, too, isn't it?"

"I know. You're thinking, why don't I take the more expensive stuff in the master bedroom?" He bit his lip.

"How stupid of me," she said. "I should have known…they hold too many memories."

She went to the closet and looked at the coats.

"Those women are going to love you for this. These coats will bring a good price."

She took each coat and held it against herself to see how it looked in the full-length mirror on the closet door. He watched the flowing movements of her body as she stretched and turned. Clutching a fur jacket against her waist, she extended one leg and twisted to see her reflection. The pose sent a ripple of desire down his spine and into his loins.

It was the last garment, and when she hung it up and turned to him, he was caught staring at her legs. She raised one eyebrow and smiled. "Having fun?"

He smiled sheepishly and shrugged.

"Let's get back to work," she said, eyes moving around the room.

She turned and walked to the window. "I looked at that vacant unit before I bought mine, and if I were you, I'd take these curtains and drapes; they'll go well with the carpeting."

He had come up behind her to look, so that when she turned around, they collided. When his arms encircled her waist to steady her, she raised an accusing eyebrow, but he also saw a smile playing at the corners of her mouth.

Then his pulse quickened when he felt her hands move up his back. He lowered his head and kissed her softly. Then urgently. He knew that her need equaled his by the way she pressed against him, and he reached up to the back of her neck and began unbuttoning her blouse. When it fell away from her shoulders, she moved back and began opening his shirt. He looked down to watch her working fingers, slim and delicate, then up again to her eyes.

When he opened the zipper to her skirt and worked it down over her hips, it fell away to the floor. She stepped back to shed her pantyhose and blouse, then moved to the bed where she stretched out to watch him kick off his shoes and struggle out of his slacks.

In his dream, when she had come to him, her body seemed wrapped in mystery, more a promise than actual flesh. His subconscious had filled in the details. But now, standing in his shorts, looking at her in bra and bikini panties, he could see she put his creation to shame.

"You're more beautiful than I could have imagined."

"Come here," she said, reaching out to him, "you're embarrassing me."

She turned toward him as he shed his shorts and slipped into bed with her. As he drew her to him and kissed her, his hand opened the snaps of her bra, then started down her torso to her panties. She raised her hips to let him roll them down to her knees, and he used his foot to kick them off.

He wondered if he was moving too fast; he was ready, but women usually needed at least *some* foreplay to reach his level of arousal. Thinking the slow approach was better, he began exploring with his fingers the fleecy triangle between her legs. When he felt how warm and wet she was, he wondered if it was safe to proceed at will. To be sure, he decided to try intensifying her desire, bring her need for him to fever pitch.

When his fingers began to stroke, he heard her moan and felt her reach between them to push his hand away. He opened his eyes and found her looking at him through half-closed, dreamy lids.

Her voice, husky and barely audible, came to him. “I don’t need that.”

Then, moving as one, they rolled over, and at once he felt the thrill of penetration, the sense of losing himself in the depths of this beautiful woman, the partner of his dream come to life.

He wanted desperately to prolong the heady sensation of her body against his. It aroused a feeling of unity, a sense of belonging missing in him for such a long time. He buried his face in the curve of her neck, and in an effort to delay the rising passion he slowed the rhythm of his thrusts.

Then, just when he thought he had control, he felt Diane's chest swell and heard her moan. Her hips convulsed against him, and her legs crossed over his buttocks, pulling him ever deeper.

“*Oh, Paul*,” she cried, her pelvis thrusting upward.

Like the undertow of a powerful wave, her movements sucked away his will, and he erupted in a rush that seemed to last longer than it ever had before.

It surprised him that she had reached such a level of passion so soon, and he wanted to believe it was him -- his presence inside her -- that made it happen.

Her moans grew softer, and he opened his eyes to find her looking at him. He thought women always closed their eyes during orgasm.

After a while, he rolled onto his side and followed the contours of her nude body with his hand, caressing, stroking. “You're a strange one,” he said.

“I am?”

“You had your *eyes* open.”

"Not the whole *time*." She grinned. "Well, maybe most of it. I needed to see you while you made love to me. Is that so strange?"

"When you put it that way, I guess it isn't." He kissed her briefly. "Speaking of love -- and you used that word just now -- does that mean you believe it was more than just sex?"

"I'd *like* to believe it was more."

"It *was*."

She shook her head and sighed. "I promised myself I wouldn't let this happen so soon. Now I'll have to call my gynecologist and...."

Instantly, he was up on one elbow, looking down at her.

"You're *not* on the *pill*?"

"I had no *reason* to be." She glared at him then. "Is that the kind of woman you think I am?"

"Hey, don't get mad." He tried to kiss her, but she turned away. "I'm sorry…really. It's just that you're a rarity in this age of permissiveness."

"It's not *that* prevalent, so don't be so quick to judge." She faced him again. "And don't panic either; it's a safe day for me."

He tried looking contrite, but inside he was jubilant. Her admission made him feel like a kid seeing the gift of his dreams on Christmas morning. It was a welcome relief after the sudden panic and twinge of jealousy he had felt the night before, when it occurred to him that she might have a lover.

"Forgive me?"

She gave him a crooked smile. "Oh, maybe I *do* expect too much. You're right; the way things are today, I guess it would be natural for you to think I'm on the pill."

He looked into those beautiful eyes with their almost transparent gray irises, and the need to see into her mind was gone. She had opened it to him.

Following the heat of lovemaking, he felt a new glow spreading throughout his body. And while he knew it might sound premature to her, his urge to share it was overpowering.

"I'm falling in love with you," he said.

She was silent for a moment, her eyes moving over his face searching.

"Paul, you hardly know me."

"So it seems. But, for me, this isn't the first time we've made love."

She looked at him as if he had suddenly gone mad.

"What *are* you talking about?"

"I've dreamed of you."

The smile she gave him, then, was mischievous, knowing.

"Then I must confess, too...you've been in some of my daydreams."

She snuggled her head into the hollow of his neck and shoulder, where she lay quietly as he stroked the curve of her back.

After a while, her steady breathing made him think she had dozed off, then she stirred and looked up.

"Would you like to have dinner with us tonight? I can call Kim and have her get it started."

"I'd like that."

She got up, pulling the spread with her and wrapping it around herself.

"There's a phone in both of the other bedrooms," he said. "Take your pick."

He pulled the sheet over his lower body and watched her leave, taking some of the magic out of the room with her. It surprised him that he felt no craving for a cigarette. The way she took the edge off his ragged nerves, he knew it would be easy to quit again with her around.

She stepped on the trailing end of the spread coming back into the room, and when it fell to the floor, he savored the view of her naked body as she stood in confusion for a moment before making a dash for the bed.

"Lord, you're beautiful!" He gasped, taking her in his arms.

"You enjoyed that, didn't you?"

"Well, of course."

She shook her head in mock disapproval.

"What took you so long?"

"Kim was full of questions."

He pulled her close and kissed her. She snuggled against him again, and they lay quietly while he indulged himself in the warmth of a togetherness that he had missed for so long.

They spent some time discussing their hopes and dreams for Kimberly and their grandson and, in the process, found out many things about each other.

Gradually mellowing to their intimacy, Diane became relaxed and comfortable with her nudity under his exploring eyes. And, after making love again, he actually enticed her to shower with him.

It was six thirty when they left for her townhouse, he in his car following her.

When they arrived, Kimberly explained that the baby had been cranky, and she hadn't been able to start anything for dinner. "Actually, it's a good thing," she said, eyeing them suspiciously. "It would have been ruined trying to keep things warm."

Diane brushed past her. "I'll call out for a pizza. What kind do *you* like, Paul?"

He followed her, happy to get out from under Kim's questioning gaze.

"Sausage or pepperoni, but I'm not fussy. Whatever you two like is okay with me."

Kimberly joined them in the kitchen. "I never thought you'd be *this* late," she said to Paul.

Diane finished giving an order that would please everyone and hung up the phone.

"*Kim*," she snapped, "Paul had many difficult decisions to make. And we had lots of things to talk about -- not that it's any of your business."

Kim eyed each of them in turn, a smile now playing at her lips. "Okay," was all she said.

But for the remainder of the evening, Paul noticed Kim's eyes searching him and her mother for clues to what really went on during all that time at his place. He was sure she could piece it together. As he had discovered the previous night, Kim had a mind like a razor. And neither he nor Diane was very successful hiding their emotions whenever their eyes met.

When it was time for him to leave, Kim made some vague excuse to check on the baby and discreetly left them alone.

"Call me as soon as you get back," Diane said. She gave him her business card. "Even if I'm at work."

He kissed her, then felt her hands push him away, and her expression looked pained.

"Go," she said.

Paul turned to leave, then stopped and dug into his pants pocket. "Here," he said, holding up the spare key to his house, "those women who are coming for Joan's clothing will need to get into my house. I'll probably be out of town."

She took the key. "I'm glad you thought of it."

Chapter 28

The emotional high of the past two days deserted Paul the moment he walked in his back door. He went upstairs, through the heavy silence of the house, and the ghosts met him at every turn, everywhere he looked. It was almost as if he had never left.

He undressed, set an early alarm, and went to bed. Then, staring into the dark, he tried going over the surprising events of the weekend. He wished he had known of Kimberly's pregnancy sooner; maybe it would have helped him reach some kind of recovery by now. And Diane. His mind traveled through their intimate dinner when she gave him the news, then her making waffles and helping him dispose of Joan's things. He lingered over the lovemaking, his admission that he was falling in love with her.

Yes, he *said* it. But *was* he? *Really*? Could it be that, in his desperate need for someone to fill the void, he was mistaking physical attraction for love? Could anyone possibly take Joan's place? His mind went back to that wonderful woman he lost. To the years they had together.

No. Diane could never replace Joan, nor could beautiful Michael fill the gap left by Kevin. And thoughts of his life with Joan and Kevin brought back the pain and then the rage. Nothing could be resolved with their killer walking around free as the wind. He would never know peace until that bastard Tate was punished. Finally, he found sleep looking forward to tomorrow.

A noise from the street woke Paul at dawn. Still dazed, he reached, out of habit, behind him for that reassuring form, his wife. And the fog of sleep, as from a sudden breeze, was swept away by the empty space he found. Another reminder of his loss and what he must do. He lay still for a minute, staring at the ceiling, then he threw back the covers and headed for the shower.

An hour later the house was locked, and he was on his way to the neighborhood restaurant. With the morning rush over, he was able to enjoy a quiet, leisurely breakfast. He lingered over a third cup of coffee, while he read part of the morning paper that someone had left behind.

A light snow began to fall during the drive to O'Hare Airport, but with traffic light, he still arrived an hour ahead of schedule. He turned into long-term, covered parking and found a space for his car on the second level.

As usual, the airport bustled with activity, but Delta had plenty of attendants at baggage check, and in no time at all, his suitcase was on its way. The other one, with the winter clothing and the gun, was locked in the trunk of his car.

The plane took off on schedule and quickly climbed to thirty thousand feet. When the warning light went out, Paul released the restraint belt and looked out the window at nothing but cloud cover. Then he remembered that he had meant to buy a copy of Newsweek. He fished around in the pocket of the seat in front of him and found at first only the usual airline fare, but digging deeper revealed a dog-eared copy of Reader's Digest, which must have been overlooked by the cleaning crew. It wasn't what he would have preferred, but it was better than the rest of the junk.

Ignoring the cover index, he began thumbing through the pages. He was halfway into the magazine without finding an article that interested him, when he came across one with a byline that jumped out at him: Condensed from *This Year's Woman*, by Diana Adams.

He was into the second paragraph of the article when he realized it was about a mother's loss of her only child. It was written in a way that protected the privacy of the characters, but when he read that the 'child' was an eighteen-year-old high school graduate, he knew the article was about Joan. The story described the pain and suffering of the mother at the loss of her son, and the subsequent anger of seeing her son's murderer set free by the courts on a legal technicality.

The article examined the mother's hopeless dilemma of trying to accept her loss and realize closure when her son's killer escaped the penalty of justice and it ended with her tragic death after visiting her son's grave.

Paul noticed that the father played only a minor role, but this, of course, was a woman's story published originally in a woman's magazine. What impressed him most was the writer's deep understanding of Joan's suffering. And he added another dimension to his mental evaluation of Diane. Was it possible that she'd understand his need for justice? Would she sympathize with, rather than condemn him, for doing what he felt he had to do? He thought about this, then decided that only time would tell.

At six hundred miles an hour, conditions change quickly, and in the time it took to place his order with the stewardess and mix his bourbon and water, the clouds had broken up. Putting the magazine aside, he peered out the window at the ground below and saw a small lake approach, looking like a piece of broken mirror, then it flashed in the sun before moving slowly out of view.

With the bourbon working its magic spell, his mood turned wistful to thoughts of what might have been. This trip could have been a vacation, an escape from winter to the sunny south, for Diane and him. Maybe someday, when he'd be able to put this behind him....

The stewardess's voice, like the point of a dart, pierced the membrane of his reverie. "Can I get you anything, sir?"

He blinked to bring her into focus, then ordered another bourbon and water. The seat next to his was tilted back, the male occupant asleep, fortunately; Paul detested idle conversation with strangers. He turned back to the window, but the spell was gone. It would have been nice. But he could hardly call this a vacation -- a trip of convenience was more like it, a means to an end. He opened the magazine again and forced himself to read.

The plane arrived at two-fifteen, and by three he was on his way. Everything came off without a hitch; even the rental car was a roomy Chrysler product. Using the map that Fred had given him, he had no problem finding the condominium. The parking lot behind the building had separate spaces for residents and guests. He pulled into a guest slot, retrieved his luggage from the trunk and headed for the manager's unit on the first floor.

The manager was a white-haired woman, heavily made up and deeply tanned. Paul introduced himself.

She looked him over, then asked for identification.

"We're strict about security." She smiled as if to soften the abrupt request.

"That's reassuring," Paul said, reaching for his wallet and driver's license.

She glanced at the photograph, then up at him. "At least it looks like you," she said, handing it back, "mine is awful. I keep track of the cars in the lot, so I need your license plate number."

He made a face. "It's a rental; I'll have to go look."

"Never mind. Which one is it? I'll get the number later".

"It's that brown two-door," he said, pointing.

"Okay." She gave him a business card. "Hope you enjoy your stay, and if you need anything, call me."

"I'll be gone most of the time…sightseeing." He turned to leave, then hesitated. "Do you happen to know of a telephone store in the area? I need an answering machine?"

She looked at the sky and squinted. "I seem to remember seeing one in Mr. Woodward's unit." She gave him a sly smile. "If not, I've got one you can rent -- save you from buying one."

He nodded. "I'll keep that in mind."

"The elevator's through that door," she said, pointing.

Paul found his way to the third floor and let himself in. He made a tour of the rooms, leaving his suitcase in the master bedroom, then returned to the living room. The woman's memory was accurate; the phone and an answering machine were on a cabinet next to the couch. He had to admire her enterprise; with her offer to rent hers, she covered her bases, just in case.

He searched the cabinet and found the manual for the machine. It was state-of-the-art, exactly the brand he had intended buying. He should have known Fred would get the best.

The setup went quickly, and when he had it operational, he composed and recorded a short, simple message that he was out sightseeing and would get back to the caller when he returned. Then, using a page from a pad on the cabinet, he wrote the instructions for retrieving messages when using outside phones and put it in his wallet.

Although he would be here only a short time, he took care to familiarize himself with the layout; Fred would ask how he liked it, and Paul would have to rely on memory. When he was satisfied that enough details were fixed in his mind, he returned to the wet bar in the living room, made himself a drink and opened the drapes that covered one entire wall of the room.

The view of the ocean was magnificent. He could see how a person might spend months searching for a place like this, and knowing the premium Fred put on time, Paul was sure the job had been assigned to some real estate agent. When you had the money, that's what you did.

While sipping his drink, Paul committed the scene to memory. Immediately below, protected by a sea wall, he saw a patio with umbrella tables, chairs and a barbecue grill; beyond that was the beach where long, rolling waves now were breaking. He lingered just long enough to form a mental picture, then turned away.

Discounting the view, which could not be duplicated at home unless one settled for a place on Lake Shore Drive in Chicago, a condo was just a glorified apartment; Diane's townhouse was much better. He could handle most of the upkeep himself and maybe have a cleaning woman in once or twice a week. He was convinced the townhouse next to Diane's was the way to go. But now, he was hungry, so he left in search of a restaurant.

It was eight-thirty when he returned, seven-thirty Central, which meant he could make a few calls without interrupting someone's dinner.

His conversation with Ray covered his flight and a brief description of the condo. When Paul told him that he would be out most of the time, Ray joked with him about being careful.

"Used to be," he said, "the worst you'd catch was something they could cure with a couple of shots of penicillin. Not any more...now it can kill you." They ended with Ray agreeing to call everyone else for him.

His second call was to Woodward, who was relieved to hear that everything was in order when Paul arrived. Fred's opinion of the building manager was the same as Paul's.

"When it comes to making an extra buck," he said, "you really have to hand it to her. She's honest, though; I've found that out."

Fred recommended several restaurants and urged him again not to rush back.

Paul passed an hour strolling on the beach, then watched the news until eleven-thirty. He transferred six hundred dollars from the money belt to his wallet, set the alarm for six, and was in bed by twelve.

But sleep was long in coming; now that his plan was in motion, he found it hard to turn off his mind. He had a goal, upon which his future depended. The scheme was good, but it called for caution. He needed to control his impatience: the volatile ingredient that could precipitate a mistake and blow the whole plan to pieces. Eventually he turned his thoughts to plans for the next day, then drifted off to sleep.

He started the day with breakfast at one of the restaurants Fred had suggested. From there, he went to a nearby travel agency where he used an alias and some of the cash to buy a one-way ticket on a flight back to Chicago, leaving at two-thirty the next afternoon.

Then, because the odometer on the rental should reflect the sightseeing he was supposed to be doing, he turned onto Interstate 95 and drove south, down the coast to Fort Pierce. He stopped there, at a restaurant overlooking the ocean.

After a lunch of red snapper, he lingered over a second bourbon and water, but when his mood turned maudlin with thoughts of what might have been, he paid the bill and left.

On the return trip, he took Highway AlA as far as Melbourne, then switched to Highway 1 through Titusville and Daytona. He stopped often along the way to take pictures of the more interesting landmarks -- further proof of his relaxing vacation.

Back in Ormond Beach, he stopped at a pay phone to test the message retrieval feature of the answering machine. Only one call had come in, from his sister, telling him how lucky he was because the weather up north had turned nasty. Satisfied with the performance of the machine, he stopped at a service station and filled the tank of the rental. A check of the odometer when he pulled in at the condo told him he had logged better then two hundred and fifty miles.

Two items were out of the way -- mileage and exposed film.

After freshening up and a change of shirts, he made a drink and returned Connie's call. She said they had freezing rain that was changing to snow. He offered sympathy while carefully avoiding sounding smug concerning the beautiful weather he was enjoying. To her questions about how he had spent the day, he made vague references to local sights rather than divulge the details of his excursion.

That mileage was to reflect a longer period of sightseeing.

For dinner, Paul chose one of the restaurants from Fred's list of recommendations. The hostess directed him to an intimate booth close to the bar, but separated from it by a planter room-divider. It offered a view of bar patrons coming and going, and near the end of his dinner, he felt his pulse quicken when a striking brunette passed by. The woman's figure and the shape of her face and hairstyle triggered memories of Diane.

Turning slightly in his chair, he followed her out of the corner of his eye as she joined a man sitting halfway down the bar. Paul knew his attentions had not gone unnoticed when he saw the woman's escort scowl at him. He lowered his eyes and turned back to his food.

He finished his meal filled with thoughts of Diane, then returned to the condo.

CHAPTER 29

It seemed crazy to be packing summer clothing to go north at this time of year, but Paul thought he would draw attention traveling without luggage. The object was to create a low profile, make himself as close to invisible as possible.

It was noon when he rode the elevator down to the exit door. He walked along the outer edge of the parking lot, putting the cars between him and the building manager's apartment to get to the street, where he hailed a cab to take him to the airport.

This time he bought a newspaper to read on the plane. The front section was filled with president-elect Bill Clinton's choices of cabinet members, and when he turned to the editorial pages he found conflicting opinions on furnishing arms to the Muslims in the ethnic fighting in Bosnia. What worried him most about the conflict in Yugoslavia was the possibility of the United States getting involved; he thought it could end up as another Vietnam. In disgust, he turned to the sports section.

Ground temperature at the airport when the plane landed was in the thirties, and after collecting his suitcase, Paul hurried to his car, where he added the warmth of a topcoat to his sports jacket. He drove past the more expensive motels on Mannheim Road until he found a less pretentious one close to the expressway. He registered under a fictitious name and paid in cash for a week in advance.

He stayed just long enough to unpack his suitcase and hang up his clothes. In twenty minutes, he was on the expressway and headed for the city.

It was well after dark when Paul reached the stretch of Diversey Avenue mentioned in the newspaper clipping. It was considered still a good neighborhood, not nearly as nice as Paul's, but far enough west and north to escape the expanding squalor of the inner city.

He drove slowly, searching both sides of the street, until he came to a video store with an apartment above it.

Steve Tate's apartment. A fluttering sensation as of swirling leaves invaded his stomach.

Directly across the street was a parking lot for a convenience store, and, after circling the block, Paul pulled in and found a space facing the street. In the event he had been observed, he entered the store and bought a pack of cigarettes. On the way back to his car, he counted five other vehicles in the lot, but no shoppers; they were all in the store.

His car windows were tinted to the maximum allowed by law, so he was invisible to passersby. Next to the entrance to the video store was an access door to the apartment upstairs, and from where he was parked, the view was unobstructed. He could hardly believe his luck; the layout couldn't have been better had he designed it himself.

He looked at the darkened apartment, then at his watch and settled down to wait. He pulled the ashtray out of the dash and put it in his lap, then lit a cigarette while shielding the glow with a cupped hand. The fluttering in his stomach had changed to a rumble, reminding him that he hadn't eaten.

The memory of a fast food restaurant on the way there tempted him, but he put the thought from his mind. He turned sideways to stretch his legs.

With the temperature in the low thirties, pedestrian traffic was light, and he figured that those who *were* out had a destination in mind; they walked quickly, looking neither right or left. He felt it safe to assume that the few who did pass by were on mundane missions. Not like him.

Thinking about his purpose in being here -- this strange neighborhood, alone in a car that grew colder by the minute, stomach complaining for want of food -- he felt the first drafts of doubt blow in through unexpected chinks in his resolve. He shivered, though he really wasn't cold.

To shake off the spell, he reminded himself of his plan. He was there to kill the monster who murdered his son...and destroyed his wife. Where was the rage -- the hate -- to warm him, to rekindle the fire? He felt empty.

Twenty-two years of marriage -- eighteen of them devoted to raising a son -- all gone. And what was there left for him? A big old house, full of memories.

The thought of returning to it when this was done filled him with dread. He would see them everywhere, hear them in every room, but when he'd look closely or turn at an imagined sound, he'd see only the trick his mind had played. They're gone, along with all the dreams and plans. He thought of the pleasures he would never know: watching his son mature, seeing him graduate from college, embarking on a career. Kevin could have married Kimberly; she had his baby and was going to college anyway. Things could have been worked out.

The anger returned. But, more than that -- stronger -- was the feeling of desolation.

He reached for his third cigarette, but stopped; the taste in his mouth told him he was smoking too much. Besides, he needed something more solid to hold.

Putting the ashtray aside, he reached under the seat for the pouch, opened the zipper and took out the gun. It felt cold in his hand and heavy, even without the cartridge clip. He pulled back the slide and let the spring drive it forward again.

Raising it to eye level, he pointed it at the storefront across the street, then higher until the sights lined up with the apartment above.

He squeezed the trigger and listened to the hammer strike the firing pin stop. The snap he heard when steel met steel was sharp -- final; a reminder that once that hammer falls on a live shell your control ends; the projectile is launched. There is no turning back.

He lowered the gun to his lap and held it for a while, enjoying the feel of it, but when a cruising police car rolled slowly by, he saw the foolishness of his actions and quickly put it away.

His stomach growled again, reminding him that he had acted in haste tonight. He should have thought to buy a Thermos for coffee and maybe a sandwich. His watch read seven-thirty, and he debated whether he should risk a quick trip to that fast food restaurant he had seen coming here. It wasn't more than half a mile back; he wouldn't be gone more then thirty minutes.

He lit another cigarette and considered the chances of Tate coming home while he was gone. It was still early.

When his stomach rumbled again, he started the car, shifted into reverse and backed up, but, as he turned to pull away, he saw a van slow down in front of the video store. It stopped, then backed into an empty space just beyond the store.

Paul moved back into his spot and waited. He saw a man get out on the driver's side and walk around the front of the van into the light from the store. Suddenly air seemed to rush from Paul's lungs, as if through a sudden puncture. He took in a deep breath.

It *was* Tate.

Paul shut off the engine. As planned, he would let Tate enter the apartment and turn on the lights. He wanted to see the expression on Tate's face when he recognized him, when Tate realized that death was staring him in the face. Paul needed to see him fall, see the blank look of death, the glassy staring eyes. Only when this was accomplished could he put all of it to rest and get on with his life.

As Paul watched, he saw Tate open the door on the passenger side and reach in to help someone else get out. Tate slammed the door shut, and they started for the apartment entrance, both swaying slightly. It was then Paul saw the abundant blonde hair and the miniskirt.

Tate's companion was a *woman*. A blonde.

Paul saw them enter the side door, and a minute later the lights went on in the apartment. Their unsteady gait told him they had had more than just a few drinks; he figured the woman was probably a pickup Tate had met in some bar.

Paul sighed and swore silently. He felt a crush of disappointment, but that was quickly tempered when he thought of what might have happened.

What if he had gone for coffee and food and found the lights on in the apartment when he returned? Would he have been smart enough to back off -- call it a night? Maybe. On the other hand, his eagerness might have driven him to blunder in without thinking. He shuddered at the thought.

He figured Tate and the blonde would have sex, then, in their condition, probably fall asleep, so he might as well give it up for tonight.

Resigned to a stroke of bad luck, he backed the car out and pulled into the street. But on the way back to the motel, he couldn't get the episode out of his mind.

He saw two ways that it might have gone tonight, either of which would have spelled disaster. Imagining one of them, he could see the woman -- frustrated by the interruption -- coming down the stairs to see if the intruder was a rival. If she came on the scene after he shot Tate, she'd be a witness, and it would be all over for him, because he couldn't kill her, too -- an innocent party.

If it had gone the other way, if she saw him before he fired, he would have had to back off and get the hell out of there fast. Then Tate would know why he was there, and he'd come after *him.*

Of the two possibilities, Paul would have preferred the second; at least he'd have a chance. He was certain he could outwit Tate, and then it would be self-defense.

Fortunately, the timing of Tate's appearance saved him from both possibilities. But it reminded him that he had got careless tonight. He should have taken the time to review his plan before he left the motel. Maybe then he'd have thought to have dinner and buy a Thermos for coffee to keep him warm and alert. He had let impatience override caution.

He ate at a restaurant near the airport, then drove to a discount store and bought a one-quart, insulated jug. When he got back to the motel, he used the phone on the nightstand next to the bed to call the answering machine and heard his brother's voice.

"Just checking on you, Paul."

He returned the call and spent twenty minutes inventing activities he had participated in during the day. Ray, of course, wanted to know if Paul had got lucky yet. When Paul said no, Ray lost interest, and the conversation ended.

Paul went out to the car for the bottle he had left in the trunk and made a double bourbon and water, half of which he gulped down. Then, leaning against the headboard with his legs stretched out on the bed, he waited for the placid glow that would settle the mass of conflicting thoughts and emotions running around in his head.

He sat up, then leaned back again, pulled his legs up, then stretched them out again. Damn his impatience. It had driven him to the brink of disaster tonight. He drained the glass. It should be a lesson to him that he was subject to error. He made another drink and returned to bed.

With the calming effect of the bourbon working, he began sorting out his thoughts. His plan was still intact. Now it was just a matter of catching Tate alone. Tonight he missed, but there was plenty of time. Once it was done, he'd catch the next flight back to Florida where, if the police inquired, he would say he was when Tate met his demise. There was nothing to do but relax until tomorrow night.

He turned on the television and tuned it to CNN. When he had his fill of that, he switched to the late movie, but a weak plot failed to hold his interest. Then, after catching himself dozing several times, he undressed and went to bed. The long day brought sleep almost at once.

Near dawn, he dreamed he was in court, accused of murder, and a mini-skirted, brassy-looking blonde was pointing her finger at him, saying, 'That's the man I saw shoot Mr. Tate'.

A cry of guilty from the jury and the rapping noise of the gavel when the judge called for order jolted Paul awake.

Damp with sweat, he got a towel to dry himself and sat down to smoke a cigarette. A glance at his watch told him it was only six o'clock. He had always been a frequent dreamer, and most of his dreams, though often puzzling, were at least pleasant. But in the last six months, most of his dreams had been nightmares, as was this one.

Chapter 30

The dream followed Paul into the shower, reflected back at him in the mirror while he shaved, and accompanied him to a nearby restaurant where he bought a morning newspaper and ate breakfast. It was with him when he returned to the motel, where he finished reading the paper.

Like some homeless transient exercising squatter's rights, the dream had moved into his mind and was busy cleaning out the ghosts of former tenants. He saw evidence of this exorcising when he turned the newspaper over to the front page again and discovered he couldn't remember reading the lead column.

To kill time and get his mind on track, he drove back to Tate's neighborhood.

When Paul saw the van parked in the same spot, he wondered if that meant the woman had stayed all night. It was hard to tell. Tate could have taken her home or back to where he had picked her up without losing his parking space. It really didn't matter because Paul's plan called for darkness.

He drove to the end of the block, circled around the back through the alley and stopped behind the video store. Instead of a rear entrance, he saw a fire escape leading to a window in Tate's apartment. Paul smiled; apparently the city building inspectors were either too busy or they had been paid to shut their eyes. The window was boarded up. Tate had only one exit.

A moving van, blocking the alley ahead of him, forced Paul to back up until he found a space wide enough to turn around. The change in direction meant retracing his route around the front of the building, and, just as he passed by, he saw Tate's van pull away from the curb. The woman was in the passenger seat.

Paul grinned with pleasure. The trip back there today had paid off, and the knowledge that Tate had no means of escape was comforting.

He stopped for lunch and bought a magazine to pass the time at the motel.

Stretched out on the bed, he read the table of contents and found an article that he thought might offer diversion. He was wrong; it depressed him instead. It described numerous guarantees of immunity from prosecution to notorious drug dealers and offers of reduced sentences to others of their kind, already convicted and serving time, all in exchange for their testimony against Manuel Noriega. It appeared the Government's case was weak, so deals were struck with the scum of the earth to guarantee a conviction. How else could The President's decision to invade Panama, with its staggering costs in money and lives lost, be justified.

Halfway through the article and sick with resentment, Paul hurled the magazine against the far wall in disgust. He thought of the laws governing admissible evidence and how the courts could be pressured into bending them. When a conviction was imperative, it seemed anything was allowed, even the testimony of criminals and convicted felons. In the trial of his son's murderer, the evidence was ruled inadmissible and his killer went free. He got up, lit a cigarette and made a drink.

Prodded by the dream that had badgered his thoughts earlier, he took another look at his plan. Everything had gone off without a hitch. Until last night. And it occurred to him that he had been careful in working out every detail -- that is, every detail but one: the final confrontation. He could see now that he had left that vital step much too vague. He had not allowed for the unexpected. Like what happened the previous night.

He had planned to ring the bell and have the gun out when Tate opened the door. Then he'd force Tate to go back up to the apartment, where he'd make him squirm -- as he did with Kevin -- before squeezing the trigger.

Paul squinted and bit his lip. But what if it doesn't play that way? Tate's unstable, a loose cannon. What if he refuses to obey? Then he'd have to kill him there, at the bottom of the stairs. He'd love to see Tate squirm, but it wasn't that important -- seeing him die would be enough.

He frowned at the thought of another scenario, worse than the first. What if Tate acted on impulse and tried to overpower him? Now there was a strong possibility. He thought about this for a minute, then shrugged. He'd just have to be ready, that's all there was to it.

Paul managed to sleep a few hours. He awoke at six, freshened up, and went out to eat. This time he would not be hungry -- or cold. When the waitress came with his check, he gave her the Thermos and asked her to fill it with coffee.

He headed for the Kennedy, then turned toward the city and worked his way over to Tate's neighborhood. By nine o'clock he was cruising past the video store, and when he saw no sign of the van, he circled the block and pulled into the convenience store parking lot. He found a parking space with an unobstructed view of Tate's entrance door, got the gun from the trunk, where he kept it locked, and settled down to wait.

Now the craving for a cigarette became urgent, and to fight it, he opened the Thermos and drank some coffee.

Then he unzipped the pouch and took out the gun. He thought the feel of it in his hand might divert his mind, and for a while it did. But it wasn't long before the demand for a nicotine fix returned. He reached into the pouch for the magazine clip, slipped it in and drove it home with the heel of his hand. The craving persisted, so he pulled back the slide and let it snap back. Now the gun was loaded and cocked, and using his thumb, he moved the safety to 'Lock'. Eventually, he gave up and lit a cigarette.

He drank some more coffee, and while scanning the cars along the curb across the street, his eyes stopped at a dark-colored sedan parked three doors to the right of the video store. Parked in the shadows as it was, it was difficult to tell, for sure, but he thought he saw two occupants sitting in the front seat. He watched the windshield and driver's side window to see if he could detect any motion, but when three minutes went by with no sign of life, he concluded that either it was just too dark, or he was mistaken, and there was nobody there.

His mind returned to Diane and Kimberly, and that beautiful grandson of his. He thought about the empty unit adjoining Diane's, how close he'd be to them -- to Diane. Everything seemed to end with her. And, after what had happened Sunday, he knew she wanted him as much as he wanted her.

He squirmed in his seat. So what the *hell* was he doing *here*? Say he *did* kill Tate, and as far as the law was concerned, he got away with it -- *then* what? How could he go to her with this terrible secret between them? What about that thing called honesty? He'd expect it from *her*, and she had the right to expect it from *him*. What would she think of him when she learned he had killed a man in cold blood? He shook his head. He'd have to tell her.

He lit another cigarette and ran the whole thing through his head again. He was here because the court set Tate *free* after murdering his son. And Joan would still be alive if she hadn't gone to the cemetery, so Tate was guilty of that, too.

Tate robbed him of his family and went unpunished. *That's* why he was here. Like Ray had said, 'It's time for the punishment phase'.

He mashed his cigarette out in the ashtray and sighed. But what would Diane think of his version of justice? And someday his grandson would know. What would *he* think?

With the promise of a wonderful new life before him, why was he sitting here, waiting to kill someone? He should have listened to Burnett; he said to let *them* handle it -- they'd get him, eventually. He still thought the law was wrong to let a technicality interfere with justice, but taking it upon himself to correct their mistake could destroy his one chance at happiness with Diane and his new family. Was he in *love* with her? Of *course*. He couldn't seem to think of anything else.

The inside of the car was getting cold. He looked out at the strange neighborhood and again questioned his reason for being there. He was lonely -- had been for months. He could be lonely the rest of his life. But it didn't have to be like that. Diane and Kim and Michael could fill that loneliness. He looked out at the cold, dark night again and felt a tightening in his chest, as though he might suddenly start to cry.

"The *hell* with it," he said aloud. "It just isn't *worth* it!"

His hand moved to the ignition key, but before he could turn it, Tate's van pulled up. Paul sat motionless for a moment, then leaned back and waited. He knew he should start the car and get the hell out of there, but something held him. An old voice at the back of his mind was whispering…tempting him.

"This is your last chance," he heard it say.

Tate backed into a space just to the left of the store, got out of the van and headed for the door to his apartment. Then Paul's suspicion about the dark sedan became fact when he saw two men get out and walk toward Tate as he was unlocking his door.

When they came into the light from the store, Paul could see their faces, and the hairs at the back of his neck stood up when he recognized the one farthest from him. The man's name escaped him, but Paul knew it was the sergeant who worked with Lieutenant Burnett.

As they drew closer to Tate, Paul saw the sergeant's lips moving and then one hand came up, holding something that glinted in the light. It looked to Paul like he was showing his badge and identifying himself as a police officer.

Paul expected Tate to turn at the sound of the voice, but instead he seemed to freeze. The men stopped, and Paul saw the sergeant reach inside the lapel of his coat.

Paul hit the button to lower the electric window so he could hear better, and a second later he saw Tate whirl around to face the officers. At the same time, Tate's right arm came up, and Paul saw the first flash and heard the *pop*. Then three more flashes and *pop*, *pop*, *pop*!

Suddenly Paul was back in Nam, his mind racing at a speed that seemed to make everything else happen in slow motion. In one instinctive leap, he was out of the car and, with barely a glance to right or left, was sprinting across the street.

When he reached the far curb, both officers were down; one lay motionless, the other struggling to reach his fallen gun. Looming over the wounded cop was Tate, gun pointed, ready to finish him off.

Paul came to a stop, legs apart, arms extended; he held the gun in his right hand, with the left one under it for support. He was behind and slightly to the right of Tate. He estimated fifteen feet separated them.

With his thumb, he flicked off the safety, then yelled, "*Tate*!"

He yelled again. "*Tate*! You *bastard*!"

Paul saw Tate swing around, the surprised look of recognition, all still in slow motion. Then Tate flashed a savage smile and raised his gun.

An icy thrill swept down Paul's spine as he looked down the sights at Tate's chest and squeezed the trigger. He felt the jolt and heard the bang of the explosion. Tate's arm jerked upward, but he, too, got off a shot, and Paul thought he heard it whistle over his head.

Tate's gun hand dropped to his side. He swayed, and his eyes seemed to look off into the distance. But he did not go down, as Paul expected.

Maintaining his position, he watched Tate try to raise his gun, and when it looked as though he might make it, Paul fired again. This one was a headshot, and Tate dropped like a stone.

Paul looked at the officer who was lying face down and knew it was too late for him; he hadn't moved since the beginning. The other one was up on one elbow, staring at him.

"Help me to the car," the sergeant said. "I have to radio in for an ambulance."

Paul went to him. "Where did he hit you?"

"My right arm…and my hip, I think. I can't use my leg."

Paul picked him up under the arms and wrapped the good one around his shoulders. He half-dragged him to the car and helped him get in.

After the sergeant made the distress call, he turned to Paul. "We'll have a crowd of gawkers here in no time, and there's two guns out there on the sidewalk -- how about bringing 'em here before *they* get to 'em?"

Paul collected the sergeant's gun first, then Tate's, noting as he did that it was a thirty-two caliber semiautomatic, a relatively easy gun to conceal in a waistband. He had quick access to it when the cop called out to him. The other cop never got his gun out.

With the guns safely stored on the seat beside him, the sergeant turned and squinted at Paul.

"Don't I know you? I know you're not a cop, but I've seen you somewhere before."

Paul shook his head and started to move away.

"*Hey*, where you going? You can't *leave* --we need information from you."

A crowd was gathering, but when he heard a siren getting closer, Paul knew it was safe to leave the officer alone. He ran to his car, the door of which, in his haste, he had left open. Even the key was still in the ignition.

He pulled out into the street and headed west. Halfway down the block a police car with flashing lights passed him in the opposite direction, and seconds later, two more went by, sirens wailing. He thought about their reaction time when they got a call that one of their own was down, and knew his decision to leave when he did was the right one.

Working his way through the streets to the expressway, he kept his mind busy watching for traffic lights and maintaining the speed limit; the last thing he needed now was to get stopped for some minor violation.

He imagined what it must be like at that moment in front of the video store, cops swarming all over the place, flashing lights still turning. The ambulance should have arrived, and probably someone from the crime scene unit would be on the way.

He was reasonably certain his getaway was clean, but still he could not shake the feeling that he was being pursued; it stayed with him like a trailing ghost until he was safely inside the motel room.

Shucking his outer coat and the sports jacket, he unwrapped one of the plastic glasses and got the bottle of bourbon from his suitcase. But when he tried to pour, the neck of the bottle rattled so against the rim of the glass it knocked it over.

It was the same way in Nam; the few times he had come under fire he had been steady, but when the fighting stopped and the shock wore off, he would break out in a sweat and his hands would shake for a while.

He brought the bottle and the glass over to the small round table near the window, took off his sweaty shirt and sat down. Given a few minutes, he knew it would pass.

That he could be certain of, this was the third man he had killed; there might have been others, but in the thick underbrush of the jungle, when something out there moved, you fired, so you never knew for sure.

When he thought he could manage it, he poured two fingers of bourbon into the glass, drank it quickly and poured another. Then, leaning back, he sipped the second drink and let his mind drift back over the events of the past hour and a half.

He thought about the careful plan he had made and how, in the passage of just one night, it had all come apart. When he thought about the wounded officer, the name Fennelli popped into his head. That was his name, Sergeant Joe Fennelli, and when the sergeant had time to think clearly, he, too, would match the face with the name. Paul's alibi was down the tubes.

But what could he have done? Tate had shot two police officers and was standing over the wounded one ready to finish the job. No matter what the consequences, Paul knew he did the right thing. He remembered the look on Tate's face, the smile, like a crazed animal baring its teeth, a rabid beast that had to be destroyed.

The alcohol, on its mission of mercy, raced through the corridors of his bloodstream to the brain and the twitching mass that was his nerve center. He closed his eyes, and details lost in the tumult of the action came back to him in vivid flashes.

He saw Tate's chest in the sights, and again he was squeezing off the first shot, feeling the jolt of the forty-five. He remembered Tate's gun hand veer upward and the pop of the only round Tate got off, but the sound of that bullet whistling over his head was missing. That had been his imagination. He knew no one could hear a bullet in the air. He saw the distant look in Tate's eyes, the attempt to raise the gun before his own gun roared with his second and final shot.

Then he recalled glancing at Tate's head as he collected the guns, the hole in the forehead just to the left of center, the missing section at the point of exit where the bullet took out a chunk of the skull.

He shuddered and drained his glass.

It was over, but at what cost? A police officer was dead. "*Damn*," he said, with a renewed surge of rage at a justice system that had freed that monster to kill again.

Pouring a third drink, he went to the sink in the bathroom to mix it with water, then he stacked the pillows against the headboard of the bed and stretched out. He could not afford this new anger; he must think about his next move.

The festering, hate-induced wound in his soul would heal. Now he could get on with his life. Or could he? What would happen when Fennelli remembered his name? Of course he'd tell his partner, Burnett. Maybe he should try to get hold of Burnett first. He lit a cigarette and sipped his drink.

Maybe he should *stop* trying to figure out his next move until his thinking became rational. The way his mind was working now, he could make a colossal blunder.

He finished undressing, made another drink and stretched out again. That one brought sleep. And he dreamed of Vietnam.

CHAPTER 31

Paul awoke at five-thirty the next morning with pressure in his bladder and a foul taste in his mouth. A dull pounding started in his head when he got up to use the bathroom. The bourbon had done a good job of knocking him out, but he was paying the price now. Knowing the futility of trying to go back to sleep, he showered, shaved and brushed his teeth. At six he was sitting in front of the TV, smoking a cigarette and watching the early news.

Following the world and national news, the newscaster switched to the local scene with a description of a shoot-out between police and a suspect the previous night in the fifty-one hundred block of Diversey Avenue. Paul heard the man say that two police detectives were attempting to serve an arrest warrant when the suspect opened fire with a .32 caliber pistol, killing one of the officers and wounding the other before being shot and killed himself. The wounded officer was rushed to Belmont Hospital, where he was reported in stable condition.

As the story continued with minor details and no mention of him, the muscles in Paul's neck began to relax. But a moment later they tensed again when the newsman told of two witnesses, a man and his woman companion, who were questioned by reporters at the scene. The witnesses said a fourth man was involved, and, according to them, both officers had already been shot and were lying on the sidewalk when this other man seemed to come out of nowhere. They said he shot the suspect twice and helped the wounded officer to his car, then drove off in a 1992 Buick sedan. Later, when asked about the mystery man who saved the one officer's life, homicide detective, Lieutenant Douglas Burnett, declined to comment until an investigation into the shooting was complete.

When the newscaster moved on to other local issues, Paul shut off the TV. He knew it had been unrealistic of him to hope he had got out of there unseen. His mind then turned to Burnett.

The lieutenant would be looking for him by now. No doubt he'd call the house first, but with nobody there to answer, where would he turn next? His brother? Woodward Engineering wouldn't be open for hours. He thought about calling the answering machine, but it was probably still a little early for that, too.

He decided to go out for breakfast to pass some time, and when he picked up his topcoat, he felt the weight of the gun. He remembered it was still loaded and cocked. Then he was reminded again of his panic the night before when he took the gun out and saw the safety lock was still in the 'Off' position. Shaking his head at his carelessness, he pressed the magazine catch to eject the clip, pulled back the slide and shook the live cartridge out onto the bed.

When he finished his breakfast, he had the waitress at the diner refill the Thermos jug and spent another hour over coffee and the morning paper at the motel. At ten thirty he called the answering machine, and, after several clicks with no messages, he heard his brother's voice:

"What's going on, Paul? Where the *hell* are you?"

The urgency in Ray's voice told Paul what to expect. He hung up, then called the number of his brother's warehouse, but when Ray answered, the stress was gone; his voice sounded playful.

"Well, well." he said, "my *brother*, the *hero*."

"What are you talking about?"

"Come on, Paul, I know you're not in Florida."

"Who says?"

"Awright, cut the *bullshit* -- that cop, Burnett, called in the middle of the night wanting to know if I knew where he could reach you. He said it was very important, and when I watched the news this morning, I put it all together."

When Paul did not speak, Ray went on.

"*Damn*, Paul, you really surprised me. You're some cool cookie, *you* are. And here I thought you were suffering in silence, biting the bullet -- instead, you were plotting revenge all along. *Boy*, I've gotta hand it to you. You mustn't have a nerve in your body the way you went about it without once tipping your hand."

Paul cut in. "Ray, slow down, for crissake; can't you see the *trouble* I'm in?"

"*Trouble*? What the hell are you talking about? Dammit, you're a hero, and I'm proud of you."

Ray's words struck a new chord of fear in Paul's already vibrating insides.

"Have you shared your detection skills with anyone else yet?"

"No, why? What's the problem?"

"Don't you see it? I may be a hero to you --you're my brother -- but if the media gets wind of this, my name is public knowledge. Everyone will know that my being on the scene last night was no coincidence...."

"So *what*?"

"What do you mean, *'so what'*? *Think* about it, Ray. A lot of people out there won't see me as some kind of hero; they'll know me for what I was -- a *vigilante* who was ready to take the law into his own hands. They'll see me as a *stalker*, and you know the kind of fear *that* word generates today...."

"To *hell* with them; your friends will know better."

Paul almost laughed. "I don't know, Ray, you're something else."

"What do you mean by that?"

"Everything's so simple to you."

"Oh *yeah*? Well, I remember when I took Barb to see 'Death Wish'. When Bronson got mad enough to go after the punks who killed his wife and ruined his daughter, and he started shooting some of those bastards, I remember the audience getting up and applauding. And so did *I*."

"You forget...Bronson never did find the real killers. And in his rage and frustration, he became a vigilante, killing any creep who crossed his path."

"Well, yeah, but that movie made a hell of a lot of money. People stood in line to see it. And the sequels did pretty good, too. I'm telling you, people are sick and tired of the crime in our streets, and they're mad as hell at the courts for letting so many criminals walk free. You, above all, should know that."

"Okay, I'll grant you, some might be sympathetic with what I was doing -- and maybe saving that cop would win a few more over to my side, but that wounded cop was Burnett's sidekick, and he recognized me. What's Burnett going to do about me? And if the press finds out about this, he can't just ignore it; he'll have to do *something*."

"I see what you mean. That sure would stir up a hornet's nest. I remember in the movie, Bronson was one hell of a headache to the cops; they just wanted him to disappear."

"Yeah, but that was just a movie. I don't know what Burnett's going to do." Paul sighed in the silence that followed. "In any event, I have to call him. Did he leave a number with you?"

"He said not to talk to anyone but him." Ray gave Paul the number. "You sure this is the right thing? Hell, maybe you should just disappear."

"I couldn't do that. Not *now* anymore."

"Whataya mean?"

Paul sighed, then told Ray about his meeting the previous Saturday night with Diane, including his decision to look at the vacant unit next to hers.

"Well, I'll be *damned*," Ray said, "a *grandson*. That's terrific news. Now I understand why you can't just walk away. You think this thing with you and Diane could develop into something really serious?"

"That's the impression I got."

"*Go* for it. It's the best thing that could have happened to you. *See*, I told you that woman had her eye on you."

Paul ended the conversation with an agreement that Ray could tell Barbara all about his meeting with Diane, but nothing else.

He poured the last of the coffee and called the number Burnett had given Ray.

"Homicide, Burnett speaking."

"This is Paul Becker, Lieutenant."

"Where *are* you?"

"I'm holed up in a motel near the airport."

"Okay," Burnett said. "*Go home* -- I'll meet you there in an hour."

Paul was unprepared for such a brusque message.

"You hear me okay?"

"Yes."

"Then just *do* it."

The abrupt conversation left Paul wondering. It certainly didn't tell him what to expect of their impending meeting. He gathered up the few items he had unpacked, loaded his suitcase into the trunk and drove off leaving the key to the room in the door.

The drive home was a blur to him. He tried not to think of what was coming, but his mind churned through one possibility after another. He knew it could have been worse. There was still a remote chance he'd get through this unscathed. At least Burnett hadn't ordered him to turn himself in.

He parked his car at the curb as a signal to his neighbor that he was home, emptied his trunk, and carried his bags into the empty house. For a moment, he just stood in the entrance, unable to decide what to do. Then he carried the suitcases upstairs, but left them unopened.

He opened a dresser drawer where he had stored pictures of Joan, picked out his favorite one, and took it to his son's room, where he put it next to one of Kevin. He sat on the bed and gazed at their faces and smiled. "Well, it's done. Kevin…Joan, you are avenged".

Paul remained in Kevin's room until the doorbell chimed. Then, steeling himself, he went downstairs and let Burnett in.

CHAPTER 32

Burnett sat down on the couch and leaned forward, his back stiff, elbows on his knees. This was a different Burnett; the one Paul remembered would have leaned back and stretched his arm over the backrest in a show of relaxed confidence. The change added to Paul's anxiety.

"Can I make you a drink?" he asked, hoping to ease the tension.

When Burnett shook his head, Paul sat down across from him and waited.

"From the way you left the scene last night, I get the impression you want to avoid publicity."

Although it was said as a statement, Burnett raised his eyebrows on the last word, and Paul knew a question had been put to him, an experimental probe to test the air.

"That's right," he said.

"Okay then, here's my offer." Burnett paused to fill his lungs. "I'll issue a statement to the press that we found the shooter. I'll say the guy was on his way home from a pistol range where he was practicing target shooting. I'll say the guy just happened to pass by as Sergeant Fennelli flashed his badge, and he stopped because he'd never seen an actual arrest before. He says when he saw the suspect shoot the officers, he knew he had to help. He was just doing his duty as a good citizen and wants to remain anonymous."

"Will the press buy it?"

"They'll have to. Nobody got your license number, so there's no way for them to come up with a name."

Paul was having trouble believing it was going to be that easy.

"Does that mean I'm off the hook?"

"Do you agree with the story I'm going to tell the news hounds?"

"Yes."

"Okay. Then I guess you're...'off the hook', as you say." Burnett leaned back then, and swung one arm over the back of the couch. "I just went off duty…now I'll have that drink you offered."

Paul grinned. "What'll it be? I'm drinking bourbon and water."

"Sounds good."

When Paul returned with the drinks, he saw that Burnett had his long legs stretched out and crossed at the ankles, and the lieutenant's relaxed posture helped to ease his own taut nerves.

"You could have been *killed* last night," Burnett said.

"I could have been killed in *Nam*, too, but I wasn't."

Burnett raised his eyebrows. "*So*, then at least you weren't *completely* untrained."

"I had a little experience."

"When your bother said you were on vacation in Florida, I knew you planned that as your alibi, but still, you took a hell of a chance."

"I couldn't live with the rage and hate any longer," Paul said.

Then he went on to tell Burnett about Diane and his grandson, and how he had decided to abandon the plan.

"I was going to forget the whole thing, but when Tate pulled up in his van, I waited. Then I saw Sergeant Fennelli and the other officer, and the next thing I knew, Tate was shooting. I just acted on instinct."

Burnett shook his head. "Funny thing, fate."

"By the way, how *is* Fennelli? I figured the other officer was dead."

"Yeah, one bullet hit him in the neck, severing an artery; he was dead in a matter of seconds. Fennelli took one in the hip and one in the right arm -- he lost his gun with that one. But he's doing okay…told me to tell you thanks."

"One thing still bugs me -- what made Tate start shooting?"

"Tate killed the owner of an electronics store when the guy surprised him during a burglary. Fennelli was there to arrest him on a murder warrant. This time we had a reliable witness who wasn't afraid to testify. And Tate *knew* it. I told you he'd screw up eventually, didn't I?"

"Yeah, you did," Paul said. "Too bad he had to kill two more people first."

Burnett winced and Paul knew he had struck a nerve. Then Burnett drained his glass and got up. "As a police officer who's sworn to uphold the law, I'm bound to oppose vigilantes." He spoke the words with a frown, then the set of his mouth changed to a crooked smile. "But, off the record, I'm glad you were there." He stuck out his hand, and Paul shook it. "I hope your life gets better. Maybe that woman and the new baby will make it happen."

Paul walked with him to the door.

"If there's ever anything Fennelli or I can do for you," Burnett said, "just pick up the phone."

He turned and started for his car. "So long Becker, and thanks again."

Paul watched Burnett's car pull away, then went to his study and called his brother. Ray was disappointed that Paul would be denied the hero status Ray thought he deserved, but he did agree they should keep the story of the shooting a family secret.

Next, he called Diane and caught her as she was about to leave for lunch.

"Paul! What a *surprise*. How's that problem coming along?"

He almost said, 'What problem'?, forgetting the lie he had told her. "I'm not in Florida. I'm here."

She was silent for a moment, then she said, "Your voice sounds strange, is something wrong?"

"Nothing's wrong, *actually*. Depends on your viewpoint."

"Paul, you're scaring me. Something *is* wrong."

"Look, it's too complicated to explain over the phone. Can I see you tonight?"

He heard a long silence, then, "I don't like the sound of this...where are you?"

"I'm at home."

"I'm taking the rest of the day off. I wouldn't get anything done this afternoon wondering what this is all about, anyway."

"You're going to just leave the office?"

"There's nothing I have to do that can't wait until tomorrow. See you in a little while -- 'bye."

He had counted on more time to think of what he was going to say. But actually, he was glad she didn't want to wait until that night. Better to get it over with quickly, and find out now if he was going to lose her.

He thought about that possibility and winced. What he needed was something to occupy his mind for an hour. Then he remembered the rental car. He wouldn't be returning to Florida now, so he should call them. But the keys to the car were in Woodward's condo. They'd probably object to having duplicate keys floating around. He'd have to call the building manager. Her card was in his wallet.

When he got her on the phone, he said an emergency had come up at home, and he would not be returning. When he asked her to let the rental agency know where the car was and have the keys for them when they arrived, she balked. She protested that Daytona was a toll call and it was inconvenient for her to have to be home waiting for them.

He wasn't surprised. Even Fred said she was always ready to make an extra buck.

"Look," he said, "I'll send you a check for twenty dollars."

"Thirty," she countered.

He almost laughed. "Okay, thirty."

He went upstairs and unpacked, but before he could put anything away, Diane was ringing the doorbell.

CHAPTER 33

Paul let Diane in and hung her coat in the guest closet. He noticed her businesslike dark-blue, knee length skirt, jacket and white blouse. She looked beautiful in everything.

"Thanks for coming," he said, leading her toward the living room. "How about a drink?"

She raised an eyebrow. "It's a little early for me."

"A glass of wine, maybe?"

"Paul, I just want to know what's going on. The way you sounded on the phone, I felt something is troubling you."

He let the silence build while he tried to decide the best way to start. Perspiration was wetting his shirt under his arms.

"Did you watch the early news this morning?" he began.

"No," she said, frowning, "why?"

"Two policemen were shot trying to serve a warrant on that guy who killed Kevin."

"The Tribune had that story; I read it this morning at the office. Two witnesses said a man in a '92 Buick..." She broke off. Her eyes opened wide, and she sat down suddenly on the couch, one hand clutching her chest over her heart. "Oh, my *God*." She blinked several times. "Paul, don't tell me that was *you*? "

Paul saw his blunder; he had wanted to ease into the telling. But he underestimated the agility of her mind.

He sat down next to her. "Diane, let me explain. Hear me out before you pass judgement. Please? "

She stared wide-eyed at him, but didn't speak, and he used her silence as an opening.

"I guess it all started that day Kevin's killer walked out of the courtroom a free man."

He paused, groping for the right words, but then she found her voice.

"I read about it in the papers and wondered how you must have felt. I know I thought it was a terrible miscarriage of justice. But...."

"Yeah," he cut in, "I was angry and frustrated with a system that could let that happen. But I lived with the anger for months because of Joan -- she couldn't handle the loss -- she needed me. Then, when she was killed coming home from visiting Kevin's grave, something snapped in my brain. This guy Tate -- this *mad dog* that the courts turned loose -- had done it to me *again*."

She winced and shook her head.

"I was full of rage and frustration. It lived with me day and night. I tried to bury myself in my work, but the hate was a festering thing inside me. I saw Tate as a rabid beast that had to be destroyed. But I couldn't come up with a plan that wouldn't destroy me in the process." He paused to study her reaction. "Then, when my boss offered to let me use his condo in Florida for a vacation, I knew I had the perfect alibi...."

He hesitated when he saw a frown and her eyes narrow down to mere slits.

"I know," he said, "I lied to you. But that's the *only* thing I lied about." He saw the frown disappear, but then her eyebrows went up in what could only be an expression of skepticism. "Anyway, I went to Florida and laid down a trail, including an answering machine to insure the illusion. Then I returned to Chicago and staked out Tate's apartment."

He stopped and reached out to take her hand, but she pulled away from him and seemed to huddle within herself. Her reaction spurred him to panic; he realized he had been going too fast. It was time to get to the part that he hoped would quell the fear, or revulsion -- he didn't know which -- mirrored in her eyes.

"*Now*," he began, "this is the part that is so important to me -- to *us*. You *must* believe me." He hesitated, then leaned slightly toward her and put as much urgency in his voice as he could summon. "When I sat in my car last night, waiting for Tate to show up, I was thinking about you...and Michael. I realized that I could lose you if I went through with my plan to see my own justice. Then I decided I needed *you* more than I wanted revenge. I changed my mind." He waited for a reaction, but, still, her eyes were filled with doubt. "In fact, I had my hand on the key to start the car, when Tate's van pulled up. I knew I should leave, but *something* -- I don't know what it was -- told me to wait. Then I saw the cops heading for Tate, and saw him start shooting…well, I couldn't just sit there and do nothing. When I saw Tate standing over the wounded cop, ready to finish him off, I reacted instinctively...."

Paul broke off and watched her for what seemed an eternity. Then he said, "Well?"

Diane seemed to shake herself, as if she were coming out of a trance and only now realized that he had stopped talking. Then she stood up.

"Paul..." she said, "...I just don't know. I don't know what to think. This has all been a little too much for me."

Her face look pinched, lips compressed, as if she were suffering through something quite unpleasant and wasn't sure what to do about it.

Paul wanted to hold her, try to reassure her, but he refrained. "Do you believe me?" he pleaded.

She sighed. "I don't know what to believe." She started toward the door. "I just know I have to get out of here."

He walked with her to the door. "Please, Diane," he said, "don't let this destroy us. Don't let this be the end of the new beginning I thought was starting."

They were at the door, and she opened it. "Paul, I'm sorry," she said, "but I just have to go."

He reached for her, but she pushed by him and started for her car. She didn't look back. Then her car was pulling away, and he watched it until it was out of sight before going back into the house.

He went upstairs to the master bedroom and sprawled, face down, across the bed. In his mind he still saw Diane's retreating figure, her car moving inexorably down the street and out of sight. Loneliness, like some malignant tumor, seemed to spread through his entire being, squeezing the very life of him out with its overpowering presence. Never had he felt so alone.

Then the recriminations began. He should have let the police deal with Tate. Who appointed him judge, jury, and executioner? Why had he allowed his frustration to get so out of control that it turned to rage?

He did it because the law didn't do its job -- the answer he had used from the start. Well, now he was paying the cost. The new life he thought was about to begin was over.

He thought about having a drink, but cast it out of his mind. In his present state he knew he wouldn't be able to stop with just one or two.

Then it suddenly came to him that he wouldn't be buying that townhouse next to Diane's. That was out of the question, now. Where was he going to live? Des Plaines -- where his brother was? He wondered if there were townhouses in that area. He should give his Realtor a call.

She answered on the second ring. “Northwest Realty,” she said, “how can we help you?”

“Sharon?”

“Yes.”

“This is Paul Becker.”

“Mr. *Becker*, are you back already?”

“Yeah, something came up and I had to get back early.”

“I'm glad you did. I was worried that I wouldn't be able to reach you, and the sale on your house is scheduled to close a week from tomorrow. The buyers want to know when they can take possession -- they're rental lease has expired, and their apartment is rented already.”

“Oh, boy,” Paul said. “I haven't found anything yet.” He didn't want to tell her he hadn't even started looking.

“Did you plan to stay in the city? Maybe I can help you.”

“No. I want to go suburban -- maybe Des Plaines or Park Ridge.”

“Oh.”

He could hear disappointment in her tone.

“I have a Realtor friend in that area. I could give her a call and see if she has something you might be interested in. What are you looking for in a house?”

“I was thinking of a townhouse -- something small enough that I could handle. Two bedroom max.”

“That shouldn't be too difficult. I'll get in touch with her and have her call you. Okay?”

“Fine. And thanks.”

“The details on the closing are in the mail. You should have them today.”

Fortunately, he still had some vacation time left to go looking. But it wasn't something he cared to do, especially in his present state of mind. This wasn't supposed to happen.

A glance at his watch told him it was after four already, and he went to the bar in the dining room. Maybe a drink would spark his appetite. Just one.

With a bourbon and water in hand, he went to the kitchen and opened the refrigerator, then the freezer. He wasn't really hungry, and he didn't want to go out to eat, either. Finally, he called out for a medium size pizza.

The pizza arrived at five-fifteen. He put it on the table, sat down, and stared at it. He got a beer from the refrigerator, opened it, but didn't drink. Then he thought about the gun he had put back in the basement. He should get rid of that damn thing. No telling what he might do when the loneliness became unbearable.

He went upstairs and started to put his clothes away, then, when he opened the closet, he saw that Joan's clothing was gone. The spare house key with a note of thanks was hanging from one of the empty hangers. That brought back memories of that day with Diane when she made breakfast for him and later when they made love.

He stopped putting his things away and went to the den, turned the television on, sat down and stared at the images on the screen. What was he going to do with himself, now? Everyone would think he was crazy if he went back to work early.

Thirty minutes later, he still was sitting in the den, staring at the TV screen, when the doorbell chimed. He swore, then got up and went to the door. This was not a good time for company. Maybe he could get rid of whoever it was. He sighed and opened the door.

Seeing her was like an electric shock. He stood there, stunned, mouth open.

Diane's eyebrows rose, then she smiled weakly. “May I come in?”

Only partially recovered, he stepped aside and bid her enter with a gesture of his arm. She went straight to the living room and sat down on the couch. Unsure of himself, Paul chose a chair opposite her and sat.

"I've had some time to think," she began. "Went straight home and ... did a lot of thinking."

He watched her, but kept silent.

"I think I've come to know quite a lot about you, Paul -- that is -- in the short time we've had together." She stopped and smiled. "And I've come to a conclusion. You may not agree with me, but I don't believe you could have carried out your plan. I don't believe you're capable of cold-blooded murder. I believe you would have decided against killing Tate even if I had never come into you life."

Paul opened his mouth to speak, but she raised her hand and shook her head. "Please, let me finish."

He smiled and shrugged.

"I'm saying you're not capable of cold-blooded murder. But, of course, when you saw those police officers in trouble, you -- the Paul I've come to know -- did what you felt you had to do."

She got up and came to him, reached down to his hands, and pulled him up. Paul looked into her eyes and wondered about this woman who seemed to know him better than he knew himself. Was she right? Would he have abandoned his plan even if she hadn't come into his life? He decided that was a question nobody could answer.

"What you did was *dangerous*." she said. "You could have been *killed*."

Paul smiled. "That's what Burnett said."

"*Well*? He was *right*; you could have. You faced an armed man who had killed before."

He put his arms around her waist. "I faced armed enemies in Nam, too."

“True,” she said, “but then you were under *orders*. Your government demanded you kill the enemy. Last night was different, you had a choice. Anyway, what you did was brave. At least you saved one officer's life.”

“That reminds me,” he said, “Burnett gave me a break…if news of my involvement got out, he'd be forced to take some kind of action against me. So, let's keep this story in the family, okay?”

“I like the sound of that.”

He kissed her.

The phone rang then, and he answered it in the kitchen.

“Mr. Becker? This is Sally Bender of Parkside Realty. Sharon just called to tell me you're looking for a townhouse out this way.”

“Oh.” Paul said, watching Diane, who had come to stand beside him. “Listen,” he said, looking into Diane's eyes, “I'm really sorry to have put you and Sharon to the trouble, but a townhouse I had been interested in before is now available, so I won't be needing your services after all. But thank you for your quick response. Yes, goodbye.”